TO LOVE AGAIN

Cindy fumbled with the keys and dropped them twice before she managed to get the door open. Still, she didn't look back at him. Maybe by the time she finished making the call, he would have changed his mind about waiting for her and be gone. "That's rotten," she told herself. "The man helped you. He got inside the dumpster for you. Now that you don't need him, you want him to disappear." Even though she was the only one who knew what she had been thinking, she still felt ashamed.

What is wrong with me? He was just a stranger who, lucky for her, had been here when she needed him. She picked up the phone. To him she was just a woman who did something stupid. *He only hung around to ease his conscious.* She shook her head. It didn't matter why he helped her. Lucky for her he did. *What kind of office does he have?* She never even noticed what was in the building. The entrance into this lot was from the other end. She had been so focused on her shops that she had barely glanced beyond here. She called the road service and gave her location.

BOOK YOUR PLACE ON OUR WEBSITE AND MAKE THE ARABESQUE ROMANCE CONNECTION!

We've created a customized website just for our very special Arabesque readers, where you can get the inside scoop on everything that's going on with Arabesque romance novels.

When you come online, you'll have the exciting opportunity to:

- View covers of upcoming books

- Learn about our future publishing schedule (listed by publication month and author)

- Find out when your favorite authors will be visiting a city near you

- Search for and order backlist books

- Check out author bios and background information

- Send e-mail to your favorite authors

- Join us in weekly chats with authors, readers and other guests

- Get writing guidelines

- AND MUCH MORE!

Visit our website at
http://www.arabesquebooks.com

TO LOVE AGAIN

Alice Wootson

ARABESQUE

★BET BOOKS™

BET Publications, LLC
http://www.bet.com
http://www.arabesquebooks.com

ARABESQUE BOOKS are published by

BET Publications, LLC
c/o BET BOOKS
One BET Plaza
1900 W Place NE
Washington, D.C. 20018-1211

All Kensington Titles, Imprints, and Distributed Lines are available at special quantity discounts for bulk purchases for sales
promotion, premiums, fund-raising, and educational or institu-
tional use. Special book excerpts or customized printings can
also be created to fit specific needs. For details, write or phone
the office of the Kensington special sales manager: Kensington
Publishing Corp., 850 Third Avenue, New York, NY 10022,
attn: Special Sales Department, Phone: 1-800-221-2647.

First Printing: October 2002
10 9 8 7 6 5 4 3 2 1

Printed in the United States of America

ACKNOWLEDGMENTS

Belated thanks to Karen Thomas for taking the chance on me; to Gwen (Word Diva), my information source, for her guidance; to Deidre Knight, my agent, for her perseverance on my behalf; and as always to Ike.

One

Cindy Granger set the bowl of her special potato salad into the carrier beside the tossed salad. She closed the insulated compartment and set the bowl of still warm fried chicken in its own section on top. She smiled. Doctor or not, Harry loved her fried chicken. Her smile widened as she closed the top without packing any dessert. If things went according to her plans, they would be too busy for dessert. She sighed. It had been too long.

When Harry first took the position as head of the neurology department at Blaine Memorial Hospital two years ago, at least once a week she'd surprised him with a special lunch in his office. The first time had been impromptu, but after he told her how much it helped him relax after he performed a tough operation, her bringing lunch to his office had become a regular part of their weekly schedule. She frowned. When had they stopped? And why? Her frown deepened. She remembered.

One morning before he left the house, Harry had told her that she shouldn't bother, that he had a meeting. The next week she had something planned. When *was* their last special lunch together? She shook her head. Too long ago. How had they gotten so far apart?

She tucked the silverware and cloth napkins into the side pocket of the case and smiled. Some traditions were worth reclaiming.

She wiped the gray granite countertop one last time,

hung up the dishcloth, grabbed the case with the food, got the small case with two wineglasses and slipped a bottle of chilled wine from the refrigerator into the case. Then she went to recapture the early romance of her marriage. All she needed to complete the scenario was Harry.

She drove the ten miles to the hospital, anticipating lunch with Harry the whole way.

Her smile was still in place when she zipped into the empty spot next to Harry's car in the hospital parking lot. One of the perks of being married to the Chief of the Neurology Department was having your own re-served parking space no matter how seldom you used it.

Despite the slight drizzle oozing from the dark May clouds and making the day gray, she kept her smile as she removed the two containers from the trunk of her car. *This is just what Harry and I need.* It had been a long time since she had done this.

Maybe it would bring back the spark in their marriage. They had been so happy in the beginning. She frowned. When had it gone into hiding, anyway? She shook her head. *No matter. We'll discover it again.* Optimism rode the elevator with her to the offices on the third floor.

She stared at her keys and frowned. Which was the key to his office? She shook her head. It had been so long since she had used it. Finally, after trying one key that didn't fit, she inserted the right one. The door swung open and she took the containers inside and set them on the table in front of the couch in the outer office.

Soft music flowed from the back where his office and three examination rooms were located. She frowned and apprehension sprouted inside her, but curiosity led her to follow the music.

She stopped outside the last examination room. The door was open just enough for her to see the examining table. It wasn't a patient on the table and what Harry was doing could never be considered a medical examination.

"Oh, Harry," drifted from Nina, his nurse, and reached Cindy. *Harry and Nina?* This could not be real. It was too much like a scene from a soap opera. Cindy stared through the tears that started to leak from her eyes. If she stared long enough maybe this bad scene will disappear and reality will show up.

"What are you doing here?" Finally, mercifully, Harry noticed her. He got off Nina, but didn't hurry to zip his pants.

I just picked up those pants from the cleaners yesterday. Now they'll have to go back.

Nina moved, but Cindy's stare was stuck on Harry.

"I asked you what you are doing here." Harry buttoned the last button on his shirt. His glare stopped the flow of Cindy's tears. She took a deep breath and swallowed the tears waiting for their turn. "I came to bring my husband lunch." She was surprised at how calm her voice was when her world was tumbling down.

Harry's face flushed beneath his copper-color skin as if he had sat in the sun too long, like that time they'd gone to Jamaica in their happy life.

"You should have let me know you were coming." He picked up his white coat from the floor.

"I didn't realize that I needed an appointment to see my husband." As she said the word "husband," she allowed her stare to move to Nina, who stood beside the table. "Does your wife need an appointment to see you now?" She took a little pleasure at the way Nina's gaze slid from hers at the word "wife." "Did your *nurse* need one?"

"We'll talk about this at home."

"Get her out of here." If Cindy's words had been any softer she would have been the only one who heard them. It had the same effect as a shout on Nina, who scrambled toward the door but stopped in front of Cindy. She clutched her shoes to her as if they were a shield capable of protecting her from whatever Cindy planned to do.

Cindy considered her options before she stepped aside to let Nina escape. If Cindy's own husband didn't honor their marriage vows, how could she expect Nina to? Besides, Nina wasn't worth going to jail for.

Cindy heard Nina drop one of her shoes. Then a desk drawer in the outer office slid open, followed by the door opening and closing. The whole time, Cindy stared at Harry.

"Cindy—" he took a step toward her.

"Don't come near me." She held her place and he moved back. The hurt that had the tears waiting to fall had disappeared and a new emotion took its place.

"Let me explain." He straightened his jacket, looking sheepishly at Cindy.

"This is one of those self-explanatory cases." A harsh laugh escaped from her, but it had nothing to do with humor. "The doctor and his nurse. What a cliché. Couldn't you be more original in your choice of sluts?"

She left the room before he answered and went back to the waiting room even though she didn't have anything to wait for.

"Cindy . . ." Harry was behind her, but he gave her plenty of space. "Look, things just aren't working between you and me. You have to realize this. We never should have gotten married."

Cindy slowly opened the small container. Her hurt that was new a few seconds ago was replaced. "You were the one"—she removed a wineglass and threw it against the wall—"who insisted"—the second glass followed—"that we were meant for each other." She took out the bottle of wine, looked at it, and put it back. "This is too good to waste on you."

"That was a long time ago."

"Yeah. A whole four and a half years ago." She unzipped the food container. "After Dean Carter introduced us, *you* chased *me*." She removed the lid from the potato salad. "I told you that I wasn't interested in a relationship." She scooped out a handful and plopped it onto the desk calendar. She nodded as the spot from the dressing spread across May. "You convinced me that we were destined to be together." A second handful of potato salad landed on the bookcase, followed by one on the file cabinet. "You could hardly wait for me to graduate." She placed another scoop on the arm of the dark brown leather couch and was sorry that it wasn't white silk.

"Don't do . . ."

"Get away from me." She smeared salad onto the other arm of the couch. "Why didn't you leave me alone when I refused to go out with you?" A piece of potato fell to the floor. She picked it up and set it on top of the last scoop. Harry just watched. She continued the litany of their relationship. "You came to Cheyney every weekend after we met, just to visit me." She paused to glare at him. "When I refused to sleep with you, you said you would wait. That it would make our wedding night sweeter." She blinked hard. "Who was your Nina back then, Harry? Who was taking care of you, huh? Why didn't you marry her instead of messing with my life?"

"I did love you. I . . . I thought we could make a good life together; that you would be ideal for me. I swear, I did love you."

"You also swore to love, honor and cherish. So much for your oaths." She held the half empty bowl as if she had forgotten that she held it. "I guess you figured that I'd make a suitable wife to parade in front of your society friends. Is that it? Is that why you had me fly out here to Cleveland to meet your mother? To see if she agreed with your choice?"

"I . . ."

"I don't want to hear it. Not another lie. Not even what you would call your truth. I can't believe anything you say ever again." She emptied the bowl onto the seat and spread it out as if the leather were a platter on a buffet table. "Or maybe you wanted me because I wasn't interested in you." She looked at him. "Is that it Harry? Was I forbidden fruit?" She closed her eyes for a second and took a deep breath. "Did you marry me because that was the only way you could get me?" She set the bowl in the middle of the couch. "Is Nina your latest forbidden fruit?" She laughed. "She certainly wasn't as hard to get."

"Cindy stop this." Harry pointed to the couch. "Are you crazy?"

"A little." She nodded. "Maybe more than a little. Anger does that to people."

She opened the tossed salad and drizzled the oil and vinegar dressing over it. Then she took the salad utensils, slowly tossed the greens together, and instead of putting the salad into bowls, she began to slowly and methodically sprinkle the greens and tomatoes over the antique oriental rug. "Don't come any closer," she warned Harry when he started toward her.

He backed away again as if the salad tongs she was holding out were a sword. Then he watched her empty the bowl. He stood staring at the greens covering the floor and oozing dressing.

Cindy scanned the room as if to make sure that she hadn't forgotten anything. "The chicken goes back home with me. You don't deserve it, Harry Granger. And you don't deserve me."

She fastened the bag, took it, the wine container and her shattered pride and left the office without looking back.

By the time Harry got home an hour later, Cindy had indulged in a cliché of her own: Harry's clothes were stuffed into every piece of his luggage and every box she could find. What she couldn't pack was piled over the suitcases by the front door.

"What's this?" Harry stopped inside the door and stared at his clothes as if they were foreign matter.

"You're too smart to play this dumb."

"We need to talk."

"You're right. You're late, but you're right. Come into *my* living room and sit down. If you were company or a friend, I'd offer you something to drink, but since you are neither . . ." She let her words trail off as she walked slowly to the wing chair where Harry usually sat. She heard him follow. He was trying to get comfortable in the other chair when she turned to face him.

"Talk."

"I admit I should have come to you a long time ago." Cindy didn't say anything so he continued. "I didn't plan this. None of this." He hesitated as if groping for words. Cindy refused to help him find them. "Maybe it's good that you found out." He stared at her, but the intimidation that his stare usually held was missing. "Nina is pregnant and I want a divorce so she and I can get married." He let out a hard breath as if he had just set down a heavy package. His stare slid to the floor as if he were as ashamed as he should have been.

"Pregnant? Nina is pregnant?" Cindy stood.

"Yes."

"This can't be the same Harry Granger who said he wasn't ready to be a father when I mentioned having a baby."

"We didn't plan this."

"It just happened. You have no idea how. The pregnancy, I mean. Not the affair." She crinkled her nose. "The word 'affair' sounds too decent for what you did." Her eyes narrowed. "Or are you going to tell me that you had nothing to do with that either? That some evil genie

forced you to move into the gutter to find a female dog
to play with?"

"Look, Cindy. That's not necessary. Nina and I . . ."

"You're going to defend her? You're going to act like
she's the one who's innocent in this mess?"

"You know you and I are through." He took a step toward her.

"Don't you come any closer." She held her ground
and folded her arms across her chest. "I do now."

"It's over between us. It has been for a long time."

"Why didn't you say something to me about that?
Don't you think I needed to know?"

"We haven't . . ."

"By 'we' do you mean you and I or you and Nina? Or
you and somebody else?"

"Why make this difficult for everybody? Nina is . . ."

"Don't mention that name in my house."

"Your house?"

"It is now." Cindy clenched her teeth then took a deep
breath. "I don't intend to make it difficult for you. You
can have your name back for free. I don't want it anymore. Let's discuss the rest. You want a divorce? What
are you willing to give up to get it? This house is just for
starters. I don't intend to be the only one paying for
this." She tightened her arms across her chest and
shifted her weight. "Have you heard of the television
show *Let's Make a Deal?*"

"What do you want?" Harry had never sounded hum-
ble before. Cindy was surprised that it didn't make her
feel happy.

The hands on the grandfather clock in the hall
marched loudly around the face while Cindy thought.
She wanted her peace of mind back. She wanted tran-
quility. What she didn't want was Harry in her life. Of
the things on her wish list so far, this last was the only
thing he could give her.

By the time Harry had loaded his car with his clothes and left, Cindy felt drained. She had gotten every material thing she had asked for: the house, enough money to start her own business and support it for five years and generous alimony. She had earned every penny of it. She had stayed home to play Doctor Harry's wife instead of developing a life of her own. She wasn't sure if it was desperation or guilt that made Harry agree to her demands. It didn't matter. The result was the same. Her financial independence and the chance to start over. What she hadn't gotten was the peace of mind that she wanted.

After Harry left, she should have felt vindicated, victorious. Instead, all she felt was miserable.

She went upstairs and stopped in the hall outside the master suite. Then she trudged past and into the back guest bedroom. She swallowed hard and curled up on the blue satin bedspread. She hugged a pillow to her and finally let go of the tears of humiliation that had been building since she had walked into the examining room and was confronted by the scene that changed her life.

She closed her eyes, but the image of Harry and Nina on the examining table kept appearing in her mind like a scene stuck on replay.

Two

Marc Thomas breathed a sigh of relief as he locked the office door behind him. The late April afternoon sunshine would have been appreciated anywhere; in Detroit it was a blessing. Too many April mornings had been greeted by a snow covering that stayed for days holding low temperatures with it.

He got into his Lexus, grateful for more reasons than one that none of his little patients had an emergency today. He smiled. He couldn't remember when he had left this early on a Friday. The other doctors always kidded him about nobody else needing keys since he always opened and closed up the practice's offices anyway.

I hope Tori doesn't have plans for tonight. Lately it was as though the only way he could get to spend time with his wife was if they made an appointment. Between her physical therapy patients and his pediatric practice, one or the other was always away from home. He smiled again. *Not tonight, though. Please, not tonight.*

Marc stopped at the florist shop two blocks over and bought a bouquet of forty-five yellow roses. He could never remember what yellow roses signified to people who knew things like that; he only knew they were Tori's favorite since about a year ago.

"Forty-five?" The saleswoman repeated the number.

"That's right: forty-five."

She stared at him for a few seconds, shrugged, then

left to fill his order. He smiled. Forty-five; one for each month of marriage.

While he waited, he used his cell phone to order dinner. Lil's was a favorite of both of them and Lil's delivered. His mouth watered thinking about the smothered pork chops, candied yams and collard greens. He wasn't going to even think about the sweet potato pie he'd ordered for dessert or he'd drool all over the flower shop. A silly grin appeared. One can never have too much of sweet potatoes. Besides, they might not get to it until tomorrow.

The woman came back, repeated the number, then gave him the roses in two bunches. Carefully he carried them out and placed them on the floor on the front passenger side. He would never give Tori less than perfect flowers.

He made himself obey speed limits on the drive home. If he got a ticket it would eat up any time he gained by speeding. Another forty-five minutes and he'd be home. Half an hour after that . . . He forced himself to lighten up on the gas pedal. *One step at a time, Marc. One step at a time.*

Traffic wasn't light, but it was light enough for him to allow his mind to wander ahead. Maybe tomorrow morning, late tomorrow morning if things went according to his plans, he could bring up the subject of having kids. He frowned as he remembered the last time he had mentioned it, about two years ago.

"I'm not ready to be tied down by a kid," Tori had said.

"We could hire a nanny to help out," he had offered.

"Do you know what having a baby does to a woman's body?"

"You'll get back in shape. Look at your mother. No one would ever know that she had five children. Besides, it wouldn't matter to me." Marc grimaced as he remembered her reaction to that.

"It's not your body. Men always say things like that, but

then they start looking at other women. Besides, that's not the only reason. My practice is just building. *You* can practice medicine no matter what your physical condition. Physical therapy is different. As the name implies, it's physical. Pregnancy would limit the therapy that I could do and I'd be hampered for months before and after. Aside from all that, I just don't want a baby."

"You didn't say that before we got married. We mentioned having two or three kids."

"I changed my mind." She had glared at him. "People change their minds all the time. Not every woman needs a baby to feel fulfilled."

"I know that. But I thought we were on the same page with this. Maybe if . . ."

"I don't want to talk about this."

She had left the dining room. Marc had let the subject go, but he'd promised himself that he would bring it up at another time.

This was another time. The only children he saw belonged to somebody else and he was tired of it. He loved his patients but he wanted kids of his own. He sighed. If men had biological clocks as women did, his was ticking. And the ticking was getting louder with each patient he saw.

He maneuvered his car to the off ramp and headed to their home in Grosse Point.

He was smiling when he drove into his detached garage behind the house and parked beside Tori's Beamer. She was home. Part one was in place. He had to juggle the flowers and his key, but he didn't let that chase away his smile.

The phone rang as he got to the kitchen. Please don't let it be an emergency for me or an appointment for Tori, he thought as he reached for it.

He opened his mouth to answer it when Tori's, "Hello" sounded from the bedroom phone.

"Hey, Sweet Thing."

Tori's deep giggle at the words sounded like a foreign language to Marc. It had been a long time since he had heard any kind of happiness from her.

Marc wanted to put down the phone, but he couldn't. It was as if he had stumbled into an old radio drama and he was one of the characters. Not a quiz show, though. He didn't have to guess who's voice had cut through his marriage. He could recognize his friend Al's voice anywhere.

"So what are you up to and what are you wearing?" Al's chuckle poked at Marc. "I'd rather hear the answer to my last question first, please. Better still, why don't you come on over and show me." He laughed again. "Of course you won't be wearing it or anything else for long." His voice lowered. "Do you know how much I want you right now? Last week's fix has long worn off."

"You are a naughty man." The giggle that followed her words hurt Marc more than a punch.

He held the phone away from his ear. *I should say something.* He shook his head. *What do you say when you find out that your best friend is getting it on with your wife?*

He thought of a bumper sticker he once saw: "My best friend ran off with my wife. I miss him." At the time he had thought it was funny.

He quietly hung up the phone, picked up the roses and walked over to the wastebasket. Carefully, he stood the roses up in the container as if arranging a floral display. Then he headed for the bedroom.

Scene of the crime, ran through his head. Was it? he wondered. *Had she brought Al here to our bed?* He didn't want to know the answer to that. It wouldn't take much to push him over the edge, and that would do it. How could he expect loyalty from his friend when he didn't have it from his wife?

He went upstairs slowly, trying to give himself time to regain control. Anger pounded in his head. Counting to infinity wouldn't help. His wife and his best friend. You couldn't find much more of a stereotype than that. *They're not worth it, they're not worth it.* He tried to swallow his anger and prayed that, by the time he reached Tori, he could convince himself of that.

"How long?" He stopped in the doorway because he didn't dare go any closer to her.

Tori, leaning against the headboard, jumped when Marc walked into the bedroom.

"How long what?"

If he hadn't heard Al for himself, he would almost believe her innocence. "I would ask who you're talking to, but I'm not in the mood for any lies."

"I don't . . ."

"Cut the crap." He bunched his hands in his pockets, forcing them to stay there.

Tori stood and Marc noticed that she had on the black silk and lace teddy that he had given to her last Christmas. Had she mentioned that Marc gave it to her when she answered Al's question?

"Please don't come any closer, Tori."

"Marc . . ."

"I'm going out. When I get back I want you gone. Go to Al, go to a hotel, go to Hell. I don't care as long as you're out of my house."

He turned and left his marriage. There wasn't anything left worth saving anyway.

He walked for two reasons: One, he didn't trust himself to drive safely and, two, he needed to get rid of the anger that was still threatening to explode inside him. He speeded up his pace. He wanted to hit something, hurt something, destroy something the way his marriage had just been destroyed.

He got to the end of the block and turned the corner and broke into a jog. How long had they been cheating on him? He ran toward the next corner. And what difference did the time factor make?

He continued to run. *How could I not notice that things had reached this point? Things have been strained between me and Tori.* He shook his head. *But this. I never dreamed that this was going on. How could I have been so stupid? There must have been clues.* He rounded another corner. *And I missed them all.*

Three

The only light escaping from the stores in the small strip mall in West Philly came from an as yet unopened store. Cindy Larson, owner, worked furiously inside her shop, too busy to look outside and notice anything. She had been unpacking inventory and stocking shelves since before eight this morning; just like yesterday, and, except for a quick lunch, she was still working at getting her store ready for the grand opening. She took a deep breath. In two days. Two short, quick days. She shoved away her panic as she climbed down the stepladder and walked over to the older woman whose face gave a preview of what Cindy would probably look like in twenty some years.

"Mom, go on to church." Cindy brushed off her hands. "If you don't leave now you're going to be late for choir practice and you know Mrs. Long won't like that."

"But, Cindy, look at all this work yet to be done." Helen Larson pointed to her left, but it didn't matter which way she pointed. The view was the same on both sides: Boxes, most opened but not emptied, and some still sealed, filled the aisle of the soon-to-be "The Bridal Shop." The shelves in the other half of the store, "Crafters' Delight," were already stocked.

"I can't help but look at it."

"I swear, it's a wonder that we can find air to breathe among all this stuff."

"It's not 'stuff,' Mom. It's my inventory." Cindy

grinned. "Of course, I have to admit, right now it does look more like 'stuff.'" They both laughed. "And I hope it doesn't take as long to finish as it looks like it will. A lot of it is empty boxes."

"Do you really think you can sell these?" Helen Larson held up a pack of strings of black pearls. "For a wedding?"

"Black and white weddings are always popular. Remember Sonya Dyson's wedding last year?" Cindy set the pack on top of the others in the display box on the shelf. Strings of tiny red pearls filled the box next to it.

"I remember." Helen shook her head as she touched a red pearl. "Call me old-school, old-fashioned or just plain old, but I still have trouble with black, and red too for that matter, for a wedding. Weddings should be light. Otherwise it seems like tempting bad luck."

"I got married in peaches and cream. It doesn't get much lighter than that." Cindy sighed and shook her head. "Still, look what happened to my marriage."

"That was the exception. If you're marrying a no-good man, the wedding color scheme won't make a bit of difference. You could get married in white with white flowers and decorations and your attendants dressed in white and it wouldn't matter."

"That's what I'm saying." Cindy nodded. "Black is okay. Purple and green plaid with touches of yellow would be okay, too, if the groom is decent." Cindy stared at an empty shelf before she blinked. "That's the hard part. Finding a good, or even an okay, man to marry."

"Baby, that skunk that you used to be chained to showed his stripe almost two years ago. It's way past time to get over him."

"I am over him. I even dumped his last name and took back my own."

"If you're so over him, then how come you've been living like a nun since you moved back here?" Helen shook her head. "Now, don't get me wrong. There is nothing wrong with nuns. I admire them for their sacrifices for their religion. That rat, Harry, however, is as far from a religion as you can get unless you count Devil worship."

"I've been busy since I got here. It takes a lot of time to find a suitable location, get all the necessary paperwork done, get the store modified, order stock, hire helpers, buy—"

"I will grant you that setting up and opening a business takes a lot of time. However, you have to eat sometime, yet when young Brother Gibson invited you to dinner a few months back, you turned him down without a bit of hesitation. Crushed the poor man's spirit."

"Most likely only his ego was hurt. I'm sure he got over it. I'm not going out with somebody just to keep from hurting his feelings." She shrugged. "He probably just moved on to the next eligible, or maybe not so eligible, woman."

"See, now, that's what I'm talking about. Brother Gibson isn't like that, and before Harry, you would never have thought, let alone talked, like that. You won't even let me introduce you to Jean's son. He's a nice man, a very nice man."

"Before Harry I was naive. That dirty dog was an education in the nature of men."

"At least we agree about what Harry is, but I don't agree about him being an example of how men are." She stared at Cindy. "Your father and I were married for thirty years. He never cheated on me." She smiled. "And I never cheated on him." She picked up a spray of miniature pink roses. "You know, women do their share of running around, too. Now take Jean's son. You two have something in common. He's divorced, too." She fixed Cindy with a stare. "He caught his wife cheating on him."

"So you think two losers might make each other winners?"

"I think two nice people deserve another chance to find a soul mate."

"I know that women run around, too, nowadays." She blinked hard and sighed. "Things were so different back in your and Dad's day."

"Every generation thinks that. There are people of all ages who don't know what a commitment is. They've always been around."

"Anyway, it's not worth trying to sift the wheat from the chaff. There's not enough wheat and too much chaff."

Helen frowned. "I'm not sure what Reverend Dent would think about your analogy. I do know he'd disagree about there being no good eligible men out there. Or women."

"He's a minister. He's supposed to be hopeful about the nature of people."

"He's also a realist: He knows there are good folks and cheaters among both sexes. He would just emphasize the good." She touched Cindy's arm. "Which is what you should do. Why not just meet him?"

"Who?"

"Jean's son. What would be the harm? You never know. You might hit it off."

"I told you. I am not looking for someone. I am happy with my life just as it is. Besides, he's a doctor."

"So?"

"Been there, done that, you know the result."

"After all of my setting good examples, my daughter is prejudiced. I have raised a bigot."

"I am not prejudiced."

"What do you call a bias against an entire group of people?"

"When we're talking about letting one back into my personal life, we call it learning from our mistakes." She frowned. "How did we get on this subject anyway?"

"I'm trying in desperation to convince you not to give

up looking for a good man. There's one out there for you, but you have to be receptive."

"I'm busy. And I'm not looking."

"If you don't seek you will never find."

"That's okay with me. Some things are not meant for everybody." She set a display box of small easels on the shelf at the end of the row. "Maybe I'll get a cat."

"Don't you dare." Her mother glared at her. "You will not be one of those women who substitutes cats for children."

"I'm talking about one cat, not a whole litter. It would be company."

"A cat is not company; it's a cop-out. Another person is company. A cat is no substitute for a man in your life and in your bed."

"Mom." Shock filled Cindy's voice. "How can you talk like that?"

"I'm speaking the truth." Helen stared at her. "And it should go without saying, since you know me so well, that the man should be your husband."

"I'm not getting married again, and it's okay if I don't."

"I don't want to accept that, and it's not okay. If you don't find somebody soon, I'll never be a grandmother."

"Mom . . ."

"That's the order of things, you know: You have a child, then, after the child is old enough, he or she gets married. Then, after the proper length of time has passed, your child has a child. That's how people get to be grandparents." She stared at Cindy. "Which all of my friends are. I did my part. Now it's your turn."

"I can't believe you. You sound like a kid asking for a toy for Christmas."

"I feel like a kid living in a tenth-floor apartment in Center City asking for a Clydesdale horse for whatever."

"At least you realize how ridiculous your request is."

She frowned at her mother. "What is it exactly that you're asking for?"

"I'm only asking you to keep an open mind when you meet an eligible man. Don't close the door on him until you're sure that you don't want to let him in. There's no harm in that. Okay?"

"Go to choir rehearsal, Mom. You're really going to be late."

"If you didn't believe in love, why did you open a bridal shop and start your wedding consultant business?"

"You asked me that before and my answer hasn't changed: I chose this because there are a lot of women who do believe in love. I've done my research. Anything connected to weddings is a highly lucrative business if it's done right. There will always be women chasing the rainbow, hoping to find a treasure at the end." She sighed. "Owning my own shop is my treasure. Besides, I'm not just counting on the bridal shop; I have the craft shop, too."

"I can see that part. Crafting is a big hobby. Look at all of the television shows about crafts. They have a whole channel on it. If something exists, somebody has a show teaching you how to make it. You always did like creating things, so that shop was a natural progression." She shrugged. "I guess with your double degree in Fine Arts and Business, you know what you're doing. A bridal shop for before they get married and a craft shop for afterward." She fixed Cindy with a stare. "After they give grandkids to their parents, they can bring the kids in to learn how to make projects, too." Cindy sighed and shook her head slowly, but she let her mother continue. She ignored the hard stare sent her way. "At least you know what you're doing as far as your business decisions are concerned. I'll give you that. Now as far as your personal life is concerned. . . ."

"Mom, please don't go there again."

Helen sighed. "All right. It doesn't seem to be doing any

good anyway; at least not tonight. I won't make any promises about not trying in the future." She looked down the aisle. "Are you sure you can finish this by yourself?"

"It only looks this bad because of the empty boxes and packaging materials scattered around. I have all day tomorrow and Andrea and Debbie will be here to help me. You'll be here after school, too, right?"

"As soon as I send the little darlings home."

"Then don't worry about this and go before you become the first to get kicked out of the choir at First African Baptist."

"Do you want me to at least take some of these empty boxes out?" Helen frowned and shook her head. "There sure are a lot of them."

"No, Mom, but thanks. I can handle them."

"If you're sure . . ."

"I'm sure. Go to church." She and her mother hugged.

"Don't you stay here too long tonight. Remember tomorrow is another day and whatever other clichés are appropriate. I'd also remind you about all work and no play making Jill just as dull as Jack, but I'm sure you don't want to hear that, especially since I'm not just talking about tonight. So I'll let it go."

"Thank you. I appreciate it."

"At least I'll let it go for *tonight*." She smiled at her only child. Cindy shook her head, but she smiled back. Then they both laughed.

"I love you, Mom."

"I loved you first." She kissed Cindy's cheek.

Arm in arm, they walked to the door. They hugged once more before Helen left. Then Cindy walked back to where they had stopped stocking the shelves. She hoped that what she had told her mother was true: that there wasn't as much to do as it looked.

"I must have been out of my mind when I set this Saturday as opening day," she said. She shook her head. "I'm so off the deep end that I'm even talking to myself."

She looked at the boxes surrounding her. Then she pulled the tape from a box and began putting tiny white floral sprays on the shelf next to the pink ones.

She worked her way down the aisle, grateful that she had drawn a diagram and that she had set the boxes beside the shelves where the contents would go. That would save some time. She tried not to think of the conversation she had just had with her mother, but her mind went there anyway.

Mom just doesn't understand. Cindy looked at the place she had just filled. Then she shifted the white ribbons and maroon ribbons so that they contrasted rather than blended with the other colors already on the shelf.

Dad was Mom's first love and they were still so much in love when he died four years ago that everyone could see it. She sighed. *They don't come like that anymore. They went the way of the dinosaurs.* She frowned. *I wonder if there are any theories of what happened to the good men. That would be more helpful than anything about creatures that disappeared before people came along.* She shrugged, took the last roll of ribbon from a box and put it on the shelf.

Good, faithful men have probably always been an endangered species. Mom just doesn't know it because she got lucky her first time around.

Cindy worked her way down another aisle, methodically changing empty shelves into possibilities for brides-to-be. As she reached the end of the row, her stomach rumbled and she looked at her watch.

"Nine o'clock." She looked back at the row she had just completed. Aside from the last group of empty boxes cluttering the aisle, this one was ready for customers. "Not bad for a day's work."

She arched her back and then rolled her head from shoulder to shoulder to try to get the kinks out. Then she began packing small boxes into larger ones to lessen her trips to the dumpster.

She took the empty boxes toward the front of the shop. There she looked at the clutter waiting for her and sighed.

The countertops and cashier aisles were also stacked with boxes. She should have gotten rid of them as she emptied them. Or she should have at least started earlier so she could have used her mother's help. She frowned. She should have done a lot of things earlier. One thing she should have done was put Harry's behind out of her life. Better still, she never should have let him into her life in the first place. *Don't go over that again.* She shook her head. *It's just going to end the same way.*

She shook Harry away, propped open the door and dragged a set of boxes outside.

Back inside, she walked to the rear of the store and peeked into the small room off to the left at the back of the bridal shop. Plastic-covered gowns hung from the racks on both sides; white and colors not in the rainbow billowed out into the room as if trying to see what was going on. The large table in the middle of the room held several sewing machines, and a small table to the side held magazines and pictures of other gown choices.

Mattie Dalton's Bridal Gown Shop was ready. Cindy smiled. Mattie was the piece that really made this a one-stop shop for women with dreams tied up in wedding plans. *Gowns from Mattie and the rest from me.* Cindy's smile disappeared and a sigh escaped. Then she shrugged. *Whatever floats their boats.*

When Mattie had approached her, Cindy had been working on how to ensure that the women who came to her wouldn't have to run around to different stores. Mattie provided the solution. Cindy's smile returned. Everything the brides-to-be needed was under one roof. Her roof. Mattie's made the slogan true. Cindy grabbed another set of boxes and started clearing the aisle in that section.

After I put all of the boxes and packing materials into the Dumpster at the end of the strip mall, I'm out of here.

When she made each trip, she had to stand on tip-toe to get the boxes to go inside the container and even then she had to throw them. Only a couple bounced back to her. If Mutombo ever wanted to practice his jumpshot some place other than a basketball court, this was an ideal place.

She lost track of the number of trips. Just as well. Counting wouldn't lessen the number and it might make her more tired, as if that were possible. She stretched her arms up as high as she could and rounded her back. In spite of her tiredness, she smiled as she dragged what she hoped was the last of the boxes and wrappings out of the store.

Her new bottle of lavender-scented bubble bath was calling to her from home and she couldn't wait to answer it.

After managing to get the last batch to stay in the dumpster, Cindy went back inside to take a final look around. With the aisles cleared, she could see how much they had accomplished in the past week. She smiled again.

Owning her own business was no longer just an idea in her head. Cindy's Shops were a reality; and they would be opened as scheduled the day after tomorrow even if she had to spend tomorrow night here. She smiled.

Customers responding to the print ads in the neighborhood newspapers and flyers and ads on local radio stations would not be disappointed. She frowned. At least not about her opening as scheduled. She hoped they would be just as satisfied after they saw her merchandise.

She also hoped that sales figures would show that combining a bridal shop with a craft shop made for good business.

She picked up one of the flyers left over from those that were distributed in the neighborhood earlier in the day. She smiled at the slogan covering the top half of the blue paper: "Cindy's Shops: The Bridal Shop: From 'Yes' to 'I Do' Under One Roof." The bottom half advertised the craft portion of the store: "'Crafters' Delight: If We Don't Have What You're Looking For, We Have Something Better.'" At the very bottom was an announcement of the first workshops scheduled for next week and the invitation to pick up a list of planned workshops for the next month for both stores.

She was not going to think about the two workshops she had to run: one for brides-to-be on Wednesday night and one for kids on Saturday morning. By that time next week, she'd be more rested. She stretched. *I hope.* She smiled. She loved doing crafts. After things settled into a routine, she'd add a workshop for general crafters if there seemed to be an interest.

She put the flyer back on the counter and shrugged. She had no control over customer response now. It was too late to change anything even if she wanted to. Either they came, or they didn't.

She went to the door but stopped before she went out. She shook her head. Then she went to the tiny office at the back for her purse. Good thing it's attached, she thought as she tapped the side of her head.

As she got into the car, she thought again about relaxing in the tub. Too bad she didn't have a way to shorten the forty-five minute trip to Mt. Airy. She sighed. She'd better be happy that she didn't have to travel City Avenue in rush-hour traffic. That would have at least doubled the time it took to get home from West Philly.

She settled herself under the seat belt and turned the key. Nothing. She wasn't going to count the soft click the car made as a real sound since it was not a substitute for the engine noise. She tried again with the same result.

Frowning didn't help. Neither did trying a third time and then smacking the steering wheel. The idea of taking a soothing bath in an hour disappeared.

She reached for her cell phone, trying to be grateful that she at least had road service. Her gratitude slowly faded as she touched the empty holder. *Where did I have that phone last?* She traced her steps mentally and remembered. She had used it to verify that the clown would indeed be there on Saturday for the craft shop and that the model dressed as a bride would be there for the bridal shop. Cindy frowned. When she finished the calls, she had put the phone on her desk next to the not-yet-connected store phone. On her desk.

She sighed as she left the car and went back to the shop. She reached into her purse for the keys to the store. Her middle tightened when she found nothing but space in the outside pocket where the keys belonged. She checked her pants pockets. Then she checked the rest of her purse. She did not have the keys. Where had she put them?

She went back to the car and methodically took everything out of her purse. Then she searched the seat and the floor, hoping the keys had fallen out. In desperation, she searched the space between the passenger side seat and the door. Sometimes things dropped into the little spot there. She shook her head. But not this time.

She sat back and did her Trace Your Memory exercise again. A sinking feeling made her stop. She had two possibilities and neither one made her happy. Either they were with her cell phone and the two were keeping each other company on her desk, or they had dropped into one of the empty boxes; one of the boxes that she had tossed out.

She looked out at the Dumpster. The term "Dumpster diving" came to mind. It was not a pleasant thought, but it didn't go away. She got out of the car again and looked around the mall.

Why did malls look so sinister after the shops were closed and the streets were deserted? She sighed. One of her choices for a location had been a mini mall with a restaurant. Right now that other location seemed like a better choice.

The only sounds seemed to come from streets blocks away. She felt as if she were the only one awake in the neighborhood. What was she going to do? Walk to a pay phone and call her mother from rehearsal? Call the road service? Where was a pay phone, anyhow?

Why wasn't there one in this mall? Tomorrow she'd call the phone company and find out. Didn't they know that people did dumb things like this and that they needed access to a phone?

She glanced to the sidewalk that, in spite of the street light, looked dark and forbidding. She couldn't leave here. She needed those keys. She didn't have time to wait for a locksmith to come tomorrow. The only way she could get the store ready in time was if she started early tomorrow morning.

She sighed again and looked at the giant Dumpster. It looked bigger. And higher.

Four

Cindy looked around again as if she could wish for daylight and it would appear. She sighed. Might as well add dozens of people to the list. She shuddered. She wasn't sure if she should be happy or scared that the mall and the streets were quiet and empty.

She took a deep breath and headed for the dumpster. *Why does it have to be so big? And so high?* Throwing things in had been easy. She stopped in front of it. Taking them out was another matter altogether. How was she going to get inside? Maybe, if she could reach the bar part way up, she could use it for a step.

The thought of climbing inside made her shudder. If she could get into her store she could get a ladder. She shook her head. *If I could get into the store, I wouldn't need a ladder.* She chewed on her lip. *If I had my phone I could call Mom.* She shook her head again. She still had to get inside the Dumpster; that was the only way she could get the keys back. Still, her mind searched for possibilities. She stared at the giant container again. She had to get inside.

"Is something the matter?"

Cindy whirled around at the sound of a deep voice. "What did you say?" Where had he come from? As scared as she was, why hadn't she heard him coming? She held her purse close to her chest as if it were a shield. Or a weapon. A weapon. She slipped her hand into the pocket at the side of her purse and wrapped her fingers around the small cylinder attached to her ring of house keys. She eased the bunch into her coat pocket. At least she had pockets.

She tried to remember the instructions for using the can of Mace that her mother had talked her into buying. All the while she stared at the stranger.

"Are you all right? I asked if something was the matter." The man stopped walking toward her when Cindy took a step backward.

Cindy stared at him. He didn't look like the type who would harm anyone. Then she thought of the serial killers that had been caught. All of them looked respectable. Some even wore suits and ties. Judging books by covers had been disastrous for a lot of people. She glared. Even her. That was partly how she got involved with Harry. If he had looked like the toad that he was, would she have let him into her life? She'd like to think that she looked for inner beauty, but you can't lie to yourself and be believed for long.

She backed up another step. Had those killers stalked their victims first? She tried to remember. She did, but it didn't help. Some had, but some had killed whomever had been unfortunate enough to cross their paths. She backed up again and looked at her car. *Can I make it? And then what? The stupid car won't start.* She stared at him again.

His dark blue coat made him look taller than he probably was. She let her gaze travel up to his face. No. He *was* tall. A whole lot taller than her five-foot-eight. And he had the long legs to go with his height. There was no way she could outrun him.

"Miss? What's the matter?"

"What are you doing here?" Cindy pulled out the can of Mace and pointed it at him.

"My office is over there." He pointed to a building on

the other side of the narrow strip of grass separating the two parking lots. All the time he stared at her.

"It is, huh?" Cindy was still exploring her options, which were too few. Run and . . . What? Where? If by some miracle she reached the car, then what? How strong was the glass in the windows? Would he go find another victim? Or would he be mad enough to try to get her?

"Yes, it is."

"What is?"

"My office is in that building over there."

"How do I know that you're telling me the truth?"

"Why would I lie to you?"

"What kind of business do you have that's open so late?"

"What are *you* doing here?"

He had the nerve to question her. "If you must know, I was working in my shop."

"I might ask you the same thing about your business being open so late. It's just as late for you as it is for me."

"I open on Saturday so I have a lot of work to do. I"— she frowned at him—"Why am I explaining things to you?"

"Because I asked." He smiled. She shook her head. Harry had a nice smile, too.

"I asked you first." How could such a little can of Mace be so heavy? She frowned. Was Mace one of those heavy elements she should have learned about in chemistry class?

His stare held hers. Then he shrugged. "Look. I just finished working on some records. I came out to go home when I saw you. I figured you must have some kind of trouble or you wouldn't be out here this time of night in the deserted parking lot all alone."

The Mace was getting heavier, but Cindy kept her hand out in spite of the tremors creeping in. "My car won't start."

"If you intend to use that Mace, you'd better turn it around or, if you use it, you won't be able to see to drive even if your car was any good."

"Is that a variation of 'Who is that behind you?' so I'll take my gaze off you so you can grab me?"

"You shouldn't watch horror movies or crime shows if you're that impressionable."

"I'm not impressionable." At least not anymore. "And my car *is* good."

"Then why won't it start?"

"I don't know."

"Did you call somebody?"

Cindy hesitated. *If he was harmless, why would he ask that?* She stared harder at him. *If she lied, and he left, who might come along next?*

"You didn't. Why not? Are you a mechanic? Don't you see how deserted it is out here?" He shifted positions. "Either use the Mace or put it away. Your hand must be tired."

"No, I am not a mechanic." The Mace felt as if it had gained ten pounds. She glared at him. "I left my phone inside my shop."

"And?"

"And I can't find my keys."

"How did you get into your car? Did you leave it unlocked?"

"Of course not. I have better sense than that. The keys to the shop are on a separate ring."

"And the keys to the shop are inside. Do you want to use my phone to call somebody to bring you your extra set?"

"I don't know if the keys are in the shop or not. I don't think they are."

"What do you mean, you don't know?"

"I think I might have thrown them out in one of the boxes." She pointed to the Dumpster.

"In there?"

"Yes. In there. At least I think so." She wondered if she looked as sheepish as she felt. "And I . . . I don't have a spare set."

"How could you not have a spare set? And how did your keys end up in the Dumpster? How could that happen?"

"You don't have to use that 'You must be stupid' tone of voice. If I knew how it happened, I'd have prevented it, wouldn't I?"

"I guess so."

"You guess so? Do you think I'd put myself in a dangerous situation with a stranger who might be a serial killer on purpose?"

"No. I . . ." He shifted positions and frowned at her. "Did you just call me a serial killer?"

"If the shoe fits . . ." Cindy inched closer to her car.

"It doesn't." He glared at her. "Listen, lady, I saw a woman in a deserted parking lot and thought she needed help." His chin jutted out. "I am not now nor have I ever been a serial killer."

"I didn't say you were."

"Just the same as." He turned to go.

"Wait." He turned around but Cindy didn't say anything.

"Yeah?"

"I . . . I need to search through those boxes and I can't reach them."

"Are you asking for help from a serial killer?"

"I didn't . . ."

"Come on. The sooner we start the sooner we find your keys and the sooner we finish. I'll try to control my killer urges until you're gone. I'll be like the troll under the bridge and wait for the next one."

"I didn't mean to imply . . . That is, I . . ." She stopped stammering and looked at him. "Thank you."

"I'm only doing this because if I don't and I look in the paper tomorrow and see where a young woman was killed tonight by a real"—he stared at her—"a real serial killer, I don't want your murder on my conscience. Besides, it might be bad for my business. Nobody but curiosity seekers would come here, and they'd quit after a while. Then the whole mall would die because some woman threw her keys into a Dumpster." He headed for the Dumpster. "Are you coming or not? They are your keys. The least you could do is help look for them." He walked a few more steps then turned to look at her.

Cindy closed her mouth on her response. A bird in the hand was better than no bird at all. She stared back. Then she followed him. If he meant to harm her he would have done it already.

She watched as he used the handle for a step as easily as if it were a curb. By the time she reached him, he was holding the first box.

"Move out of the way." He dropped a batch of nestled boxes after she moved to the side. "Check inside as I drop them to you. If we're lucky, they'll be in one of the last boxes you got rid of."

She dragged the boxes out of the way and separated them. "If I were lucky, I wouldn't have lost the keys in the first place."

"You didn't lose them." He dropped another set down. "You threw them away."

"By accident. It was an accident." She repacked the first set and started searching the second.

"Whatever you say." Another group of boxes hit the ground. "Besides, if you weren't lucky, a serial killer would have come along instead of a good Samaritan."

"That's true." She repacked the second set of boxes and shoved them beside the first set.

"How many of these came from your shop?"

"All of them so far." She dug through the packing material in another box.

"What kind of business do you have?"

"I own a double store: a craft store and a bridal shop."

"Bridal shop? You sell wedding gowns?"

"Typical male response. There is more to a wedding besides the gown."

"I'm in the Dumpster searching for your keys and you insult me? How many women would do this for you?"

"My mother."

"Mothers don't count when it comes to helping their children. They're obligated."

"If I knew your mother, I'd tell her that you said she doesn't count." Cindy set more boxes aside.

"Do you always twist words around? When you aren't throwing away your keys, I mean."

"I didn't . . ." A box hit the ground and another sound besides cardboard hitting the concrete escaped from it. "Wait a minute." She pulled the large box closer. Then she took out a smaller box. A still smaller box was inside that. "I thought I heard a clink."

Slowly she eased a wad of packing paper from the box and was rewarded with a clunk. "Here they are." She held them in the air as if she had just won a contest and they were the victory trophy. "My keys. I knew it." She twirled around in a circle. Then she smiled up at him. "I won't need a locksmith. Do you know what they charge?"

"No, I can't say that I do." He climbed down and landed beside her. He stood there and brushed off his hands. She didn't move away. "I've never thrown away my keys," he continued. "If I had, I'm sure I would have had a spare set." He brushed his hands again. "Do you know that Tony's shoe repair shop down at the corner makes keys?"

"I know, but I've been too busy. I'll get a set made tomorrow." She was too grateful to get angry at him. "Thank you." She held out her hand.

"Are you sure I'm safe enough for you to get close enough to touch?" He didn't wait for an answer. Instead he took her hand and held it. What was supposed to be a handshake lasted way beyond the time limit for that. They both pulled away at the same time. "We'd better clean up this mess." He nodded toward the boxes spread out all around.

Cindy looked at the boxes. They looked like a tower of giant building blocks had toppled. "Yeah. I'm not even open yet. I don't want the trash removal company to get mad at me."

"You go make your call. I'll start on this."

"You sure? I put them in the Dumpster before. I can do it again."

"Am I back to serial killer status?"

"No. It's just that"—she shrugged—"you've spent so much time helping me already."

"Do you want me to leave you here alone?"

"No." She answered before he finished the question. Then she shrugged. "But I thought you might have somewhere to go."

"Go make your call."

"Okay." She turned away then turned back. "I won't be too long."

Marc watched her go. He did not like what he was feeling. Did she realize that she had a little wiggle that showed even when she wore baggy sweatpants? He frowned. Tori had a wiggle, too, although hers had been deliberate. Probably still was. Planned. Calculated. Meant to attract the attention of any male in her vicinity. *Is that how she caught Al? Or was it simply a case of a player attracting another player?* He shook his head. It didn't matter. The result was the same. Besides, that was a long time ago. Tori was out of his life and, he had thought, off his mind.

He began packing small boxes into larger ones, glad for something to do. It wasn't hard work, but maybe physical activity would block any mental activity.

Who was this scatterbrained woman? He threw the set

of boxes he had just finished into the Dumpster and grabbed some more. And what did he care?

He glanced toward the store, glad that he couldn't see her. Was her face as beautiful as he thought, or was it that the light was dim and he couldn't see her imperfections?

He threw another set of boxes away and looked at the light directly above him. It was almost as bright as day. Why couldn't she be plain looking? What he needed was somebody with *inner* beauty. *No, no, no.* He dropped a box. *I am not looking for anyone, period.* He picked the box back up. Not inner nor outer beauty, but especially not outer beauty. He glanced at the store again. Did he see a dimple when she finally smiled? He held a box as if he couldn't remember whether he was taking it out of the Dumpster or putting it in.

Why did he have to pick this night to work on his patients' records? He sighed. What would have happened to her if he hadn't been here? Who would have come along? He tossed a box into the Dumpster and smiled. He couldn't imagine her climbing into a Dumpster and crawling around in the trash. If she had somehow managed to get into the Dumpster, how would she have gotten out? Would she have been stuck until morning? He laughed even though he felt guilty. Then he laughed again. Had anyone ever had to spend the night in a Dumpster? His laughed eased into a smile. He was glad she hadn't had to.

Five

Cindy fumbled with the keys and dropped them twice before she managed to get the door open. Still, she didn't look back at him. Maybe by the time she finished making the call, he would have changed his mind about waiting for her and be gone. "That's rotten," she told herself. "The man helped you. He got inside the Dumpster for you. Now that you don't need him, you want him to disappear." Even though she was the only one who knew what she had been thinking, she still felt ashamed.

What is wrong with me? He was just a stranger who, lucky for her, had been here when she needed him. She picked up the phone. To him she was just a woman who did something stupid. He only hung around to ease his conscience. She shook her head. It didn't matter why he helped her. Lucky for her he did. What kind of office does he have? She never even noticed what was in the building. The entrance into this lot was from the other end. She had been so focused on her shops that she had barely glanced beyond them. She called the road service and gave her location.

"Ten or fifteen minutes," the woman had said. "We have a truck in the area."

After repeating what the woman told her, and thanking her profusely, she accepted the fact that she had gotten a break in this mess. Then she went to the entrance of the store.

She watched as the man threw a box into the Dumpster, and she couldn't help but notice how easy it was for him; no struggling, no wasted effort. *Does he work out?* She shook her head. *What did she care? She wouldn't see him again.* She shrugged. *Well, maybe one more time.* She'd go over to his store tomorrow and thank him again. Without his help she would have . . . What? Spent the night scrunched down in the car hoping nobody would notice her or that somebody wouldn't decide to try to steal the car?

She kept her keys in her hand and went outside. She was glad she didn't have to find out what would have happened without . . . She frowned. She didn't even know his name. She shrugged. That was easy to fix.

She walked over, put her purse into the car after making sure the alarm was in valet mode, then went to help with what was left of the boxes.

"How did you make out?"

"Great. They said ten or fifteen minutes."

"Where are they? Around the corner?" He stopped moving boxes and stared at her. *Yeah, she's just as beautiful as I thought, even with the smudge on her cheek and her hair escaping from a scarf.* He tightened his grip on the box. He'd lose his "Knight to the rescue" status if he tried to wipe the smudge away. For a few seconds he was tempted to risk it.

"Is something the matter?" She frowned.

"It's nothing." His common sense returned and he threw the box away.

"She said that a truck is in the area."

"Who said?"

"The receptionist at the road service office."

"Oh." He grabbed another box without looking at her again. "We'd better hurry and finish then."

"Yes." Cindy stuffed a box into another and lifted it.

"Here, let me do that." He took it from her.

"But I did it . . ."

"I know you did it all by yourself before." He stared at her. "And look what happened. Who knows what you'll throw away this time." He took the box from her and tossed it into the container.

"That was an accident."

"I hope so. I hope you don't make a habit of throwing away keys or anything else that you want." He stared at her. "You know we had this conversation a few minutes ago."

"Look, I—"

"I'm just kidding about you throwing away good stuff. Hand me that other box. We're on a deadline here."

"Oh." She handed him the box and looked around. Two more and nobody would ever know they had emptied the container. She pulled the last two over and watched as they disappeared inside. She smiled when he climbed down and turned to her.

"Thank you. I don't want to think what might have happened if you weren't here."

"Have I lost my serial killer status?"

"I'm sorry about that." She shrugged. "My mother always accused me of having an overactive imagination."

"Apology accepted. I know it's late, but there's a little diner two blocks over and it's open all night. Do you want to go have a cup of coffee or a late-night snack?"

"Do you realize that I don't even know your name?" She frowned. "What kind of store do you have anyway?"

"It's not a store, it's an office." He held out his hand. "I'm Marc Thomas. What's your name?"

"I'm Cindy Larson. What kind of office is it? Are you a real estate agent?" She placed her hand in his.

"No. It's a doctor's office. My three partners and I have our practice over there. We've been there for a few years."

"A doctor's office? You're a doctor." She pulled her hand from his.

"That's what my license says."

"And that's your office over there."

"Yes, our office is over there." He frowned at her and put his hand down to his side. "What's the matter now?"

"Nothing." A doctor, and a charming one at that. As Yogi Berra said, "It's déjà vu all over again." She shook her head. No way. He wasn't getting that close to her. She put her hand into her pocket. "Thank you, doctor."

"Doctor? Even my little patients add my name to my title." He smiled. "I'm a pediatrician."

"That's nice." She glanced down to the street. "I wonder where that tow truck is."

"It's been barely ten minutes since you called."

"Oh. Yes." She glanced at him. "Look. I'll understand if you want to leave."

"Are you saying that you'd rather wait here alone than with me?"

"No. I . . ." A tow truck pulled into the lot and stopped beside them. Cindy was glad that she didn't have to finish her answer.

After making sure that he was in the right place and verifying her insurance number and the problem, the driver opened the hood. Cindy watched as he attached wires to her battery.

"I guess you'll be okay," Marc's voice was low.

"Yes. Thank you again, doctor."

"My name is Marc. 'Doctor' is my professional title, not my name." He walked away. He quickly covered the distance to his car, got in and never glanced back at Cindy.

She watched his car leave the parking lot. A doctor. Why did he have to be a doctor? Why not anything else except a doctor?

She walked over to her car and looked under the hood as if she could see the battery charging. She tried not to feel regret. After all, she hadn't spent much time with him. What could she possibly regret? She blinked hard. What might have been, was the answer. She shook her head. *There is no "might have been." I don't care what he is, I don't want him in my life.* She glared. *Or anybody else.*

She sat in her car and waited. The driver had come quickly, but she still felt as if he had gotten there too late.

In fifteen minutes she was on her way home. The idea of a relaxing bubble bath wasn't as appealing anymore. A doctor. He was a doctor. A nice doctor. She frowned as she drove down Fifty-fourth Street. Harry had been nice, too. Helpful. Harry had fallen all over himself being accommodating when they first met. Look where that led. She sighed. Why couldn't Marc be a realtor as she had thought?

She turned north to City Avenue, no longer in a hurry to get home. Usually she thought of her home as cozy and friendly. Tonight the words empty and lonely came to mind.

Marc kept his car within the speed limits as he drove home. *Typical female. Use you to get what they want and when they have it and they have no more use for you, they dump you like Cindy did her trash.* He stopped for a red light. *Just like Tori had dumped me.* He shook his head. That wasn't true. Tori hadn't dumped him. She would still be using him if he hadn't found out what she was. A horn blew behind him and he moved through the intersection.

In spite of his efforts, large eyes in a beautiful face kept coming back to him. Finally he let Cindy stay. It was time to quit letting Tori affect his life. She had moved on. He could do the same. He frowned. Couldn't he?

What does Cindy have against doctors? Whatever it is, it's important enough to make her slam the door on me.

He turned off City Avenue and onto Lincoln Drive and headed toward Mt. Airy still wondering. His frown remained as he reached his house on St. Martin's Lane and pulled into his driveway. Was it worth trying to find out?

He went into his empty house still thinking about it, but he had already decided. He had a full schedule tomorrow morning, but after that he'd drop by her shop. He didn't want anything from her except an explanation. He'd come right out and ask her. He was known for being straightforward. He picked up the mail from the floor under the mail slot. His attitude marched back.

First, I go over to see if she needs help and she accuses me of being a serial killer. A serial killer, of all things. Not a carjacker. Not even a rapist. A serial killer. He dropped his keys into the basket on the hall table. *But do I let that stop me? Oh, no. Being the good guy that I am, I still hang around and offer to help her find her keys that she threw away.* He jerked off his jacket. *How many people do I know who threw away their keys?* He glared even though there was nobody to see it. *None, that's how many.*

He hung the jacket in the hall closet. *I climbed into the Dumpster for her. Anything might have been in there: garbage, dead animals. Rats.* He frowned. *Dead people. That has happened.* His face relaxed. Now his imagination was as bad as hers. He shook his head. *Garbage would have been bad enough. A Dumpster. I climbed into a Dumpster. Who knew what was underneath the mountain of boxes, most of which she threw in there?*

He checked the answering machine and was glad that the red light was steady. He was on a roll and didn't want to be stopped.

She found her keys. Thanks to me, she found her keys. Still I offer to wait around until the mechanic comes, as if I don't have a life. You don't have a life, a little voice reminded him. You work, you go to church, you watch a little television and that's it. Once a week you have dinner with your mother. Your mother. He frowned. *That doesn't have anything to do with anything. I don't want anything from her except an explanation. I earned that. Digging in that trash bought it for me.*

Tomorrow, after his last patient left, he'd go right over there and get it.

He got ready for bed, still thinking about seeing her tomorrow and looking forward to it. Only to hear her explanation, his mind added.

Cindy finally gave up waiting for the bath to soothe her mind and climbed out of the huge clawfoot tub. She wrapped the red bath towel around her and blew out the candles. Her muscles felt relaxed enough to continue with their job again tomorrow, but her mind was another story.

Why couldn't he have his office somewhere else? Why had she been so friendly? Because he seemed like a nice guy. Why hadn't she asked in the beginning what he did? Because she was focused on her problem. She appreciated his help. Really she did. Something terrible could have happened to her if he hadn't come over. Still, she wouldn't have been so friendly if she had known. She shrugged.

Truthfully, she hadn't been very friendly anyway. At least not at first. She dried her legs. Later was different. Something seemed to kick in between them. When he asked her to go with him for a snack she had been about to go. She shook her head. *Stupid. Harry should have taught me better, but no. I must have a defective cautious gene. Maybe it was replaced by stupidity.*

She finished drying off and opened the lavender-scented lotion. It was a good thing she had asked who he was, or rather what he did. It would have been awkward to be sitting in a restaurant with him when she decided that she didn't want to know him better.

Just as well she found out. She didn't need any more

turmoil in her life; opening the business provided enough. She didn't need the problems and complications that come with having a man in your life at any time, but especially right now.

She pulled on her red T-shirt nightgown and climbed between the cotton sheets, trying to ignore the chill. Next week she'd have to get out the flannel sheets. She'd need the warmth they gave to her bed.

She turned off the light. Although she had the whole bed to herself, she stayed on the side she had always used when she was still with Harry. She turned over. Some habits die hard. She scooted to the middle. She could choose whichever side she wanted. She could even choose to sleep in one of the other bedrooms, if she wanted. This was her bed in her house and she didn't have to share either with anybody.

Usually that fact gave her satisfaction. Tonight it just made her feel more alone.

The lavender's reputation for helping to relax a person was in question tonight.

Six

"Coming." Cindy scrambled down the short stepladder at the far end of the ribbon aisle. *Debbie and Marie must have forgotten to take the keys with them when they went to lunch. I know it isn't Andrea and Vera. They left later.* She frowned. *Been almost there.* The extra sets she had made this morning should keep it from happening again.

She thought about the night before. A doctor. She sighed. Just one step above serial killer status. She shrugged. It didn't matter. If he stayed on his side of the grass strip and she stayed on hers, she'd never see him again. She moved past the ladder.

The knock sounded again and she rushed to the front of the store. Maybe it was her mother. She had said that she'd be here around this time with their lunch. Cindy smiled. One of the perks of owning a business near the school where your mother taught. She shrugged as she turned down a side aisle. Just answer the door and quit speculating. She had too much to do to spend time wondering who was locked out or to be thinking about last night.

Just as the knock intruded a third time, she reached the door but didn't open it. What was *he* doing here?

She hesitated, then she unlocked the door. After what he did for her last night, she couldn't ignore him. She let him in and stepped aside. When he came in, she moved even further away from him.

"What are you doing here?" She folded her arms across her chest.

"Good afternoon." Her hair had escaped from the clip holding it back. Another baggy sweat suit—today she had chosen royal blue—covered her. What would she look like in something that fit? Would she ever let him find out? Did he want to get that involved with her or anyone again? He frowned. *No. I just want the explanation that she owes me.*

"Good afternoon. What are you doing here?" She glared.

"What's with you and doctors?"

"What?"

"You were ready to go out with me last night." He held up a hand when she started to speak. "No. Don't try to deny it."

"So, you're a mind reader, too."

"No, I'm not. If I were, I wouldn't be questioning you. I do know enough to know when a woman is interested in me and you were."

"You must be either a mind reader or conceited. You're probably used to women falling all over themselves trying to get next to you." Cindy shook her head. "Conceited or a mind reader. It doesn't matter which."

"Women falling all over themselves to get next to me? If we weren't having a different conversation I'd take time to laugh at how ridiculous that is. But you're not going to distract me that easily. You were ready to go with me," he insisted, "until I said the 'D' word."

"The 'D' word?"

"Doctor. When I told you that I'm a doctor, suddenly I was pushed below serial killer status; way below."

"I'm busy. I don't have time for this. Don't you have a patient waiting or a golf game to go to?"

"I'm through with patients until later this afternoon

and I don't play golf." He leaned against the wall. "You're avoiding the issue again. Why?"

"I am not interested in you. Is that so hard to believe?"

"You were." *Why am I pushing this?*

"I have work to do." The look she threw at him dared him to disagree.

"I climbed into the Dumpster and picked over trash for you."

"I know. I appreciate it. I really do. I don't know what I would have done if you hadn't come over."

"If you appreciate it so much, then show it."

"How?" Cindy stiffened and her face tightened. *Here it comes: the catch. Give them enough time and all men want something. Well, Doctor Marc can just go find somebody else to fill his wants.*

"Tell me why you changed your mind." *Let it go, Marc.* He ignored his own advice. *All I want is an explanation. Then I'm through with her.*

A knock on the door made them both turn. Cindy opened the door.

"You probably thought that I forgot all about"—Helen stared at Marc—"What are you doing here, Marc?"

"Talking to the owner of the new business on the block. What are you doing here, Miss Helen?"

"This new business owner is my daughter." She handed Cindy the bag of Chinese take-out. "Oh. That's right. Your office is near here, isn't it?"

"In the lot next door."

"You know each other?"

"For a couple of years now."

"How do you know him?"

"It's a long story. I'll explain later." Helen's glance slid to Cindy. "Why don't you have lunch with me and Cindy? There's always too much food in Chinese take-out and I bought enough for an army." She shifted her glance to Marc as she took the bag back.

"I'm sure Doctor Thomas has something to do." Cindy dared him to disagree.

He took the dare. "I'm free until three-thirty."

"You probably don't like Chinese food." She glared at him.

"It ranks right behind soul food in my favorite foods column." He reached for the large bag. "Let me carry that. It looks a lot heavier than empty boxes." He stared at her. "Chivalry has taken a hurting, but it isn't dead yet, is it?"

"No." How much mileage was he going to try to get out of Dumpster diving for her?

"Lead the way." Instead of moving, she stared back at him.

"Come on, Cindy. I'm on a tight schedule." Her mother took her arm. "I assume we'll eat in your office."

Cindy stared from one to the other. Then she walked slowly to the small office at the back as if hoping that, by the time she got there, she would have thought of the words to make him change his mind and leave. She didn't and he didn't. She took a deep breath. Lunch. It's only lunch; not a commitment of any sort.

"I have to get another chair."

"Allow me." Marc set the bag on the table set for two and got the folding chair leaning against the wall. He placed it at the end of the small table in the middle of the room.

"I have to get out another plate."

"Oh, for goodness sakes, don't make such a big production out of it." Her mother took the package of disposable plates from the shelf behind Cindy, took out one and set it on the table. She shook her head, took out another paper placemat and set it down as well.

"You may as well sit down." Cindy glanced at Marc.

"I know I taught you better manners than that, but I'll excuse you today on the grounds that you're probably still tired after the long day you put in yesterday." She frowned at her. "Go ahead and sit. The food is getting cold." Marc held her chair and, after she smiled at him, Helen sat next to Cindy at the small table.

They held hands for the blessing. Then Helen picked up a container and put a spoonful onto her plate and passed the cardboard box to Marc. "Dig in," she said as Cindy just sat there.

Cindy took the box from Marc, being careful not to touch his hand. She knew she was being ridiculous, childish. She shook her head. No, not childish. A child wouldn't be in this situation.

"So, how did you two meet?" Helen bit off a piece of broccoli.

"I'd better let Cindy tell it." Marc tilted his head to one side as if waiting to hear Cindy's version of the story. He listened as she told it exactly as it happened. What she didn't tell was why she was through with him before anything started.

"You threw away your keys."

"Accidentally."

"Of course accidentally. I didn't think that you did it on purpose."

"I'm tired of hearing that. How do you know Marc?" Cindy didn't even look at him. Maybe if she ignored him he'd disappear.

"I told you about Marc. He's Jean's son."

"Jean's son? You never mentioned that he was"—she shook her head—"That he *is* a doctor."

"I didn't?" Helen shrugged. "I guess it never came up."

"Yeah, right."

"She won't tell me what she has against doctors."

"Her ex-husband is the head of the neurology department at Blaine Memorial Hospital in Cleveland. Harry Granger has a reputation for being one of the top men in his field."

"I've heard of him."

"I guess everybody in the medical field has, especially after he developed that new procedure for removing brain tumors. It's my understanding that he's a brilliant doctor: He's expected to win the Nobel Prize for medicine some day. He was just terrible as a husband."

"That's enough of the ancient history for today, Mom. I doubt if Marc wants to hear this."

"On the contrary, I find it very interesting."

"You do?"

"Yes, Miss Helen, I do." He smiled. "It clears up some questions I had."

"What kind of questions?"

"You two can stay here." Cindy quickly took her things to the wastebasket. "I have to get back to work."

"Just questions." Marc shrugged and dumped his trash. "I'd better let you ladies get back to work. I have somebody coming in for an interview for the nurse vacancy."

"A nurse."

"You say it like it's a disease. Yes, a nurse. Nurses work with doctors, you know."

"I certainly do know that. I've seen the proof of that for myself."

"Don't tell me. You have something against nurses, too? Is it the whole medical profession? Are pharmacists included? How about orderlies and medical technicians?"

"The explanation behind that is another long story, Marc." Helen patted his arm. "Maybe one day Cindy will tell you." She nodded but avoided eye contact with Cindy. "Jean told me that Marisha, your nurse, is going on maternity leave."

"Yes. The vacancy is supposed to be temporary, but I won't be surprised if she decides to stay home with the baby afterward. Her husband is an engineer and makes a good living so, unlike a lot of new mothers, she has that option."

"I know her parents have to be looking forward to having a grandchild. Grandchildren must give such pleasure." Helen shook her head slowly. "Of course, I have to speculate since I haven't been so blessed." She stared at Cindy. "At least not as yet. I haven't given up." She sighed heavily. "I'm sure you know what they say about hope springing eternal."

"Mom . . ."

"Just making an observation, baby."

Marc looked from one to the other. "I'd better go. While I wait for the nurse to show up, I have a few things to do before I see patients this afternoon." He looked at Cindy. "I'll be seeing you. You take care, Miss Helen."

Cindy was tempted to add the childish, "Not if I see you first," but she didn't. Instead she followed him silently to the door.

Marie and Debbie were at the door when Cindy and Marc got to it, so Cindy got away with a curt "Good-bye." She didn't even take time to add good riddance in her mind, as Andrea and Vera returned too.

"I've got to get back to school, too." Helen had followed the other two to the door. "My class will be lined up in the yard when I get there. If I'm not on time picking them up, Louis acts like he doesn't know how to behave." She shook her head. "Sometimes he acts as if five is his age instead of his grade." She kissed Cindy's cheek. "See you after school."

Soon Cindy was back up on the stepladder straightening the boxes of extra supplies stored above the shelves and hoping they would soon be needed to replace shelf stock.

She had to admit that having lunch with Marc hadn't been so bad. But she didn't intend to do it again.

* * *

So that's it. Marc frowned as he made his way back to his office. *She marries a jerk who happens to be a doctor and so every other doctor is just like him? I guess if he were president she'd have the same opinion of all presidents. He shook his head as he crossed the grass. Think of another example, Marc. That one is too close to the truth.*

He unlocked the door. Why was he pushing her? Why did he feel the need to convince her how wrong she was, that he didn't belong in the same category as Harry Granger? He frowned.

I'm not interested in a relationship with somebody who obviously doesn't intend to let me get close.

He got the files for his afternoon patients from the cabinet. *I've been down that path with Tori, chasing after her like some lovesick kid. I should have let her go in the beginning.* He frowned. *Before the beginning.* He shrugged. Of course he had found out afterward that she had been after him first; she had just let him think that it was his idea. He released a deep breath. That part was okay. He didn't have a problem with a woman going after a man that she was attracted to. His problem was with the cheating, with the going after another man when you still had a ring on that special finger. Too bad he found out so late.

He shrugged as he closed the file cabinet drawer. If he could find a way to bottle twenty-twenty hindsight, he'd make more money than the U.S. government had in the treasury. Maybe even more than the amount of the national debt.

He opened the folder of his first patient. He needed to let it go and move on. If he was as ready as he thought he was to let a woman into his life again, he'd find her.

Or she'd find him. He'd rather take a long time to get it right than to rush into strike two. He sighed. He knew he wasn't ready yet and had no idea when he would be. What he was ready for, though, was to get Tori out of his thoughts completely.

He had finished reviewing the patient records when a young woman walked in.

"I'm Denise Nelson." She held out her hand and Marc took it. "I have an interview for the nurse's vacancy."

"I'm Dr. Marc Thomas. Please come in." He led her to his office. "I have a few questions about your application."

"Is something the matter?" Denise stopped in the hall. "I thought the job description looked as if it had been written for me. I know this is my first job in private practice, but I think I can handle it."

"There's no problem, Miss Nelson. Just a few minor details that I'm sure we can work out. We realize that this is your first job not in a hospital and that's all right with me and my three partners. Come on. Let's go over the questions."

Twenty minutes later Marc walked Denise to the door.

"I'll see you on Monday."

"I'm sure I can handle the job." Eagerness filled her words.

"I wouldn't have hired you if I didn't think so. I do think it will be helpful for you to shadow Marisha next week so you can see the routine in action. That way things will go smoothly after she goes on leave. Of course, after Marisha leaves, Janie, our other LPN, and Lisa, our receptionist, will be on hand to help you with any questions."

"Okay. Whatever you say. You're the doctor." She smiled. "I'll see you on Monday, bright and early."

"Not too early." He smiled back. "It won't do any of us any good if the office isn't open when you get here."

"That's right." She laughed. Then she grabbed his hand and pumped it up and down. "Thank you. I really appreciate your giving me this job. You won't be sorry. I promise. You'll see."

"I'm sure we won't be sorry."

Marc smiled as he watched her go. He hadn't seen that much enthusiasm about a job in a long time. He shrugged. She hadn't been that long out of nursing school. He hoped she kept her eagerness.

Seven

Cindy stretched and glanced at the clock: 6:45. She had gotten to bed after twelve, awakened several times, pushed thoughts of Marc Thomas from her mind each time, and yet here she was, awake an hour before the alarm was set to go off. She smiled. Feeling like a kid on the first day of school, she jumped out of bed and hurried to meet the day.

"Today my first customer will arrive, today my first customer will arrive." She sang the words over and over as she went down the hall to the bathroom, not caring how childish she sounded. She frowned as she brushed her teeth. *Customers. Plural. I'll be happy for all of them, but I need more than one; a lot more.* She closed her eyes. *Please let there be a lot more than one.* She frowned and opened her eyes, thought some more and then closed her eyes again. *And make Marc Thomas stay in his own space.*

Twenty minutes later she stepped outside her house and took a deep breath of the late October air. Crisp and fresh. Beautiful. A perfect day to go to the opening of the new store. She got into her car and smiled all the way to the shops.

Once there, she was so busy with last-minute things that she almost didn't have time to think of Marc. Almost.

"Leave me alone," she muttered once at a persistent image of a wide smile in a dark honey colored face.

"Did you say something, dear?" her mother called from further down the aisle.

"It's nothing, Mom. Just talking to myself." *Get a grip before somebody else benefits from your hard work.*

"That's supposed to be okay as long as you don't answer." Her mother's chuckle skipped down the aisle.

"If you only knew," Cindy muttered, this time low enough so that she was the only one who heard.

Cindy worked her way down the row, straightening displays that were already perfect.

"Enough." Her mother stood beside her. "I'm through making work. Everything is as okay as we can make it."

"You're right." Cindy dusted off her hands even though they weren't dirty. "All we need . . ." A knock on the door interrupted her. "I'll get it. It's probably my salespeople." She grinned. "Doesn't that sound wonderful—my salespeople?" She glanced at her watch and hurried to the front of the craft store.

She reached the door and stopped. Her mouth opened, but nothing came out. People, mostly women, stood in a group, a large group, outside the door, just behind Andrea, Debbie, Vera and Marie.

"Wow." She just stared. Then she looked at her watch. They weren't supposed to open for another fifteen minutes. *Wow.*

Andrea's stare met hers and made her move. Quickly she let in the four women. "We'll open in a couple of minutes," she said to the crowd. "Give us time to get set up." She turned away but turned back. "Thank you for coming." Then she waited until Marie and Debbie were ready at two of the cash registers in the bridal shop and Andrea and Vera were in place in the craft shop. *If each woman outside bought just one thing. . . .* She shook her head. *Stop before you jinx things.*

Her mother came to the front and went to the third

register in the bridal shop. Cindy took a deep breath and opened the doors early.

Customers rushed in as if the free gifts for the first fifty customers were worth millions. Cindy smiled and savored the crowd. Then she got too busy to enjoy what was happening in her shops.

After the initial rush, she switched Marie to the craft shop. In spite of the directory hanging over each aisle, she had to answer many questions about where particular items were located. She had gone to the back with a customer when she heard her mother greet somebody.

"Am I glad to see you. I need your help." Cindy frowned and went back to the registers. She centered her frown on Marc.

"We need Marc's help."

"For what?"

"This customer says there aren't any more peach flower sprays on the shelf. We need somebody to get another box down."

"He doesn't work here."

"What does that have to do with anything?"

"He's a doctor. He has patients. He doesn't have time."

"He's a neighbor willing to lend a hand."

"I'm here, and able to speak for myself."

Helen looked at Marc. "Good. You are willing to help out in an emergency, aren't you?"

"That seems to be my job lately." He met Cindy's stare. "I can get the things down myself."

"Where can I find gold stars?" A customer stopped beside Cindy. "You know, on thin gold wire? I looked, but I saw just about every color except gold. There is an empty box between the blue and the silver ones. Maybe you don't have any more gold?"

Cindy stared at the question showing in Marc's eyes and sighed. "I'd appreciate your help," she said, hating to let each word go. "The boxes are above the other sprays. The color is printed on each box."

"Okay. I'll see what I can do."

"The gold stars? Do you have any more?" The customer reminded her as Cindy stared at Marc for a few seconds more.

"I have some in stock. I'll get them down for you." Cindy led her back to the proper aisle, glad for something to do besides watch Marc walk away.

Cindy was busier than she had dared hope. She lost track of the number of times during the morning that she had to take down cases of additional stock as display boxes on the shelves emptied. She felt as if she were doing a different kind of step aerobics than the ones in exercise class, but she didn't complain.

A couple of times she saw Marc at the other end of an aisle doing the same thing. She frowned. She owed him again. Her frown deepened. She didn't like owing him.

At one o'clock Cindy went to the front of the store when Marie called her. A delivery man held a huge tray and a large bag from the nearby deli. The meats, cheeses and salads reminded Cindy that nobody had stopped for lunch. She looked at them longingly and shook her head.

"I should have thought to order this, but I didn't. Sorry. You must have the wrong place."

The man looked at the slip taped to the plastic wrap. "It says: 'Congratulations on your store opening. Welcome to the neighborhood.'" He shifted the tray. "It has this address on it, so it must be for you."

"I ordered it." Marc stood beside her. "I figured nobody over here would have time to go get lunch."

"Thank you." Cindy shook her head. "And thank you for helping out. It looks like I owe you again."

"I don't keep score." He stared at her. "Do you?"

Cindy shrugged. "I don't like owing somebody."

"It's okay to need help." His stare softened. "Payback

isn't always a dog." He smiled and Cindy's mind emptied of all coherent thought. "A wise songwriter once said 'Everybody needs somebody sometime.' It's true."

"I know." She shrugged.

"I have a patient in fifteen minutes. I only came over to tell you to expect the deli tray so none of you would have to worry about lunch. I thought you might be too bogged down with customers to leave." He laughed. "I forgot to do the one thing I came over for."

"That's because my mother pounced on you and drafted you as soon as you came in the door."

"No harm done. Glad I could help." He smiled again. "At least it didn't involve getting dirty." He winked at her and his stare dared her to react to it. "See you."

He left before Cindy could decide if she wanted to give a smart answer or just look sheepish.

"I have never met a more stubborn, nor a more infuriating woman in my life," Marc muttered as he made his way to the office. He paused as he reached the narrow grass strip.

Maybe we should see about getting a walkway paved between the two lots. He frowned. *Not necessary.* He didn't intend to come this way again, and he doubted if Cindy would. *What got into me to make me wink?* He frowned. *I never winked before in my whole life.*

He shook his head as he walked the few feet that took him to his side of the grass. She had acted as if she was afraid that he was interested in her. He scowled. *She should be so lucky. I am a nice guy. A nice guy who isn't interested in having her in my life.* His scowl hardened. *Or anybody else. Women are nothing but trouble.*

"Your patient is here." Denise smiled and handed him a file as soon as he walked into the office. "You're not late, Mrs. Fulton is early," she added when he looked at his watch. "I told her that."

"Denise, never criticize a patient for being early."

"I suggested that," Lisa said.

"Where's Marisha?"

"She was rubbing her back so I told her that I'd get this one for you."

"Is she all right?"

"She says she's okay." Denise chewed at a fingernail. "About Mrs. Fulton, I'm sorry. I just didn't want her to think that you're not busy."

"She's been bringing her kids here since we opened. She knows how busy we are."

"I'm sorry." Denise sniffed. "Really sorry. I . . . I didn't mean any harm."

"I know you didn't. It's okay." He patted her shoulder. "Give me a minute and then send the Fultons in."

"Yes, doctor."

He frowned as he went to the back office for his blue coat.

He had four patients and each time Denise brought him the file for the next patient, she apologized again. By the fourth patient, his patience was disappearing. *This is her first day. She's new at this,* he told himself as he tried to calm down. *She'll be fine once she gets used to the way we do things.*

The customers slowed to a steady stream. Cindy was busy, but not too busy to think about a devastating smile on a golden brown face. Thinking wouldn't cause any trouble: It was a lot safer than doing. She frowned. Which she didn't intend. Not with Marc; not with any man ever again. No one ever got hurt playing it safe. *He winked at me. How did he dare do something so juvenile?*

She moved slowly down the aisle, filling sparse displays where needed.

Around 5:30 P.M. the shops got busy again. Several women came in to take advantage of Cindy's special opening price for her wedding consultation services, so she had to leave the cash registers.

When she finished with each woman, she took them to Mattie and left them discussing wedding gowns and attendant dresses.

Cindy couldn't prevent the feelings of regret that filled her as she remembered her own wedding. She hoped these women had better luck than she had in having their dreams come true.

"Are you as tired as I am?" Helen asked. It was after eight o'clock, the four cashiers and Mattie were gone, the store was finally closed, and Cindy and Helen sat on top of the counters at the front of the store.

"Yes," Cindy answered. A wide smile spread across her face. "Isn't it wonderful?"

"Speaking as someone who wants her daughter to succeed, the answer is 'Yes.' Speaking as somebody whose feet are killing her, I refuse to answer on the grounds that I may hurt my only child's feelings." She smiled. "Congratulations, baby. You did it. You are now the owner of the highly successful new shop on the block."

"Don't jump to that conclusion yet, Mom. One great business day, especially the opening day, does not a financial success make."

"That's true. However, it is okay to allow yourself to feel optimistic about it. Savoring the fruits of your labor is not a sin." She hopped down. "What else do you have to do tonight?"

"Not another blessed thing."

"Beautiful answer. Let's blow this joint and go get something to eat."

"You've been watching old gangster movies again."

"They don't make them like they used to."

"Some people would think that's a good thing."

"Not my daughter, though. She had better taste." She smiled. "What about going to Ida's?"

"That heavy food might keep me up all night." She smiled.

"But it's worth it," her mother finished. "I wonder if Marc's still in his office. Maybe he wants to go with us."

"He's a pediatrician. His patients are in bed."

"Not if they are sick. He might still be over there."

"You're not too tired to keep trying, are you?"

"The least we can do is offer to repay him for what he did."

"Make him a cake. I'll pay for the ingredients."

"Cold. And brutal. You definitely didn't get that from me." She shrugged. "You always did get cranky when you were tired."

"Mom."

"You go get our purses and lock up. I'll go check on Marc and meet you out front."

Cindy sighed and watched her go. Then she shook her head as she went to her office. Surely Marc was gone by now.

"His office is empty." Helen stared at Cindy. "I guess you got a reprieve."

"You mean a pardon," she corrected her. She had no intention of going over to Marc's office herself. "The restaurant is on the way, so we should both drive. Meet you over there."

She waited until her mother got into her car before she slid behind the wheel of her Taurus.

At least I don't have to see Marc Thomas again. Why wasn't she sure how she should feel about that?

She pulled out of the parking lot behind her mother. Another doctor. Why did he have to be a doctor?

Eight

"Have I told you how happy I am that you came back to Philly?"

"A time or two, I think." Helen settled into a desk in Jean's classroom.

"I can't believe that of all of the elementary schools in Philadelphia, you picked this one for your assignment." Jean unzipped her insulated lunch bag.

"Seems like a variation of that line from Casablanca, doesn't it? Of all the gin joints . . ." They both laughed.

"You know, if we had stayed in touch or if you had at least come back home after college, we wouldn't be looking at this situation with our kids. Four years together at Girls' High School should have meant enough for us to keep in touch." Jean sighed.

"You know how busy young folks are when they are trying on a new life filled with freedoms." Helen took a container from her bag.

Jean nodded. "Especially when we were in love with a capital 'L.'"

"That's true." Silence, weighed down with memories, hung in the air between them. "It's been four years, but I still miss Marcus as if it were last week." Helen's eyes had a faraway look.

"I know what you mean. Steve's been gone for seven years, but sometimes the loneliness is almost too much to stand."

"Yeah."

Somebody walked past the room and pulled the two women back to the present.

"Speaking of the situation, I'm not giving up. I like to think that if Cindy and Marc had known each other as they grew up, they would have developed deep feelings for each other."

"Yes." Jean nodded. "But on the other hand," Jean said, "the opposite could have happened. They could have looked on each other as brother and sister and then where would we be?"

"Right where we are now: getting older and with no prospects for grandchildren anywhere on the horizon."

"That's true."

"Okay." Helen set her napkin down. "Talking won't cut it. What are we going to do about this?"

"I don't know." Jean sighed and stared at her sandwich. "You know Barbara Edwards just got her third grandchild?"

"I heard. She told me after church yesterday. A girl this time." It was Helen's turn to sigh. "She wasn't trying to rub it in or to make me jealous. She was just so happy. Not only did she have another grandchild, but this time it's a girl; the first girl in her family in two generations."

"If you and I don't do something, we won't have any future generations."

"Where did we go wrong?" Helen didn't expect an answer.

"Maybe we should have had more kids."

"You mean not put all our eggs in one basket, so to speak?"

"I mean we should have put more than one egg into play at the right time."

"You are so terrible." Helen tapped Jean's arm.

"I speak the truth."

They both laughed. Then they sighed at the same time as if somebody had given them a signal.

"That's not it," Helen said. "Barbara has only one child. Her daughter just picked the right number in the marriage lottery. She took a bite of her sandwich.

"When you and I were at Girls' High, daydreaming about our futures, we dreamed about large families," Jean said. "I talked about four children; two of each. In all fairness, we didn't do that part well." Again they sighed together. Then Jean shrugged. "We can't undo the past. Besides, Barbara has . . ."

"Yes, I know. She had only one child and look at her," Helen said. "Three grands." She shook her head. "I thought that all we had to do was get Cindy and Marc together. All those times we tried to get them in the same place at the same time and didn't succeed we were so frustrated. We couldn't even get them to meet."

"Now they have." Jean stared into her coffee cup. "For all the good it did."

Helen shook her head. "You should have been at the store on Friday. I don't know when I saw anything so ugly."

"I was happy when Marc graduated from medical school. Now I wish he had gone into engineering. Or teaching. Or to law school."

"Not law school. Cindy still talks about Harry's lawyer." She gathered up her trash. "I don't know where she got her fussiness from."

Jean stared at her and Helen stared back. Then they laughed. "Okay, maybe I do have an inkling about where she got it."

"The real question is: What are we going to do?"

"Dinner next Sunday at my place. I'll cook, you think of a way to get Marc to come with you. You have almost a whole week to come up with a plan." Helen gathered her things. "Maybe it won't be so hard since he insisted on eating lunch with Cindy and me on Friday."

"You don't know my son. You said that Cindy obviously didn't want him to stay? That's probably the only reason why he insisted on staying. He's got an ornery streak running through him that would make a country mule envious."

"He probably got it the same way Cindy got her fussiness." She hesitated. "But we won't go there. We'll just work around it."

The first bell rang and they went to the yard to meet their classes.

As they went down the stairs, Jean's mind sifted through one idea after the other seeking a foolproof plan. In the end she decided to go with the universal appeal to men: the promise of a delicious meal capped by homemade dessert. She could honestly swear that Helen's pound cake was the best she had ever tasted, including her own Aunt Jane's.

Business at the stores was brisk enough to make Cindy's concerns about succeeding disappear. There was enough business to keep the clerks busy, but not enough so they couldn't handle it all. Cindy even had enough time to make samples of favors and place tags and decorations for her Wednesday evening bridal workshop. By the end of the day she went home and was asleep before the eleven o'clock news.

Before she opened on Wednesday, she put the kits they would use on the workshop table. When six o'clock came, she was glad she had done so, the store had been so busy.

Eight women had registered, but two more showed up, which was okay since Cindy advertised that last-minute registrations were welcome. At exactly six o'clock she started the workshop.

"We have a lot of possibilities for decorations for every phase of your wedding." Cindy looked at the ten women sitting around the long table in her workshop and smiled. They had introduced themselves and wore name tags. "I thought I'd show you the samples that I made up." She held up a miniature easel and passed it around. "These come in plain wood, but they can be painted to match your color scheme. These others things can be adapted as well."

"What if we have something in mind, but you don't have a sample?" one of the women asked. "And what if I have no idea how to make it, either?" she added timidly.

"Then we decide on something else," one of the other women said.

All of them laughed, including the woman who asked the question.

"Not necessarily, Olivia," Cindy said after the laughter faded. "If you can show me one, or draw a picture or at least describe it in detail, we can probably come up with something that will please you." She passed around the samples of favors and answered questions about the cost of materials and the time it would take to make them.

"One option is to have me make the items, but you can save a lot of money if you do them yourself." She stared at them. "And if you decide to make them yourself, no calling me the day before the wedding begging for help."

"How about two days before?" Everybody laughed.

"I can't find any elves to help, Kim, so two days' notice isn't enough. I'd suggest that you call in favors, draft relatives, bribe friends—whatever it takes to get as much help as possible."

"Competent help," Rosa added. "I have a friend who had her fiancé help her and it almost caused the marriage to end before it began."

Cindy laughed with the others, but the remark about marriages ending stirred up bitter memories. *When will Harry leave me alone?*

* * *

At eight o'clock the workshop ended, and Cindy walked the women to the door. Six of them had decided on their favors and were going to buy the materials and get started, but Cindy talked them into thinking about their choices for a few days to make sure.

When she left the shop she was surprised at the envy she was feeling at the women's happiness. Had she been that happy planning her own wedding? She sighed. She hadn't planned her wedding; Harry's mother had. Right down to the color of mints in the little silver favor baskets. She frowned. Cindy couldn't blame Harry's mother completely. *I let her do it.* She sighed. *It wouldn't have made a bit of difference. I'd be right where I am now even if I had done everything myself.*

The week had been busy, but on Saturday morning Cindy bounced out of bed eager for the day's activities to begin. Her first kids' craft workshop was scheduled for ten o'clock. She hoped the kids would be interested in the project she had chosen.

The Saturday morning workshop was as different from the one on Wednesday evening as she had expected it to be.

She looked at the fifteen kids and five parents sitting around the table and wondered if she should cut it down to a dozen total from now on. She took a deep breath. She'd know whether to change her numbers by the end of the day.

She showed the kids the plastic pails shaped like pumpkins that they were going to paint and decorate. The pails could be used for either decoration or for Trick or Treat goodies. Cindy distributed the supplies and materials. That part of the activity went well. Then Janice, a five-year-old, insisted on painting her pail purple.

"You can't have a purple jack-o'-lantern," Lynn, one of the other kids, said.

"I can make it any color I want to. It's mine." She looked at Cindy. "Isn't that right, Miss Cindy?"

After Cindy agreed, Monique decided on blue. "My favorite color," she explained.

After that, except for Lynn, it was as if orange had disappeared from the paint selections.

The kids worked intensely, ignoring each other. Cindy had to help with details several times, but the kids handled most of the decorating alone. Maybe fifteen kids wasn't too many. Cindy smiled through the rest of the activity.

The cleanup was finished and it was time to leave when a voice behind her caught Cindy's attention.

"Wow."

Cindy looked up as the familiar voice reached her. "What are you doing here?"

"Why is that always your greeting to me? What happened to 'Hello'? I know Miss Helen well enough to know that you didn't learn that from her."

"Hello." She put her hands on her hips. "What are you doing here?"

"I came for a schedule of your workshops."

"You're not going to be a bride and you're not interested in crafts."

"How do you know what I'm interested in? You never gave yourself a chance to find out." He fixed her with a stare. "Besides, I wasn't interested in seeing the interior of a Dumpster, either, yet I ended up getting up close and personal with that one out there." He pointed toward the parking lot.

Cindy sighed. "Do you ever intend to give that a rest?"

Marc shrugged. "Maybe. Over time. Traumatic experiences take a while to get over." He stared at her. "But, with effort, it is possible to get past them. I think I'm making great progress with mine."

"Doctor Marc, look at my pumpkin."

"It is not a pumpkin," Lynn corrected. "It's a jack-o'-lantern. Isn't that right, Miss Cindy?"

"It's mine. I can call it what I want to, can't I, Miss Cindy?"

"Look at mine, too, Doctor Marc." Monique pointed to her royal blue creation.

"They are all beautiful. They look like a rainbow spread out on the table." He met Cindy's stare. "My patients."

"Are the pails dry yet?" a parent asked.

"We used fast-drying paints, so they should be. I suggest you set them on newspaper on the floor of the car, though, just to make sure."

By the time the parents who had stayed took their children, the other parents had come for the rest. Cindy looked at the paper-covered table and smiled. Kids' craft workshop number one had been a success.

"So. What do we do next week?"

"What are you doing here, Marc?"

"Ah, progress. I am no longer addressed as Doctor Thomas."

"My mistake." Cindy put the last paint bottle into the plastic case and snapped the lid into place.

"We're human. Mistakes are allowed as long as you don't dwell on them and let them ruin the rest of your life." He smiled. "Besides, that's not a mistake. That's one step forward. Progress. Progress is a good thing." He reached for the box. "Let me help you with that."

"I can do it myself." She stared at him. "I don't want to be hearing about how you did this for me for the rest of my life. I don't want to owe you."

Marc eased the box from her hands. "I promise not to mention it again, and it won't go into the debt column." He stared at her. "Besides, I don't keep score. If you do, consider this a freebie." He lifted the box. "You get the brushes and paper towels." He frowned. "Get a move on, woman. We're wasting valuable time, and I have patients coming in this afternoon. Where do you want these?"

"I didn't ask you to . . ."

"Uh-uh." He shook his head. "Never turn down free labor. Where does this go?"

"Over here." Cindy shook her head, but she led him to the shelf at the far end of the room.

"Now." She turned to him after the materials were put away. "Why did you really come over here? To bug me?"

"I told you. I need one of these schedules."

"You do crafts?"

"Maybe. Depends on what they are."

"You have patients on Saturdays."

"I made a deal with my partners to have Saturdays off."

"Saturday has to be a busy day for a pediatrician."

"It is. I had to give up Monday and Tuesday evenings, but I have something important to do."

"My workshop?" Cindy frowned.

"Granted that's important, but not just that." He fixed her with a stare. "I know somebody who's interested in crafts."

"My crafts are geared toward kids. I doubt if an adult would be interested." She wanted to ask if it was his girlfriend, but she didn't. *What do I care?* She clamped her teeth together so the question couldn't escape.

"I'm talking about a kid. I have a little brother who likes to do crafts."

"I thought you were an only child." Cindy frowned.

"Not that kind of little brother. You know: The Big Brothers of America? I met my Little Brother for the first time last Tuesday after he got out of school. Kevin is nine and interested in art and crafts. He likes sports, too, and we'll be going to some games, but he's really enthusiastic about making things. I thought your workshop might be ideal for him."

"Oh. OK."

"I'll be seeing you.

Marc held out his hand and, without thinking, Cindy slipped hers into it.

The store noises drifted into the workshop, but they were quiet enough not to distract the two people facing each other, poised as if on the edge of something.

Footsteps were coming toward the room, but they didn't register with Cindy. It took a voice to break the spell.

"A customer wants to know if we have any more of those . . ." Debbie stared from Cindy to Marc and back to Cindy. "Sorry. I didn't know"—she frowned—"I didn't mean to interrupt. I mean . . ."

"It's OK." Cindy pulled her hand away. How long had they been standing like that? She glanced at Marc, who looked as confused as she felt. She tore her gaze away and looked at Debbie. "What?" she swallowed hard. And took a deep breath. Maybe that would help her find her senses. "What is it you need?"

Debbie asked about a stained glass kit. Cindy told her where to find them. Then Debbie left them alone.

"I need to . . ."

"I have to go . . ."

They spoke at the same time as if both were trying to deny what had happened. What *had* happened?

"I'll show this schedule to Kevin and probably come register him." He smiled at her. "Little people await me." His smile softened. "I'll see you next week."

"Yeah." Cindy stood in place, glad she wasn't at home and had to walk her guest to the door. She frowned. If she were at home, Marc wouldn't be there. They'd never get that close.

She sighed. He did have a great smile. *Do I want Kevin to want to do the crafts or not?*

* * *

On his way back to the office, Marc tripped over the curb as if it hadn't always been there. It was a good thing the office was right next door or he might have gotten lost on the way back. He shook his head.

Man, she looked good. His "Wow" hadn't been for the surrealistic jack-o'-lanterns. Cindy in sweats that looked two sizes too big had been appealing. Cindy in a skirt and blouse that were the correct size was too much. Her breasts made themselves known behind the red silk blouse, not making it look as if they needed more room, but obvious enough to make you want to see them without the covering. He shook his head. To make him see them without the dressing.

His hands itched with wanting to feel her generous breasts fill them. What kind of bra was she wearing? Lacy or no-nonsense cotton? Was it red? He shook his head again. Those hips that revealed her heritage and said "Yes, I am a woman." Ample. Wide enough so a man would know he was holding a woman when he wrapped his hands around them.

His pants tightened painfully. He looked around. He was in front of the cleaners shop in the lot on the other side of the office. He smiled. He was definitely over Tori. In fact, his mind was asking, "Tori who?"

Marc walked to the end of the row of shops and forced his mind to the patients whom he would see this afternoon. *This changing his mind's focus had to work. I don't have time to go home and take a cold shower.*

In spite of his physical discomfort he smiled. *All I have to do, now, is get her to move past her failed marriage the way I've pushed mine to the past.*

Nine

The church sanctuary buzzed with Sunday worshipers greeting people they hadn't seen since last week. Cindy reached her mother and the two hugged.

"I wasn't sure that you would be here this morning." Helen unzipped her choir robe.

"You should have known that I wouldn't skip service."

"Not normally, but I also know that you have had a busy week." She turned to hug Mrs. Jones and Cindy did the same. Then they faced each other again.

"Busy does not begin to describe this past week."

"And you loved every minute of it."

"And I loved every minute of it." Her wide smile made her mother's smile match her own. "I just can't explain the feeling you get from owning your own business."

"How was the workshop yesterday morning?"

"Busy." Cindy shook her head. "There's that word again."

"Did you have many attend?"

"Fifteen kids plus five parents."

"Oh, my. Twenty people and mostly little people."

"My thoughts exactly when I saw all those folks sitting there waiting for me to do my thing."

"Was it successful?" She pulled off her robe and draped it over her arm.

"It must have been. One little girl asked if we could have a second one during the week."

They stopped to speak to Mrs. Willis and hug her.

"You didn't give in, did you?"

"I haven't lost my mind completely yet." Cindy laughed. "I handed them copies of the schedules and told them they had to wait until next Saturday. The sad little faces almost made me change my mind, though. I still might reconsider for the summer."

"You would never make it as a teacher." Helen's glance slid from Cindy. "Did Marc stop by?" Helen fussed with the top sleeve of her robe, smoothing out the wrinkles as good as any iron could.

"Why do you ask? Did you tell him to stop by?"

"Why would you think I would do something like that?"

"Because I know you."

"I can truthfully say, standing right here in the church sanctuary, that I did not ask Marc to stop by your store. I just thought he might have decided to be neighborly and welcome you."

"He did that already. You were there. Remember?

"I remember." She stared at Cindy. "So. Did he?"

"Yes."

"And?"

"And what?"

"What happened?"

"He asked for a workshop schedule and I gave it to him."

"That's nice."

"Quit beaming, Mom. He didn't get it for himself."

"Then for whom did he get it?"

"He joined Big Brothers of America and his Little Brother, Kevin, likes to do crafts."

"Oh." Helen frowned and shifted her robe to her other arm. "So he won't be coming, huh?"

Cindy stared at her mother. "He'll be doing the crafts with Kevin as one of their activities together."

"So he will be coming?"

"I'll talk to you later this week."

"Wait a minute." She grabbed her arm. "You're coming over for dinner, now, right?"

"I don't know. I was planning to get some take-out on my way home. I'll just kick back and watch the Eagles game."

"You can't do that."

"Why?"

"Because I already cooked. I assumed that you were coming." She frowned at Cindy. "You know my home cooking is better than anybody's take-out." She touched Cindy's arm. "I even made a sweet potato pie and a pound cake." She straightened and stared at her. "You can watch the game at my house."

Cindy sighed. "OK, but let me go home and change first."

"No, you don't. I know you. You'll go home, get comfortable and call me and cancel."

"Oh, all right." Cindy sighed again. "I'll see you at the house."

She hugged Deaconess Swindell on her way out and left the nearly empty sanctuary. She shrugged. She could relax almost as easily at her mom's as at her own home.

"I'm here." Cindy called as she stepped on the marble floor inside the first door of the foyer. "Where's the woman who used guilt to get me here?" She took off her coat, hung it in the roomy hall closet and proceeded through the second door.

"I'm out here." Her mother's voice came from the kitchen.

Cindy smiled as she reached the first of the pictures of her great-grandparents and then her grandparents. Aunts and uncles and cousins appeared in other photographs. These pictures had lined the hall for as long as she could remember, no matter how many times her mother had redecorated the house. Cindy recited each name as she stood before it.

"Where are you?"

Her mother's voice tore Cindy's attention from the pictures. "Something smells delicious in here." She started toward the kitchen again.

Her mother greeted her halfway down the hall. "I hope it tastes as good as it smells."

Cindy smiled. "You know it always does." She sniffed again. "Pot roast. Did you put mushrooms in it like the last time?"

"After the way you raved about it, you know I did." She led the way to the living room. "I turned on the game, but the last time I looked, the Eagles were losing by three."

"It ain't over until the clock reads '00' at the end of the fourth quarter."

"Since I'm off duty as Mrs. Larson, schoolteacher, and I know that you know better, I'm going to let that 'ain't' slide."

"Thank you so very much. Anything I can do?"

"I promised that you could 'kick back,' as you called it, and watch the game. Besides, I have everything under control."

Cindy went into the living room, glanced toward the dining room and stopped before she reached the sofa.

"Why is that table set for four?"

The game forgotten, she went into the dining room and stared at the table as if looking at it could change it. Her mother came and stood beside her as if she were seeing the table settings for the first time.

"Oh. We're having company." She waved her off. "Go ahead and watch the game. It sounds like somebody just scored."

"Somebody scored at church with her persuasive speech."

"Since when did you become antisocial?" The doorbell rang before Cindy could respond. "Please get that, baby. I have to take the bread from the oven."

Cindy took her time getting to the door. She wasn't clairvoyant, but she knew who was there.

"Hi, Cindy." Jean Thomas took a few steps forward and hugged her. "I haven't seen you in too long a time." She stepped back. "Do you know my son, Marc?"

"I know him." Cindy stared at him.

"Hi, Cindy." His smile almost made her thaw. If it were anybody else's, it would have.

"Hi, Jean. Marc." Helen came to the door, but she didn't look at Cindy. "Come on in. I can't afford to heat the outdoors."

"I'll come help you in the kitchen." Jean handed her coat to Cindy.

"You told me that you didn't need help."

"Something came up. Show Marc into the living room. He likes football, too."

Cindy watched the two women rush away as if something dangerous was chasing them. She turned to Marc.

"Did you know about this?" Cindy asked after their mothers disappeared into the kitchen.

"Mom told me she was taking me out to dinner." He shook his head. "I guess I should have asked her where. I didn't have a clue until I saw your car outside." He stared at her. "If you'll see that Mom gets home, I'll leave."

"You can't leave."

"Why not?"

"You're my mother's guest. Come on in." She took his coat and hung it next to hers.

"You're not going to leave, are you?"

"I don't want to get disowned, and I don't want them to gang up on me."

"What are we going to do?"

"For the time being, tell me you like, or least tolerate, football."

"That's my second middle name."

"What's the first?"

"Mom said she was heavily sedated when they asked her my name."

"That bad, huh?"

Cindy smiled at him. Marc blinked hard, but he managed to process her question and an answer. "In my years of searching, I haven't run across, any worse. I'd change it, but a child should have *something* to use to send his mother on a guilt trip."

"This situation is enough to make me wish for a terrible name, too." She shook her head. "I don't think it would work on my mother, though."

"It hasn't worked on mine yet, either, but I keep hoping. Where's the television?"

"Just follow the cheers; I assume they're coming from the game and not from our parents, but with Mom, I wouldn't bet on that."

"Same for mine."

She led him to the family room down the hall and off to the left and he didn't complain about following her. He wished the hall were longer and the television were farther away, maybe a block or so. It was difficult, but he managed to let a little more space form between them. The view was almost ideal. Ideal would be if the only thing she wore was her beautiful brown skin. He inhaled and hoped the breath would cool his heating body, but he doubted it. Her perfume was too enticing. His dark brown pants tightened, but he kept looking at her and imagining any way.

Her royal blue skirt followed the beautiful contours of

her body before quitting just above her knees. He wished he could thank the designer, probably a man, who first got women to accept short skirts. The matching suit jacket, trimmed in black, didn't fit as close to her body as the skirt did, but that was OK. He remembered the shape of the top part of her body from that red silk blouse that she wore at the workshop. His body tightened even more at that memory. Did he ever remember.

Cut it out. You're acting like a teenager. He shook his head. Right now, if he matched his hormones with any teenager, the doctor would win. He took another breath and tried to think of something else; anything else. Finally, mercifully, they reached the family room and he made his attention move to a safer subject.

"This is a nice room."

A deep green and cream floral sofa sat in front of the large middle window in the bay. Deep green brocade swags joined matching drapes, which were fastened back from the three windows in the bay by antique pink and white floral pins. The other large window in the room matched the three. Cream wallpaper with tiny green and yellow stripes covered the walls. Wide plaster molding formed large rectangles forming frames along the walls, with gold rosettes at each corner. A print depicting an African American scene was hung in each of the five built-in frames on one wall and the three on the other.

Marc walked over to the large print in the middle. "'The Banjo Player.' I love this print. I have a copy in my house."

"It's one of Mom's favorites." Cindy touched the edge of the gold frame. "She changed the color scheme in here about five years ago, but the prints stayed."

Cindy moved to the first of two green chairs flanking the sofa, but she didn't sit. Instead she moved on to the sofa.

"The whole house is beautiful. I love these old Victorian stone houses. Builders don't add these details to new houses." Marc pointed to the wide plaster molding running along the top of the wall penning in the ceiling.

"They can't afford to. Do you live in an old house?"

"Yes, I bought it as soon as I moved here. It's on the west side. You?"

"A few blocks from here. When I was house shopping, I didn't think I couldn't afford one of these, but a couple who was divorcing was anxious to sell." She shrugged. "Their misfortune was my gain."

"Did you grow up in this house?"

"I was five when we moved here."

"I'll bet you spent a lot of time on that wraparound porch."

"That swing in the corner was my reading spot. No matter how high the temperature, it catches a breeze from either the front or the side."

"Mom told me that this street was declared the prettiest one in the city by some national magazine that features Victorian houses."

Cindy laughed. "Mom said that she and some of the neighbors decided that they had better pay more attention to the lawns since the whole world is watching and they now have a reputation to uphold." She laughed again. He liked the new sound. "Go ahead. Sit down, or did you decide not to stay?" *What did that note in her voice mean? Did she still want him to go, or had she changed her mind?* he wondered.

"I'm staying."

"Well, let's see if the Lions are wishing they were playing somebody else, anybody else, this week." She sat in a corner of the couch.

Marc hesitated, then he sat in one of the chairs, the one with the better view of the couch.

"Have you been here before?"

"Never been invited before."

"Now I know why Mom wouldn't let me go home from church today instead of coming over here."

"Those two women should not be allowed to communicate with each other."

"Do you have any clout with the school administration?"

"They can't force transfer anyone without a reason. Meddling in their children's lives is not a reason." He stared at her. "At least not to the school administration."

"Why did they do this now? I've managed to hold Mom off for a long time."

"I know you heard about their friend's third grandchild."

"Barbara Edwards." Cindy nodded. "I get a report every day." She sighed. "Let's watch the Eagles beat up on the Lions."

"Don't be too sure about that."

"That's right. You used to live in Detroit until you came to your senses." She frowned at him.

"You sound like one of those bloodthirsty fans. Do you paint your face green and white when you go to the games?"

"I always watch from the comforts of a home. How about you? Did you wear a blue and white face in Detroit?"

"Not even once. I didn't want to look ridiculous."

"Standing in a Dumpster was enough, huh?"

"Now who won't let it go?"

"Guilty." She smiled again. "I guess we won't hold being from Detroit against you, especially since the Lions are being tamed so thoroughly today."

"I appreciate that." His voice softened. "I already have enough to overcome."

Cindy stared at him. She opened her mouth, but closed it without saying anything. Then she forced her gaze to the television. *Is he still looking at me?*

* * *

Marc had no idea who had just made the play that had the fans sounding as if they were trying to burst into the living room. He wasn't looking at the television. *She is beautiful. My imagination was not exaggerating.* Her eyes crinkled at the corner and her full mouth formed a smile as he watched. The Eagles must have done something important. He regretted that he didn't have the right to touch his lips to hers, sample her sweet mouth, take her mind off the football game and move it on to a one-on-one activity. He shifted in the chair, glad for the high arms. He didn't even wonder what happened to get her excited. Right now, the only thing he cared about was how to get her to get past what he was.

He frowned as the path his thoughts were taking to a possible future became clear.

Do I really want to go after a woman who doesn't want me within seeing distance of her? If I get her to change her mind, then what? Spend the rest of my life trying to prove to her that she didn't make a mistake about me? He shook his head. *No way. This time I let* the woman *decide that she wants* me.

He turned his attention to the game. The Lions were playing like dead men who wanted nothing but to lie down. He tried to care.

"I don't hear anything except the game," Jean said.

"Do you think they're both still in there?" Helen glanced at the kitchen door even though she knew she couldn't see the living room.

"I wouldn't mind if they both left, as long as they went together. What I'm afraid of is that there's only one of them in there."

"Cindy wouldn't dare leave," Helen said. "She promised to have dinner with me. Of course, that was when she thought it was just the two of us."

"I don't think Marc would leave me, but after this, I don't know. Do you think we did the right thing?"

"Don't wimp out on me now. Desperate situations call for desperate measures. If we didn't do something those two would be our ages and regretting that they would never have grandchildren."

"I can't stand this not knowing."

"We can't hold off serving dinner. I told Cindy it was ready when she got here."

"United front." Jean locked her arm with Helen's. They each took a deep breath as they marched into the living room.

"Are you two ready to eat?" Helen smiled. Cindy and Marc were both engrossed in the game, but they were still there.

"It's about one minute to halftime. I want to see the Eagles score one more time." Her mother looked at the score posted in the corner of the screen.

"Twenty-eight to three? They're winning twenty-eight to three and you want to watch them score again? I didn't know my child was so vicious."

"I'm not vicious. The Eagles have to get the Lions while they're down. If Detroit ever gets it together we might be in trouble."

"I'm glad to hear you admit that." Marc dared to look at her.

"I know how to be a gracious winner."

"It's only halftime. The Lions might roar back."

"Yeah, and our mothers might decide to quit meddling in our lives." She glared at her mother.

"Since this is Sunday and we have company," Helen said, "I'll let that one go. Come on," she said as time ran out on the half. "Dinner's getting cold."

"You sit there, Cindy." Her mother pointed to the chair at one side after they got to the dining room. "Marc, you sit at that end, next to Cindy." She felt Cindy's glare.

"What?" she asked. "A man should sit at the end of the table. It's his proper place."

"When did you become a chauvinist?"

Helen ignored the question. "Let's hold hands so I can say grace. Cold gravy is not a pleasant thing, nor are cold mashed potatoes."

"Amen" echoed around the table and Marc reminded himself that he was finished chasing women who didn't want to get caught. He forced himself to let go of Cindy's hand.

During the meal Cindy answered questions about the past week at the store.

Did she know how her face lit up when she talked about her stores? Did she have any idea how tempting it was to take her in his arms and taste her lips right there in front of both of their mothers? He glanced away from her. Their mothers weren't the ones who would mind. He frowned at the string beans on his plate. He wouldn't have been able to stop at tasting her mouth, anyway.

Marc forced his attention back to reality instead of wishful dreams. He did smile at Cindy as she talked about the bridal shop but he shook his head. How could she run a shop for brides and plan weddings if she was so against letting a man get close to her? He pushed his attention back to what she was saying.

"Already I've been hired as consultant for two weddings and probably for a third." She laughed. "The last one has to wait for a small detail to be ironed out: her boyfriend hasn't proposed yet." They all laughed except for Marc.

"I still don't understand why women make such a big thing out of the wedding ceremony." Marc frowned and shook his head.

"It's a woman thing," the three women said in unison.

"You men don't need to understand," his mother added. "All you have to do is show up and look handsome in whatever we decide will go with our plans and color scheme." She patted his arm. "That part we know men can do."

"The whole male sex gets insulted, and I'm the only one here to defend it."

"We're not being insulting, just realistic," Jean said. "Tell the truth: If a man had his way, if there was any ceremony at all, he and his fiancée would go to the Justice of the Peace alone, dressed in whatever, say 'I do' and go home."

"The marriage would be just as valid," Marc said and frowned at his mother.

His mother cringed and shook her head. "You have just proven my point." She looked at the other two women. "I will now change the conversation to a safer subject to protect my son. Marc, what was your most satisfying case?"

"A Reyes-Syndrome case last week. Chuck had been misdiagnosed by another doctor and I caught it in time." He let out a heavy breath and shook his head. "For awhile I was afraid I would lose him." He shrugged. "Most of my cases are routine and I'm grateful for that. I love a noisy office: Healthy kids are noisy."

"Cindy said you have a Little Brother."

"You've been talking about me." He pinned her with a stare.

"Mom asked me if you had stopped by the shop." She shrugged. "I just answered her questions."

"Don't get defensive." He smiled at her. "I don't mind." Their stares held for awhile and their mothers held their breaths. Finally Marc shifted his gaze as if he had just become aware that he hadn't answered the question.

"Kevin is nine years old and living in a group home."

"Group home? Not foster care?" Cindy asked.

"There aren't enough foster homes for all the kids

who need them." He shrugged. "Group homes are OK. Most kids adapt. Kevin doesn't quite fit in. He's one of six boys in the home and the youngest. Sports are the only thing that matters to the other boys; they all play on one of the neighborhood teams. They spend their free time shooting baskets or playing tag football on the playground. Kevin would rather watch or read or make things. He showed me some of his things. His art projects are fantastic for a nine-year-old. The other boys don't tease him; they're very protective of their little brother. They call him their family artist."

"That's why you got the kids' workshop schedule from my shop."

He nodded. "Kevin is going to love them."

The conversation between them drifted from one subject to another. Both mothers spoke only to ask questions.

Marc had to work to focus on Cindy's words. He had never been indecisive before. Now here he was, swearing that getting involved with her would only lead to trouble, yet he was wondering how she would feel in his arms. He worked to keep a frown from forming. It wasn't appropriate to her words. It did fit his mixed feelings. Did he want to chase someone who didn't trust him even though she didn't know him? If he didn't, why was he imagining how they would be together? His frown formed in spite of his effort. Did split personalities develop this fast?

"Is something the matter, Marc?" Helen brought his thoughts back to the present.

"No. I was just trying to work through a problem."

"Can we help? Sometimes it helps to talk about it."

"Thanks, but this is something I have to work through by myself." He didn't have to work on the smile that replaced the frown. Helen asked him another question about his practice, and he had no problem keeping his mind in the present from then on.

* * *

"We'd better clean up so I can get home," Jean said after their dessert plates had been empty for awhile. "I have a set of spelling papers to grade."

"Forget the cleanup. It's only these things still on the table. Besides, when I come to your home, I don't intend to do anything except be a guest."

"Sounds like a plan."

"Haven't you two had enough of making plans?"

"Jean, you have to forgive my daughter's bad mouth. She picked up some bad habits while she was away."

"I agree with Cindy." Marc stared at his mother. She smiled at him.

"My son seems to have developed a few of his own. I guess that goes to show you: A mother's job is never over." She smiled at Helen. "We'd better go before these two freeze us with their glares. Besides, it's past time I drag my caveman son home. See you tomorrow. Good seeing you again, Cindy."

"You, too, Miss Jean."

"See you on Saturday," Marc said.

"As close as your offices are, you'll probably see each other before then."

"As you can see, my mom is like superglue when she sets her mind to something. If she were a scientist she would have developed a cure for several serious diseases or still be holed up in her lab until she did."

"I'll take that as a compliment, because I know my own son would not insult me."

Cindy shook her head, but she laughed with the others. She went into the family room to watch the second game while the others went to the door.

She didn't intend to even confront her mother when she came into the room after seeing Jean and Marc to the door. Maybe if she ignored the scheming, her mother would give up.

She stared at the television screen, but the man she was visualizing wasn't wearing a football uniform. He wore a tan shirt that molded muscles that any player on the field would envy. Had he left the top two buttons of the shirt open so she could glimpse the crisp, black hair peeking out? So she could wonder if it was as thick all over his chest? So she could imagine brushing her hands over it?

She could still see the way his whole face brightened when he talked about his patients. They were blessed to have a doctor who cared so deeply.

Would he care just as deeply about other things? About other people? About a specific person? She shook her head to try to derail that thought before it continued. *Not me. Not him. No.*

She shifted up her chair and tried to focus on the game. The Steelers, her second favorite team, were playing, but her mind kept drifting from black and gold to brown and tan.

How could she catch herself before she fell into serious trouble?

Ten

At noon on Monday Denise went to the last room to find Marc. "I'm going to lunch now, Marc. Is there anything I can do for you before I go?" Denise stood in the doorway, her hands clasped in front of her.

"No. You go ahead, Denise." Marc slipped the paper on which he had been writing into the folder and looked up at the woman who hadn't moved from the doorway. "Was there something else?"

"I just wanted to tell you that I pulled the file for your first patient after lunch." Her smile widened and she leaned forward a bit. "It's in the holder on the examination room door."

"Thank you."

"I didn't want you to have to wait when the patient came back. We get so busy."

"I know." He kept from frowning.

"Yes." She giggled. "Of course you do. You're the doctor, the reason why they come here." She batted her eyes and pushed her braids back from her face. "I guess the patients flock to you because they know how good you are." She gave him an even wider smile. "Well, I guess I'd better go to lunch so I can get back in time to help you."

"Yes. Go. Have a good lunch." His patience deserted him and his scowl showed itself.

"I will." She stared at him, oblivious to his frown, and

nodded. "Too bad you have to stay here for your lunchtime meeting with the other doctors."

"Why is that too bad?"

"I . . . I"—a frown flitted across her face, but the smile came back—"I just mean, it's a shame that you don't get to relax over lunch the way we others do. You should have the opportunity to relax before your afternoon patients come."

"I don't mind eating here. This is my choice."

"Yes, I guess it is. You can't let the other partners down." She straightened from the door frame. "I'd better go."

"Yes."

Marc frowned as she left the doorway. What was it with that woman? His frown was still in place when he went to the meeting room.

"Sorry I'm late."

"What's the problem, Marc? You have a difficult case?"

"Not the kind you think." He pulled his lunch from the refrigerator. "That woman is driving me crazy with her attention." He plopped down in his usual chair and looked around the table. Jim, Raheem and Sylvia stared back at him.

"Who?" Raheem frowned at him. "You having trouble with an anxious mother?"

"That I can handle." He leaned his elbows on the table. "Somebody please tell me that I'm not the only one who's getting smothered by Denise."

"What did she do?"

"A dozen times a day she has to stop me and ask if everything is all right, if I need her to do anything. Even if I'm in the last examination room, she makes some excuse to come back there."

"She's enthusiastic about her job. It's her first job outside a hospital."

"Is she as enthusiastic with you as she is with me?" Marc stared at Raheem.

"Hey, man, I'm probably not her type."

"See. That's what I'm talking about." Marc leaned forward. "You noticed it, too."

"She does seem to like you better. But that's all right. I realize that I'm not as appealing to some people as some other people around here are." Sylvia laughed. "Especially to those of the other gender."

"She has probably imprinted on you." Jim chuckled and sipped his coffee.

"Imprinted?"

"You know: like birds do with the first creature they see after they hatch. You're the one who hired her."

"Denise is not a bird and, if she were, she would not be newly hatched." He glared as they laughed.

"I'm serious." Marc shook his head as he took his salad from the bag. "I'd ask Janie to handle my patients' records from now on and switch Denise to somebody else, but I don't have a valid reason for the switch." He frowned. "Besides, why upset Janie's routine when she hasn't done anything?"

"What do you want to do?" Sylvia sipped her tea. No trace of her smile was left.

"I don't know. I don't want to hurt her feelings if she doesn't mean anything by her behavior." He shook his head. "I can't change her schedule because of something that might be my imagination. She hasn't really done anything. Maybe she's just trying too hard to be helpful." He sighed. "Let's leave it alone for now and see if she tones it down."

"You're sure?" Jim asked.

"Yeah. I guess that's the best way to handle it for now."

"OK, then." Jim pushed his empty plate aside. "I have a case I want to discuss." He opened the folder in front of him.

Marc listened to Jim's presentation. By the time lunch was over, he had offered him suggestions just as the others had.

When they had first opened the practice and Raheem had suggested that they close the office from one to two and meet over lunch, Marc had been reluctant. Now he wondered why he had dragged his feet. It was helpful to have three other doctors to confer with about a case.

He walked back to the examination room. Denise wasn't a case, but he felt better after having discussed her. Maybe it was nothing. He hoped so.

Denise brought his first patient in and she didn't ask him how his lunch was. Maybe he had read things wrong with her. Sometimes he did that with people. He thought about Cindy. Unfortunately, her reaction to him he had read accurately.

Monday, early afternoon, Cindy sat at her desk eating a late lunch alone. The usual lunchtime customers had left and there was a lull until business would pick up again about five o'clock.

Today, instead of spending her lunchtime processing orders or looking at catalogs for new products as she usually did, she pulled a romance novel from her purse. With her life in the mess it was in, she was hesitant to read romances, given her situation, but Debbie had raved so much about Marilyn Tyner's latest book after she started working for Cindy that Cindy had given in. She was surprised that she had enjoyed it so much. She bought one of the first books by the same author. She had a choice of several titles, but *False Impressions* was the one she chose. When she selected this book because of the title, she wondered if the author chose it because she knew Harry. She shrugged. There was no danger in reading about romance, just in trying to live it. Fiction couldn't hurt you the way real life could. She shook her head as she opened the book. Not every man was like Harry. The trick was to identify those who were and avoid them like some deadly disease. She sighed and started where she left off in chapter three.

The hero, according to the description in the story and the picture on the cover, didn't look anything like Marc Thomas, but that didn't keep his image from creeping in at key scenes. She read to the end of the chapter and stopped. She had to get back to work. She closed the book, but Marc didn't go away. His warm smile and tan face kept her company as she left the office.

It's not fair for me to be so hard on him. He's as much a reluctant victim of his mother's manipulations as I am of mine.

She went to the front of the store, wondering how long it would be before their mothers gave up. She shook her head. She wasn't sure she wanted to know. Most likely the answer was in months rather than weeks.

Wednesday came and her mother brought over lunch just as they had planned.

"Because you're teaching your workshop tonight, I figured you needed something substantial." Helen handed Cindy a covered plate. "I made meatloaf yesterday and I know how you love it. I still had string beans, so I put some of them on the plate, too."

"I do love your meatloaf, but right now I'd love anything. I got up late this morning and only had time to grab a yogurt for breakfast." She put the plate into the microwave to warm. "Where's your lunch?"

"Today is my light day." Helen pulled a salad from her bag.

As they ate Cindy carried on her end of the conversation, but she was waiting for something to happen. No way had her mother given up. She just couldn't figure out what she had in mind.

"I have something for you."

"You already gave me lunch."

"That was nothing." Helen rummaged in her purse. "Here it is." She pulled out an envelope and handed it to Cindy.

"What is it?" Cindy kept her hand on her side of the table.

"Don't be so suspicious. Take it." She waved the envelope at Cindy.

"Not until you tell me what it is."

"My poor untrusting child." Helen shook her head.

"I know you."

"Of course you do. I'm your mother. You've known me all your life." She shook her head again. "It's a ticket. One of the secretaries has a daughter acting in Freedom Theater's production of *The Black Nativity* this year. I bought a ticket for next Friday night, but I can't go."

"Why not?"

"I have something else scheduled."

"Then why did you buy the ticket for that night?"

"I forgot."

"Uh-huh."

"I'm getting old. I'm allowed to be forgetful every now and then."

"Why didn't you exchange the ticket?"

"It's too late to sell that one." She leaned forward. "What's the big deal? You've gone to their productions before. You know they put on fantastic plays."

"How many tickets are in that envelope?"

"One. Why would I buy more than one ticket?"

"I'm sure you have no idea."

"I will feel bad if you let it go to waste." She placed the envelope on the table. "You need a break. You've been working too hard."

Cindy picked up the envelope, took the ticket out and made sure that there weren't two stuck together. "Thank you. I do kind of need a break."

"You're welcome, Miss Doubting Thomasina."

"I've got my reasons. You of all people know what they are." She tucked the ticket into her wallet. "For years I kept saying that I wanted to see this production. I've heard so many people rave about it."

"Now, thanks to your thoughtful mother, you can." Helen stood. "I've got to get back to school." She gathered her things and fastened her coat. "See you Sunday for dinner?"

"My place this time."

"I will assume that's because you feel it is only right that you take a turn."

"Whatever flies your kite."

Her mother left, and Cindy went to the cash register. Debbie, her assistant manager, had a doctor's appointment and had left early, but would be back.

Doctor's appointment. Marc came to mind. *Mom must be slipping. I expected two tickets to be in the envelope and some devious excuse from her.* She shook her head. Maybe Marc had convinced his mother that she was wasting her time and Miss Jean had passed the message on to Mom. *Maybe I should ask him how he did it.*

By the time Debbie returned, Cindy had managed to keep Marc from her thoughts most of the time as she went through the shops, straightening the shelves and replenishing stock.

Later she got out the basic materials that she needed for the workshop and placed them on the table. In the schedule she had described the activity and had placed an illustration at the top of the description so anyone who came would know exactly what they would be making. Cindy didn't want anybody to waste time on an activity that didn't appeal to them.

She checked to make sure everything was there, then got back to the shelves until it was time for the session.

Cindy opened the workshop. "This is an alternative to your attendants carrying plain bouquets. I made these in two different color schemes and used different types and sizes of flowers so you could see how adaptable they are."

Cindy held up two fans with sprays of flowers fastened to them. Streamers of wide satin ribbon hung down with a flower fastened at each end. "These are easy to make and not very expensive, but it makes a big impact." She told them the cost and passed the fans to the eight women sitting around the table. Five had been at the last workshop, but were still trying to make decisions.

"Now that you've seen them, does everybody want to make one?"

"Most definitely. Have you all checked the price of real flowers?" one of the women asked and looked around the table. Comments came from the others as they all agreed that artificial flowers were a wise choice.

"Bring it on," one of the women said and the others laughed and nodded.

"Okay. Tell me your wedding colors and I'll go get the materials." Cindy made a list. "I'll bring ribbon in both of your colors for each of you so you can see which you prefer."

When she got back, the women were talking and laughing. Cindy distributed the direction sheet and the materials.

"Ladies, if your attendants are really your friends, you can have them make their own fans." She smiled at them. "If they are not your friends, why are they in your wedding in the first place?" They all laughed.

Cindy walked around the table, offering suggestions, giving help, and trying not to envy their happy enthusiasm. She also hoped their happiness lasted longer than hers had. She frowned.

Had she really been happy with Harry? Her frown deepened as she faced the answer. Why had she stayed with him until he ended it? Why had she been so in love with the idea of being in love that she couldn't face the truth until it slapped her?

"Why are you frowning? Did I do this wrong?"

Cindy pulled her attention back to the workshop. "No, Mia, I was thinking about something else."

"You're sure? I'm not known for my manual dexterity. I'm much better at saying the word than in showing it." She laughed at herself.

"Your fan is perfect."

"For real?" Mia examined the front of the fan and then turned it over. "You'd tell me if it wasn't, wouldn't you?"

"Absolutely. When folks ask you who taught you how to make this, you're going to tell everybody that it was me. Do you think I want people criticizing my ability?" Cindy laughed with the others. "Really, Mia. It's perfect."

The others agreed before they went back to their own work.

Cindy was surprised when it was time to end the workshop.

Four of the women had decided to use the floral fans for their weddings and they bought the supplies before they left.

"If you run into trouble, let me know and we'll sort it out." She watched them go and then went back to clean the workshop table.

"Another success." She sighed. "This is good for me, too. It lets me see that some women still have faith in marriage."

Maybe one day I'll catch that feeling.

At closing time, she clutched her keys in her hand and locked up. She walked to her car, only looking at the red brick building in the next lot twice.

Eleven

By the time Friday afternoon came, Cindy was check-ing her watch every ten minutes as if afraid that time would skip ahead and make her late for the play. Stop it, she ordered herself when Andrea had to repeat a ques-tion. Cindy answered her and then moved on.

She shook her head. *Just goes to show you how much I need to get a life.*

She went down the aisles of both stores checking stock. She smiled the next time she checked her watch. Forty-five minutes had passed. She went back to her of-fice to process an order.

"You gotta help me." Mia stood in the doorway hold-ing a fan. "I told you that I am manually challenged." She held out her handiwork. "I swear I followed your directions exactly. So why doesn't mine look like yours? Or at least like the one I did during the workshop. How can I teach my attendants how to do this if I can't get it right myself?"

"Don't panic. Sit down." Cindy took the fan and looked at it as she sat beside Mia. "You skipped a step." She got out a direction sheet and showed her. "It's easy to fix. Do you want me to do it?"

"No, I have to get it right myself." She touched the spot where she had gone wrong. I see, now." She stood. "You know, if I have a problem with making a simple fan bouquet, how can I hope to handle a marriage?"

"One doesn't have anything to do with the other."
Cindy stared at Mia. "Do you love him?"

"I don't have any room in my heart for any more love
for Doug." Mia's face eased into a smile. "My heart is full
beyond capacity already."

"Then you'll be all right." She patted her arm. "Just
don't try to teach him to make fan bouquets." They both
laughed. Mia thanked her, hugged her and left.

After Mia had gone, Cindy sighed. *Why couldn't I have
found a love like that instead of . . .* She frowned. *I am making a New Year's resolution right now: Harry Granger will no
longer occupy space in my thoughts.* She set her jaw tightly
and went back to the craft store feeling less weighed
down than she had in a long time.

It was now fifteen minutes before Cindy had to leave.
"I'm going back to change. Do you need anything before
I go?" Cindy asked as she stood in front of Debbie.

"No. I've got everything covered here. Go change. You
don't want to be late. I know how you've been looking
forward to this."

"What gave you a clue? It couldn't have been the way
I kept checking the time, could it? Nor maybe my pre-
occupation?"

"Both, boss." Debbie laughed. "Go change."

Cindy laughed as she hurried back to the office. She
took the red two-piece dress from the garment bag she
had brought with her and went into the bathroom to
freshen up.

"See you tomorrow morning," Cindy said to Debbie a
short while later. She smoothed the bias cut wool skirt over
her hips and slipped on her full-length black wool coat.
"You know where to find me in case you need me." She
buttoned the coat and pulled on her black leather gloves.

"Oh, yeah. I might have an emergency like"—Debbie

pretended to frown—"What kind of emergency? Maybe I won't be able to find the blue beads. Or the white ribbon. Or the . . ."

"OK, OK." Cindy shrugged. "So sometimes I worry unnecessarily."

"Don't. Your store is in good hands with me. I'll treat it like my own, but, of course, I won't sell it." She laughed. "I like the dress. Red is your color and the boots really set off the dress."

"Thanks. Don't tell anyone, but the boots are to keep my ankles warm, not to make a fashion statement."

"Your secret is safe with me. You're the boss, but I'm ordering you to have fun."

"Yes, Ma'am. I will."

Excitement stayed at a high level as Cindy drove to Broad Street and the theater. *It's been too long since I've been out.*

In spite of the cold night air, she smiled all the way into the theater from the parking lot a half block away. She mingled with the rest of the theatergoers. *I'm glad Mom gave me the ticket,* she thought as she made her way to her row.

She inched toward her seat but didn't sit when she got there.

"It looks like I asked Mom the wrong question. I asked if she was sure that she only had one ticket in the envelope she gave me."

"You should have asked her if my mother had a ticket for the seat next to yours." Marc stood and smiled at her.

"I'm sorry," they said at the same time.

"My mother said she had somewhere else to go." Again they spoke together.

"So did my mother. Sit down and pretend that I'm not here. I'll really have a talk with my mother tomorrow."

"I'm sorry for my mother's part in subjecting you to this." Cindy sat. "I'm sure you are perfectly capable of finding your own date on a Friday night. Or any night, for that matter." She stared at him. "Not that this is a date." She rushed her words. "We came separately so this is not a date."

"That's true. This is not a date."

"This is what we get for trying to keep theater tickets from going to waste."

"No good deed going unpunished and stuff like that."

"Exactly."

"You know, my mother is as much to blame as yours is."

"I'll bet they're at one of their houses right now trying to cast spells over us."

"If mom is and I find out, I'm going to tell Reverend Dent that she believes in magic."

"Maybe they're trying to pray us together."

"I'm glad the Lord makes His own decisions." He stared at Cindy. "I'm the one who should apologize for my mother. She knows how you feel about me and so do I."

"It's not you personally. I don't even know you." She shook her head. "I know I'm being illogical. It's just that . . ." She shrugged.

"I know. It's Harry what's-his-face who gave a bad name to all doctors."

"I'm not going to talk about him."

"Good, because I don't like to talk about jerks."

"I made an early New Year's resolution, one I should have made at least one year ago: No more thinking about Harry."

"Let me know if the resolution works. I have a couple of my own to try."

The lights dimmed and the talking hushed. The curtain opened and Cindy was transported by the opening scene. Soon she was lost in the play.

Later, as the lights came up for intermission, Cindy blinked to adjust to the light.

"That was wonderful." She stopped clapping as the

rest of the applause died down. "It's enough to make me forgive Mom for her manipulating." Cindy smiled at Marc. She blinked at the effect when he smiled back.

"Do you want a soft drink?"

"No, I'm fine."

"I'm not thirsty either."

Marc struggled to keep from agreeing out loud about her fineness. He didn't want to blow the fragile peace or at least cease-fire that was in place. If this were a date, he could caress her hand instead of wishing he could. He could comment on how beautiful she was in red. If they had a relationship going, he could tell her that he liked looking at her in any color. If they were really close, maybe she would have given him the privilege of taking the dress off her and caressing more than her hands.

His hands itched to touch her smooth shoulders and let the dress fall to the floor. The floor in his house; his bedroom. Or her bedroom. Or . . .

Mercifully the lights blinked and then dimmed for the next act. He hoped that by the time the play was over his body would no longer show where his thoughts were. Then he tried to concentrate on the stage instead of the woman sitting reluctantly beside him.

"That was fantastic," Cindy said over the applause that filled the theater at the final curtain. "I have got to come again next year." She touched his arm, but drew her hand back immediately.

"Me, too." Marc frowned. Her hand had been there so briefly. How could he miss it being there?

"Let's go get a cup of coffee or something. I think Gloria's over on Fairmont Avenue is open late."

"I don't think . . ."

"We have to plot our strategy. How else can we hope

to get the best of those two. We never know what they'll try next."

Cindy nodded. "I know what the saying about 'waiting for the other shoe to drop' means."

"Then you agree that we need a plan."

"Yes." She nodded again.

"Then we have to meet." The soft sounds of others leaving filled the air around them, but Cindy didn't say anything. Marc grasped for words to make her agree with him. He took a deep breath. "Look. It won't be a real date. We'll be in separate cars." He smiled. Maybe that would help sway her. He didn't let himself wonder why he was going against his own promise to leave it alone and instead was working so hard to persuade her.

Cindy's forehead creased and she looked as if she was searching for an answer to a universal problem instead of whether to go with Marc. Finally she shrugged. Then she smiled back. "You're right. It wouldn't be a date."

They left the theater together and were soon parking near each other across the street from the small restaurant. You are not on a date with a doctor, she told herself as she got out to meet Marc.

She tried not to notice how right it seemed that he should hold her elbow as they crossed the street and leave it there when they reached the other side.

"So. What's your plan?" Cindy shifted in her side of the booth and sipped her herbal tea.

"I'm not dating anyone."

"What?" Cindy frowned.

"I haven't in a long time."

"So what?"

"In the theater you said something about me having a date for Friday nights."

"Oh." She leaned back in the booth. "What does that have to do with anything?"

"I think we should start dating."

"You mean you and I?"

"Yep." He nodded. He tried to sound casual even though he didn't understand why.

"I don't think so."

"Why not? You said that you're not going to think about what's-his-name anymore."

"I'm not a charity case."

"What are you talking about?"

"I don't need for our mothers to fix me up."

The waitress chose that time to take their order. Marc scrambled for words to move Cindy's answer into the 'yes' column.

"They're not. I am. Or rather, you and I are." He leaned close. "Look, this is the only way we can get them to back off. We go out together a few times, when it doesn't work out, they consider us a hopeless case and find another project."

"You don't know them as well as you think."

"The worst that will happen is that they find somebody else to fix us up with. Unless your mother has a book full of phone numbers of eligible doctors, the next one she finds will have a profession that will be more acceptable to you."

"Marc . . ."

"Of course, the longer we go out, the longer they leave us alone. Only you and I will know that our going out won't be real dates."

"I don't know about this."

"Then you come up with a better plan." He kept his stare on her. "Well?"

"I can't." She sighed. "Okay. I'll go along with your plan. At least if they think we're dating we won't have to watch for any more tricks from them."

"We'll give it until the end of the year. Okay?"

"That long? That's almost two months away."

"You know the holidays are a prime time for fixing people up. They, of all people, feel that everybody should have somebody during the holidays. Who knows what or *who* they'll come up with for us if we don't keep it going until after the holidays." He smiled again. "Besides, if we keep it going until then, they'll be feeling so smug that when we break up they won't know what to do."

"At least for awhile." She sighed. "Okay. I could use a break from their sneakiness." She shrugged. "Let's give it a try." She shrugged again. "Want to come over for dinner after church on Sunday? Mom's coming over. We may as well start now."

"Sure. Should I bring Mom?"

"Yes. Let them both be witnesses." Cindy looked around. The only other couple in the restaurant was leaving. "We'd better go."

"I'll follow you home."

"That's not necessary."

"Humor me. I can't let my date travel at night alone."

"You don't have to pretend when we're alone."

"I'll follow you home."

"OK." She shrugged, but she was glad for his thoughtfulness. "See you Sunday."

"Uh-uh. See you tomorrow at the workshop. Remember?"

"Oh, yeah." Cindy got in her car and gave Marc time to get into his.

As she drove home she tried not to be excited about seeing him tomorrow. *It's not about you, it's about his Little Brother, Kevin,* she reminded herself. She drove toward Lincoln Drive.

And Sunday dinner is not a date, it's just part of a plan to break free from our mothers, she told herself. She frowned.

Then why was she as excited as she would be if it were a date with someone she was attracted to?

Twelve

Saturday morning came crisp and cold, the way November in Philadelphia is supposed to be. Cindy hopped from between her flannel sheets as if a May morning were waiting for her. She hurried about getting ready as if she were late.

At first she tried to rationalize herself into tamping down her enthusiasm by focusing on the workshop, but she soon gave up. She was going to see Marc. It was safe to look forward to it. As long as nobody else knew, she wasn't vulnerable.

She rushed her breakfast of hot cereal and arrived at the store earlier than usual.

"I have to set out the materials that we need to make the personalized trays. That's why I'm early," she told herself as she filled a box with fifteen kits. Only twelve had registered, but there was always the possibility of walk-ins.

She set the things on the table and got the samples from her office. Then she checked her watch. An hour before opening time. What next?

She went back to her office and checked the schedule for workshops to take her through the rest of the year and into the first week of January. She swallowed hard. It looked like such a short time between now and the new year.

What if he weren't a doctor? What if he were a lawyer? Or sold real estate? Or were a teacher? Or maybe a mechanic? She stared at the paper on the table. *If I'm not going to let Harry into my life, why am I letting him affect this thing, whatever it is, with Marc?*

She shook her head. No matter how she tried to deny it, she did feel an attraction to him. *Why does he have to be so nice?* She frowned. *And tall? And good looking? Why does his chest look so inviting? Why do I wonder how it would feel to have him hold me close?* She gave up trying to check the schedule.

Even if there had never been a Harry, she would still be skeptical. Somebody who looked as fine as Marc did and acted as nice must have something the matter with him. With a shortage of eligible men, if he is as perfect as he seems, he would have been grabbed by some woman by now. She nodded. Something had to be wrong with him. She sighed. She didn't want to be the one who got close enough to discover what it was.

Her stare was on the desk, but her mind formed a rich chocolate brown face with full lips curved into a warm smile. She sighed. She got warm just thinking about him. What would happen when she started seeing him regularly? *What am I going to do? Why did I agree to go along with his dumb plan?* She frowned. *Because I couldn't think of a better one.*

She left the office. He was probably anxious to get on with his life without interference from their mothers. He probably had his eye on some woman and wanted Cindy out of the way. He only made his suggestion to keep from coming right out and telling her that he wasn't interested. She frowned. *Why doesn't that make me happy? That's what I want, so why doesn't the idea please me?*

She drew in a quick breath at the image that formed in her mind as the words "Please me" came to her. She and Marc together. His hands showing exactly how much he could please her. Marc capturing her lips with his. Exploring her mouth with his discovering her sensitive places that had been neglected for too long; for forever. And she. She feeling her way across his chest, learning if his muscles were as firm as they looked; discovering if the hair on his chest was as crisp as she imagined; exploring to find out where the hair ended; tasting the chocolate skin covering his chest.

The buzzer outside the store sounded. It was probably Debbie and Andrea, but she didn't care if it was somebody else. She was grateful. She frowned. What had gotten into her? She shook away the image of what, or rather who, she would like to get into her. *Cut it out.* She went to open the door. *He only wants to move past me and find a woman for himself, one who isn't pushed on him.*

She let Debbie and Andrea in. She even managed to act as if she hadn't just gone on an erotic fantasy trip.

"How was the theater?"

"The performance was fantastic. You should go see it." She was not going to mention who sat beside her. And across from her later at the restaurant. She had to look on that as a business meeting. Cindy watched as the two women went to hang up their coats. Was spending time with Marc what had sparked her imagination? She hoped not. If they followed their plan, she'd be spending a lot more time with him. Who knew what her mind would do with that.

Cindy wrestled with her thoughts in between waiting on customers. When ten o'clock came, she was glad she had to conduct the workshop. Hopefully, despite the fact that Marc would be there, the concentration required wouldn't let any dangerous thoughts in.

Cindy was wrong. But she was right, too. Marc introduced her to Kevin.

"Do you really own this store? Do you get to use anything you want?"

"Yes. I do." Cindy nodded and smiled at the thin boy who was almost as tall as she was.

"Do you have oil paints, too? I mean the kind real artists use?"

"Yes, we do."

"When we're finished here, we're going to the art museum." He looked up at Marc with a grin as wide as his face. "I love Monet." He looked at Cindy. "I like to make things, too. Can we sit down there?" He pointed at the far end of the table.

Cindy wanted to kiss him for choosing the last two seats on the side. That should be far enough for her to be safe from Marc distracting her, shouldn't it?

"You sure you want to sit that far away?" Marc asked Kevin, but he looked at Cindy.

"Yeah. I can see everybody else, and Miss Cindy, too, from there."

Marc stared at Cindy a few seconds longer.

Even though he's here, he can't know what I'm thinking. And there's no way he could tell where my thoughts were before he got here. She stared back at him.

"Can we sit down before somebody else gets our seats?" Kevin's words allowed Cindy to break free. She tried not to watch as Marc followed the boy.

Those who had preregistered came in as well as two walk-ins. Cindy thought that Marc sitting so far away would be ideal, but she was still too much aware of him. The way her mind was acting this morning, if he sat in his office he would still disturb her thoughts; only maybe not as much. There was something to be said about the advantage of distance learning. *Please let my thoughts stay in the PG-13 area.* She sighed and began.

"This is what we'll be working on today." She held up a plain white plastic tray. "You get to draw a picture on it. After you paint it and you're satisfied with the way it looks, I'll put it in a special oven to set the colors, then it will be ready for you to use. It's not long until Thanksgiving, but you might not want to draw a Thanksgiving scene; you want your tray to fit in all year 'round." She started to look at everyone around the table, but her gaze got stuck when she reached Marc.

"Can I really draw any picture I want?" Faye asked.

"Miss Cindy said we could, didn't you Miss Cindy?" Lynn looked at Cindy.

"Yes I did." She handed out kits containing everything needed.

"Can I draw a dinosaur?"

"If you want to."

"I want to draw a clown. Is that all right?" La Sonya asked.

"Yes."

"Are there any black clowns?"

"Blacks work at every job you can think of. A few years ago we had a black clown at my family reunion."

"How about my dog?" Frank asked. "My mom calls her dumb dog, but I want to draw her anyway."

"Whatever you want to draw is fine. You decide." Cindy looked around at the others. Most of them had their hands up. In spite of what Cindy had said, they each asked if their idea was all right. *This isn't going to be as easy as I thought.*

"If I had a girlfriend, I could draw her picture, couldn't I?" Marc looked as if he was struggling to keep from laughing. Cindy glared at him.

"Is it okay to start now? I want to do a painting of the Japanese Bridge that Monet painted." Kevin pulled Cindy's attention from Marc and pushed the glare from her face. "Do you know that he painted a lot of pictures of the same bridge?"

They all opened the kits and, while they worked, Kevin talked about Monet. Even Lynn listened and worked quietly.

Cindy walked around the table to give help when it was needed. She hesitated when she got near Marc.

Then she took a deep breath and moved toward him. Kevin's work grabbed her attention. Cindy was familiar with the Monet painting that he had mentioned. Kevin's rendition was amazingly accurate although he used slightly different colors. Cindy smiled. She liked Kevin's version better.

"That's wonderful." She touched the edge of the tray.

"Thanks." Kevin shrugged. "I didn't get the colors exactly right, but you shouldn't copy an artist's work exactly anyway."

"That's true." She hesitated, then moved to Marc.

"What do you think?" He touched her hand and for a second she forgot what he was talking about.

"About what?" She stared at him.

"My painting, of course. What did you think I was talking about?"

Cindy looked at the tray in front of him. An oak tree spread its branches across the width and the length as if only the tray's edges kept it from growing even taller and wider.

"I didn't know you could paint."

"There's a lot you don't know about me. We'll have to fix that."

Cindy couldn't think of a smart answer. She couldn't think of an answer at all, smart or dumb. She sighed and moved to Janice, who sat on the other side of Marc. *Maybe my agreement for us to pretend to date was not one of my best decisions.*

Lynn caught Cindy's attention and the second-guessing ended. She worked her way around the table, assuring the kids that their families would love their work. After that, each time she made her way around the table, she did not stop at Marc.

"Your trays will be ready in about an hour." Cindy smiled when they had all finished. "You can come get

them whenever you want to; later today or next week."
She collected the trash as it was passed to her.

"Can we keep the leftover paints?"

"Sure. You can use them, just don't try to paint something at home and bake it. The trays are made out of a special plastic. Regular plastics melt and smoke if you heat them. You can use the paints on paper or anything else. Just remember, once it dries, you can't wash it off."

They thanked her and left. Marc and Kevin were the last to go.

"That was a lot of fun." Kevin's smile filled his face. "We're going to get lunch and then go to the museum." He frowned. "I guess you can't come with us, huh?"

"No, sorry, but thanks for inviting me." Cindy shook her head. "Saturday is our busiest day here at the shop." She smiled at him. "Have fun."

"See you tomorrow." Marc drew her attention.

"Tomorrow?" She frowned.

"Dinner. Or did you uninvite me?"

"Of course not. I'll see you tomorrow after church."

"Should I bring anything?"

"No."

"You're supposed to say 'nothing but yourself.'" He smiled at her. "I won't push it by adding a flattering adjective." He touched her arm. "See you."

Cindy did not watch him go. This dating idea was definitely not the result of her best thinking.

The store was busy until closing time, but not too busy for Cindy to think about Marc a few times; too many times.

The phone was ringing as she unlocked the door to her house. She rushed to it, wondering, as she often did, why she even set the answering machine when she only allowed it to do its job when she wasn't there.

"So. How was last night?" Her mother's voice failed at trying to sound casual.

"I'm surprised you waited this long to call."

"I didn't know how late you got in last night and I thought you might have slept a little later this morning.

"You're only calling because you gave me the ticket, right?"

"I have to make sure you got my money's worth."

"And that's the only reason. It seems I asked you the wrong question when you gave me the ticket. I should have asked if you knew who had the ticket for the seat next to mine."

"Jean had something else to do, too."

"You two probably met to plot your next move. General Patton would have been proud of you."

"Thank you. We try. Did Marc show up?"

"Didn't Jean tell you?"

"Marc wouldn't tell her anything. Kids can be so secretive sometimes.

"I wonder where we get it from."

"I'd resent that if it weren't true."

Cindy laughed with her mother. "The play was great. Thank you for the ticket."

"Did you go right home afterward?"

"No. Marc and I went to his house and I spent the night. We made mad, unbridled love until dawn. I was almost late for work this morning."

"Cindy Larson! You just met him! What were you thinking? You don't do things like that."

"Isn't that what you wanted?"

"You know it isn't. I want you to get to know each other, fall in love, get married"—she glared at Cindy through the phone—"and then have children."

"The topic of children didn't even come up. We were too busy to discuss it. We . . ."

"Stop. I don't want to hear anymore." Her mother

held up her hands even though Cindy wasn't there to see it. Then she slowly shook her head. "I never thought you would . . ."

"Don't have a heart attack, Mom. It never happened." She nodded. "But you did ask for that." Cindy laughed. "We went to Gloria's for a cup of coffee."

"And?"

"Then I came home."

"And?"

"And I'll see you tomorrow morning at church. You should feel relieved at the truth after my storytelling."

Cindy hung up before her mother could get another "and" in. She went into the kitchen to heat up leftovers, but her mind wasn't on eating. It had dug itself into the answer she had playfully given her mother.

What if it had been true? What if she had gone to Marc's house? What if she had spent the night making mad love with him?

Her body prepared itself as if not only was what she had said true, but it was getting ready for a repeat of those activities. *Activities. How can I think of lovemaking as just an activity?*

Her imagination kicked up a notch. Marc, holding her against his bare chest, the hair there teasing her breasts. His mouth would . . .

She shook her head. *That's what I get for teasing Mom.*

Maybe instead of eating dinner she should take a cold shower or run until the image left and her temperature, heart rate and body fluids returned to normal.

She shook her head and opted for the shower, but she would be surprised if it worked.

Thirteen

Sunday morning, mild and sunny, came too soon. As she went for her morning run before church, Cindy should have been wondering about the unseasonably warm temperatures and how long they would last. Instead her thoughts were full of dinner. She sighed as she jogged a block and stopped to stretch. Dinner wasn't the problem. *I've been cooking long enough not to be nervous.* She shook her head. It wasn't the idea of cooking that disturbed her; it was her dinner guests that kept her from fully enjoying the early morning. She shook her head. Guest. Singular.

She stepped up her pace as if she could outrun her doubts if she went fast enough.

She crossed the street and turned down Anderson Street. This morning she needed the distraction of street running rather than the peacefulness of the park path along Lincoln Drive.

Her distractions came from within. She set a fast pace, but her doubts kept pace with her. Marc's image even tagged along. Neither left even after she had found the zone. Was he out running at this very moment? He didn't live far. Did his route cross hers? Would she see him?

By the time Cindy had reached Washington Lane and was jogging back along Crittenden Street, she had given up clearing her mind and had almost convinced herself that dinner with Marc might not be too bad. Her mother and his would be there.

She stretched on her porch, then she went inside. *I can do this.*

"We're still on, aren't we?" Helen stood with Cindy after church.

"Of course we are. When did you know me to back out of an invitation?"

"I don't remember when you were last late for church either, but today was the day."

"I wasn't late. I got here before you marched in."

"Just barely." She kissed her cheek. "See you at the house."

Cindy made her way to the door, making sure that she hugged ten people as Reverend Dent always instructed the congregation. She smiled. One day she was going to ask how they were supposed to know when they reached ten if they didn't count as he also instructed them.

She made her way along the expressway, trying not to be impatient when the traffic getting off at the zoo slowed down the rest of the cars. She had plenty of time to get dinner ready.

She reached her house and went inside. Change clothes or not? She sighed and went upstairs. She would at least change her shoes.

She put the chicken in mushroom sauce into the oven and the collards on the stove to warm up. Then she went to set the table. She frowned as she put four place settings on the table. *Where do I want Marc to sit? Beside me or across from me?* She shook her head. She was sorry she didn't have a third choice.

"To quote you: 'Why is the table set for four?'" her mother asked when she got there.

"I invited somebody to join us."

"Anybody I know?"

"You look like a kid who got a surprise toy."

"You shouldn't tease your mother." The doorbell rang. "I'll get it." Cindy laughed as her mother almost ran to the door. Then the fact that Marc was one of the ones she was letting in made her laugh run away.

"You didn't tell me Marc was coming." Helen's smile said that she didn't care.

"And Jean is with him; by invitation, of course." Jean smiled as if she had just won the grand prize in the lottery.

"We'll take care of the part with you and me the next time." Helen hugged Marc's mother.

"I didn't think it possible, but they are getting bolder." Cindy said. Then she looked at Marc and had trouble breathing. It felt as if her breath had decided to go jogging without her. "Hi, Marc." She knew her words sounded as if she had tried to catch her breath but failed. *Residuals of my imaginings. That's all.*

"Hi, Cindy." His soft, deep words tugged at her insides. His words, coupled with the way he looked in his olive green sports shirt and dark green pants, were devastating. Cindy fought the chaos running rampant through her.

"I know this isn't my house, but come on into the living room," Helen said when neither one of the young people moved.

The two women watched as Marc eased to Cindy and kissed her cheek. Cindy stood as if the area rug under her feet had changed into a pool of quick-drying cement. She never heard Helen and Jean gasp and then sigh. If Marc hadn't wrapped a hand around her shoulder and squeezed, she might have still been there when it was time to go open the store on Monday morning. Of course, the feelings coursing through her at the warmth coming from him and spreading through her where their sides met didn't make her think about going to work. Visions of another setting swayed in her mind.

"Let me help you in the kitchen." Marc smiled and she felt herself getting more lost.

He should have saved that smile for when we're alone. Cindy smiled back, then she frowned and blinked. *Pretend. This is all pretend, a play for our mothers.* She tried to convince herself of that. She frowned. *Then why does it feel like for real?* She tried to take a step away from him, but his hand tightened. She sighed. She really didn't want to move from him anyway.

"Which way is the kitchen, sugar?"

"You don't have to help. I can. I always offer, but . . . Ow." The rest of Helen's sentence was interrupted by the not-so-gentle pinch that Jean gave her arm.

"Let's go into the living room, Helen. I want to see if Randall Cunningham gets to play today."

"Randall Cunningham?" Helen frowned. Then her face lit up as though a lightbulb had come on inside her. "Oh, yeah. That kitchen would be too small for four people, and we couldn't leave you out here alone. Besides, I'm tired from all that standing I did when we were singing." This time Helen took Jean's arm and pulled her into the living room.

"Well?" Marc still stared at Cindy.

"Well what?" She managed to ease away from him.

"The kitchen. Which way?"

"Oh. OK. This way."

Cindy led him to the kitchen at the back of the house, wishing it was as far away as the one in her friend Arlene's house across the street. She was glad that there wasn't much to do. She shook her head. For crying out loud. It was only a little kiss on the cheek.

"I like this kitchen. Did you have the granite counters put in, or were they already here when you bought the house?"

"They were already here." She frowned up at him. She could see the faint, light lines in his eyes, like spokes in a wheel. She could see where laugh lines were hinting at the future. She could see . . . Too close. Cindy stepped back. "What was that all about?" She took another step away from him.

"What?"

"That"—she swallowed hard—"that kiss." She resisted the strong urge to touch her face where he had kissed her. Was it still as warm as it felt? She shook her head. It was an innocent kiss on the cheek. The kind friends and even acquaintances used to greet each other. She frowned. Then why didn't it feel as if that's all it was? And how would she be behaving now if it had been a real kiss?

"The kiss?" He shrugged. "It was no big deal. It was all for show. Our mothers were watching. They're very smart, you know. We have to put on a good performance in order to fool them."

"We only went out once." She glared at him. "Actually, we didn't go out then. We met afterward." She moved to the stove and spooned the collards to a serving bowl. "I don't let anybody get that close after one real date. Certainly not after just going for coffee after we run into each other." She lifted the pan of rolls from the oven and moved them to the basket.

"When was the last time you dated?" He frowned at her. "Folks have taken giant leaps away from being that reserved even on a first date. You would be surprised."

"Shocked is probably more like it. Is that how your dates go? Are you speaking from firsthand experience?"

"We're not talking about me." He pretended not to notice her indignant look and her comment and went on. "Remember, we're under a tight timetable. We don't have time to waste on old-fashioned preliminaries."

"My mother would never believe that I let somebody get that close that fast. Not after my experience with . . ."

"Shh." Marc put a finger against her lips. "You're not

to say his name. Remember your resolution? You can't break it so soon."

He moved his finger away, but not before he gave in and brushed it gently across the length of her lips. He wanted to place his mouth there so badly. He wanted to pull her against him and feel her softness against his hardness just this once. He wanted to let his hands discover if her skin was as soft and as smooth as it looked. He held his breath. *She looks as if she wants the same thing that I want.* He shook his head and stepped back from her. He was never much of a gambler. He let out a harsh breath. To give his hands something to do besides get him into trouble, he picked up the closest dish.

"I'll take this out." Marc looked at the platter of chicken in his hands as if seeing it for the first time.

"OK." Cindy stared at him as if waiting for him to tell her what to do next. She picked up the collards, but put the bowl back down when the greens threatened to spill. She took a deep breath, straightened her back and picked them up again. Satisfied that they would stay in the bowl, she picked up the candied sweet potatoes with the other hand. She took another deep breath, refused to analyze what had just happened, and went into the dining room. There hadn't even been another kiss.

"Is everything all right?" Helen looked from Cindy to Marc and back to Cindy.

"Of course it is. Why wouldn't it be?"

"I don't know. You look . . ."

"That was a rhetorical question, Mom. No answer required." She went back to the kitchen before her mother could say anything more. Marc followed her, so she couldn't rub her face with an ice cube to cool it off. *It probably wouldn't do any good, anyway, as long as he's here.* She glanced at him. *And he is here.*

"I'll take this. OK?" Marc picked up the basket of rolls.

"OK." Cindy watched him leave the kitchen. *I lied. It's*

not OK. Things are a long way from OK. She got the iced tea
from the refrigerator, fought to get her pre-Marc calmness in place and went to the dining room.

"Does everybody have what they need?" She resisted
the urge to add "Besides me." What she needed was to
become immune to Marc.

"Sit down before the food gets cold." Helen motioned
to Marc. We left the end for you." She smiled at Cindy.
"Since you and Marc are just getting acquainted, we left
the place next to it for you."

"Whatever." Cindy sighed. She needed to save her
strength for the bigger battle. She had to get through
this meal.

"Marc, tell us about last night. I already heard Cindy's
version." Cindy sputtered as her iced tea went down the
wrong way. "Are you OK, baby?" Her mother patted her
on the back. If Cindy didn't know better, she would have
believed that innocent look on her mother's face. She
hoped the others did. Marc began to speak and she
dared a look at him. Her outrageous fantasy seemed
more like wishful thinking. She looked away from him
and stared at her plate.

"This was the first time I saw the production, but it
won't be the last. I think it ranks right up there with *The
Nutcracker* for a must-see Christmas production." He
smiled. "To tell you the truth, I'd rank it above. I can relate to it more." He turned his smile on Cindy. "Cindy
and I will go see it next year together." He placed his
hand on Cindy's and squeezed. "Isn't that right?"

"Uh-huh. Yes." She felt her head nod so she must have
been moving it.

"I'm so glad." Jean looked at Helen and winked.

"It should go without saying, but I'll say it anyway."
Helen smiled. "I'm glad, too."

"Maybe you two will leave us alone now?" Marc but-
tered his roll.

"What did we do?" Helen's eyes widened. "We only gave you two a little nudge. Mothers are allowed to act in the best interest of their children."

"I agree. We just helped you two get out of the ruts you were stuck in." Jean smiled as if she were waiting for somebody to hang a medal around her neck.

"I think we better let it go," Helen said as she looked at the two young people.

"This chicken is delicious. How did you fix it?" Marc looked at Cindy.

"It's nothing fancy. Mr. Campbell helped out with his cream of mushroom soup, and I just doctored it up a bit."

"You'll have to give me your recipe."

"Do you cook?" She dared a look at him.

"I've been known to fill a pot or two. Come to dinner on Tuesday and I'll prove it."

Helen and Jean were so quiet that if anybody weren't looking, they would never know that four people were in the room.

"I thought you had to work Tuesday nights."

"I can switch with Sylvia." He smiled. "My partners are very accommodating. I'm the only one of us who doesn't have a significant other. Yet." He fixed a stare on her. "Is it a date?"

Was it her imagination, or had he emphasized the word "date"?

"Yes."

"Yes." Helen looked sheepish when everyone looked at her after she made the word sound like a triumph. "I mean, I think it's good that men know how to cook."

"That's not what you meant and you know it."

"I don't know what this younger generation is coming to." Helen shook her head. She looked at Jean. "You know, when we were coming up, we would never talk to our mothers like that."

"I know exactly what you mean." Jean shook her head.

"You two need to stop." Marc looked at each older woman.

"Tell us about the kids' workshop." Helen changed the subject. "How did it go?"

Cindy, grateful for a safe subject, described the project. As they ate, she and Marc answered questions from their mothers. Marc talked about Kevin and how excited he was about the activity they did. He filled them in on Kevin's background. Then each of the mothers told about some incident with their students. Conversation flowed and skipped around the table as they finished the meal.

"Does anybody need anything else before we have dessert?" Cindy began to gather the dishes.

"I would say that I'm full, but you said the magic word: 'dessert.'" Jean chuckled.

Cindy laughed as she stood. "OK. Shall we have it in the living room and catch the rest of the game?"

"I'll help clear." Marc stood.

"It's not necessary."

"I have ulterior motives." The fork clattered to the table as Cindy picked up the platter. "On Tuesday I intend to let you help me clear the table."

"We'll just go watch the game. We'll fill you in on what you miss when you come in." Helen stood.

"You may as well clean up the kitchen while you're in there." Jean said. "I don't know about you, but I like to get it out of the way. I hate to go back to a dirty kitchen." She followed Helen out of the room.

"I'm not sure this was a good idea." Cindy frowned as the women rushed away as if afraid somebody was going to stop them. "They're like hungry sharks on the scent of blood."

"It will be all right. They're just not used to their plans working." Marc took the vegetable bowls from the table. "Has your mother tried to fix you up before?"

"Every week she suggests somebody else. I think she

has a list hidden somewhere." Cindy smiled and led him into the kitchen.

"My mother's been busy, too." He set the bowls on the table and went back for the glasses. Cindy got the bread and set it on the kitchen table.

"Let's leave everything. I'll finish later."

"We can't."

"Why not?"

"Uh . . ." Marc frowned. "It's unhealthy. Leftovers should be refrigerated right away."

Cindy stared at him. "OK, Doctor Marc." She shrugged and took containers from the cabinet.

Soon, but not soon enough for her, the chicken and vegetables were in the refrigerator. She turned to get the tray with the dessert dishes and forks from the counter.

"Not yet." Marc touched her shoulder and she turned toward him.

"What . . ."

He captured her open mouth with his. His hands eased her against him as he tasted her mouth, as his tongue danced with hers, as she got lost in the dance. Her hands crept up his chest and brushed across it, searching for the right spot, the spot to anchor her in common sense. His hands tightened around her and brushed across her back in return. The kiss deepened and Cindy got lost and common sense hid.

Slowly Marc helped her find her way out. Cindy blinked as she tried to gain control of her emotions.

"That's better." Marc's words rumbled from him. He brushed a finger gently over her kiss-swollen lips. "Much better."

"What?" Cindy was proud that she had been able to form a word and get it out. She frowned.

"They expected more than kitchen cleaning to take place. I figured we should show them proof." He took a deep breath and released it slowly. His voice sounded casual.

"Oh." What else could she say? And how could he be so unaffected by what just happened? She frowned. *Because it's nothing to him. He told you the new birds and bees story. This is no big deal to him.*

She wished she could ask him how he did it.

"I'll take this in." Marc picked up the tray. "You bring the cake."

Cindy followed him. At least the cake plate couldn't rattle. She hoped the game was tied and all kinds of scoring was going on.

She took one deep breath and then another and went into the living room. She set the cake plate on the coffee table and took off the lid. What she did not do was look at either her mother or Jean.

"Coconut cake. My favorite." Cindy made the mistake of looking at her mother. She saw her focus on Cindy's mouth before she looked at her eyes. Helen's smile could have taught a lesson to the Cheshire cat. "Do you have any vanilla ice cream to go with it?"

"Yes." *Concentrate.* She cut four crooked slices. "Do you want some ice cream, too, Jean?"

"Yes, please."

"I want coffee with mine," Helen said. "I always did like a cup of coffee with my dessert."

"It's instant."

"That's OK. Instant is good."

"I'd like ice cream and coffee, too." Marc put the cake plates back on the tray and lifted it. "I'll come help."

"No. You stay here. I'll get it."

"Don't be silly. You can't carry this and a cup of coffee."

"I'll manage . . ."

"Coffee sounds like a good idea to me, too," Jean added, "but I wouldn't want you to have to make two trips."

"Of course it does and of course you don't." Cindy sighed. The sooner she got this over with the better.

She tried to ignore Marc right behind her as she went back into the kitchen. She took out the ice cream and slid the container across the counter. "Put a scoop on each plate. The scoop is in the top drawer. I'll get the coffee." She dashed over to the stove and grabbed the kettle as soon as it whistled.

"What's the rush?" Marc took one step toward her. "Are you trying to catch the rest of the game?" He closed the space between them and took the kettle from her hands. "Or are you afraid this will happen?"

He kept his hands at his sides as he brushed his mouth across hers. Her desire to stay away from him was dissolved by a new desire. For all her ability to move, he may as well have tied her in place. She was on the verge of leaning into him when he stepped away from her. "Part of the plan, too. Let's go, Sunshine. Our mothers are waiting.

I am not going to his house on Tuesday unless our mothers come, too. She frowned and thought of the two women a world away in the living room. *Not even then.* She went back into the safety of the living room. At least it had been safer than in the kitchen.

Who knows what else he has in mind.

Fourteen

Cindy carried the tray with the cake and Marc followed with the coffee. She hoped the tray didn't reveal how rattled she was. *At least if I drop it, solid is easier to clean up than liquid.*

She set the tray on the coffee table and straightened. Her mother smiled at her from the chair Cindy had been sitting in. Marc's mother had a twin smile from the twin chair.

"I hope you don't mind. This chair is so comfortable. Besides, we thought you two would like to sit beside each other."

What can I say? Cindy frowned. *That's exactly what I wanted her to believe, isn't it?* She shook her head. *You weren't supposed to believe it, too.*

"Thank you," Marc answered as he set his tray down and handed coffee to both women. Then, while Cindy was still trying to decide what to do next, Marc placed a slice of cake in front of each of them. "Let's sit down and catch the rest of the game. It looks like your Eagles are losing." He took her hand and led her to the couch as if she couldn't find it alone. "You're supposed to say, 'It's still the first quarter. Anything can happen.' Or something like that."

He sat and tugged her down beside him. Cindy used reaching for her cake as an excuse to move away from him. He used getting his coffee as an excuse to close the space.

"This is delicious." Jean said after tasting the cake.

"Thanks. It's a recipe from an old cookbook that I found at a garage sale." Cindy smiled, glad for the new distraction.

"I like garage sales." Marc closed the inch between their thighs.

"Men don't go to garage sales." Cindy tried not to notice the feel of his leg against hers.

"That's a sexist remark. If I made such a statement, somebody would be all over me about it."

A vision flashed in her mind at an image brought on by the "all over me" part of his comment. It didn't have a thing to do with what was just said. She shifted her leg from his. It was either move or singe her leg.

"What do you have to say to that?" Her mother dragged Cindy back into the conversation. Now all she had to do was recall what she was supposed to respond to.

"Men don't go to garage sales?"

If a kiss hadn't been what started all of this, Cindy would have kissed him for getting her back onto the conversation track.

"I don't see many men at the sales I go to."

"Let's watch the game before your other foot replaces the first one in your pretty little mouth." Marc gently eased her mouth closed and brushed a finger across her lips.

He doesn't look like he's pretending, she thought as she noticed the intense look in his eyes before he turned his head away. *What a tangled web we weave . . .* The words of an old Robert Burns poem popped into her mind. It was still true. She looked at the television and struggled to make sense of what was going on.

A player on the Eagle defense intercepted a pass and was streaking for the end zone. *Too bad I can't outrun what*

I'm getting tangled in, she thought. Then she tried harder to concentrate on the game.

"This was great. Delicious food, great company and the Eagles beat the Cowboys." Jean laughed. "We have to do this again. My house next week, maybe?" She put on the coat that Marc was holding for her.

"Sure," Helen answered. "Unless Cindy and Marc would rather have dinner alone."

"Your house would be fine," Cindy answered before Marc could say anything.

"You're so enthusiastic. You must have heard about Mom's cooking." Marc chuckled. Cindy glared at him.

"While we're making plans, how about you two joining us at my house for Thanksgiving dinner?" Helen buttoned her coat.

"It's a date." Marc answered Helen, but he looked at Cindy.

When did the word "date" become as unwelcome as certain other four letter words?

"I can drop Jean off if you'd like to stay longer," Helen offered.

Marc stared at Cindy as if he could see the turmoil tumbling inside her. "I'd better leave before I wear out my welcome."

Cindy wanted to thank him, but he was to blame for this mess in the first place.

She said the proper good-byes and closed the door.

I'm not being fair, she thought as she went into the living room. *I agreed to go along with this plan.* She sighed. *It's my fault that I didn't think it through.* She stacked the trays and put the dishes on the top one. *I never considered that we would create monsters that Dr. Frankenstein would be proud of.*

She went into the kitchen. *How can this room look so innocent after what just happened?* She shook her head and set the tray on the counter. Nothing had really happened except a kiss; a real kiss. She shook her head slowly. A kiss unlike any she had ever experienced before. She felt her face warm. Then the heat spread through her body. It was so much more intense than her imaginings. She closed her eyes and recalled the feel of his mouth against hers, the taste of him as their tongues joined in a hint of what was inevitable. He held her against him, and she could feel the effect the contact was having on his body. *I'm not ready for this. I'm happy with my life the way it is.* She frowned. *Then why did she feel cheated when he moved away from her?*

She shook her head. This water was too deep and it had been a long time since she had gone swimming.

She poured a glass of iced tea, looked at it and put it back in the pitcher and filled her glass with water instead. She was going to have enough trouble sleeping without taking in more caffeine to stimulate her already tense nerves.

Marc dropped his mother off at her house and silently thanked her for not mentioning Cindy on the ride home. He had carried on a conversation with her, hopefully answered at the appropriate time, and didn't sound as if half of his brain was missing.

He turned onto Stenton Avenue. Half of his brain wasn't missing, but it sure wasn't functioning properly. It was busy holding onto Cindy Larson and her sweet mouth. He turned off the car heater and let down the window. Once he had heard song lyrics that fit right now. "Rock My World" was exactly what she had done. And this whole scheme had been his idea. She had responded. Both times. She had felt perfect against him. Her mouth was sweeter than he had imagined, and hotter, and sexier. He opened the window on the passenger side. It had taken everything he had to move away from her, when what he had wanted to do was clear the kitchen table and make love to her right there, right then, despite their mothers sitting a few feet away.

She had responded, all right, but she hadn't liked her own reaction. He pulled into his garage. Why was he doing this? Why was he chasing a woman who had come right out and told him that she didn't want anything to do with him?

He thought again about how her hands brushed fire across his chest as she searched for . . . For what? What was she looking for? He went into the house. *For that matter, what am I looking for?*

Her mouth had been so sweet, so minty, so sensual. He wanted her. Reality kicked him in the middle. He had never been interested in one-night stands. He had had a few short-term relationships, although they hadn't been planned that way. He hadn't been disappointed when they ended.

He went into the living room. Darkness filled it, but he didn't turn on the light before he sat in the recliner. *I don't want that with Cindy. I want more, much more with her. Forever might be long enough.* He imagined her there with him now. He'd take her hand and lead her up the stairs; their first time would be in bed, not on the thick living room rug, and definitely not on a kitchen table. They wouldn't rush; they would have all night. He would explore her body with a slow hand; with slow kisses. He would enjoy discovering one by one the places where her nerve endings were the most sensitive. He would taste them; savor them; take her to the threshold of pleasure and go with her. Then, when neither of them could wait any longer, he would touch the center of her desire and fulfill both of their yearnings as he filled her, as she closed around him, held him inside her, went with him to the place just the two of them could enter.

Marc took a deep breath hoping it would serve two purposes: cool his body and yank him back to reality.

She wasn't ready for a relationship, at least not with him. She hadn't gotten past the doctor thing. The only reason she agreed to see him at all was because of his desperate plan to make their mothers back off. He shook his head.

Cindy had responded to his kisses; even the first one that was only on her cheek. Then, when his mouth touched hers, she got just as lost as he had. Her body had molded against his without too much encouragement from him. He frowned. It wasn't the response of her body that had him worried; it was her mind. She still saw him as not to be trusted.

Marc shifted in his chair. He had learned a long time ago to listen to words when they conflicted with actions. He shook his head. Despite the reactions of her body, she wasn't ready for anything to develop between them. He was a doctor. He knew that women had hormones, too, and that often they acted against the woman's wishes.

He stared into the dark. Maybe he needed to look for somebody else. Maybe that was what he needed to take his mind off Cindy. He shouldn't have to work so hard, especially at the beginning of a relationship. He shook his head fast. There was no relationship with her. And there was a good possibility that there would never be. He frowned. Then why did he feel that there was?

"Hi, Marc." Denise met him at the office door on Monday morning as if she had been waiting for him. "How was your weekend?" Her smile was as wide as usual.

"It was OK." He walked to the conference room. She followed.

"Just OK? As hard as you work, you deserve more than

an OK weekend." If possible, her smile widened. "Wait right there."

Marc put his lunch into the refrigerator. Now what?

"I brought you something." She held out a bag.

"What is it?"

"Open it, silly. It won't bite." She clasped her hands in front of her and watched as he pulled a plate from the bag. "I baked a cake this weekend and I thought about you."

"No, thank you."

"You don't eat cake?" Denise's face looked as if she had just discovered that there was no Santa Claus.

"I don't care for any, thank you. Maybe one of the others would like it. Jim has a sweet tooth." He left the room.

"But I brought it for you. I thought of you as I made it."

"Hey, Marc. How's it going?" Jim walked in before Marc could respond.

"It's going."

"How was dinner yesterday?"

"Better than I expected."

"Glad to hear that, buddy." He looked at Denise. "White cake with chocolate icing. My favorite. Is it claimed?"

"You may as well take it."

"I will overlook your lack of enthusiasm since my sweet tooth is throbbing. Did you make it?"

"From scratch." She glared at Marc. Jim stared at the cake as he took it.

"Oh, man," he said as he wiped a bit of icing from the top. "That is good. I might skip lunch and go right to dessert."

"Thank you."

"You're welcome." She stared at Marc once more. "I'd better get to work. I have files to pull."

"What was that about?" Jim broke off a piece of cake and ate it.

"She brought it for me and I wouldn't take it."

"You love this kind of cake."

"I guess I'm going to have to talk with her."

"Because she brought you a slice of cake?" Jim took another taste and licked his fingers. "Man, you don't know what you're missing."

"You didn't see the look on her face when she offered it to me. I don't like the signals she's sending me."

"Then talk to her." He gave up tasting and finished the rest.

"I don't know what to say. She hasn't really said anything out of line. If I mention what I'm reading into her actions, she could accuse me of imagining things." Marc shrugged. "Maybe if I don't encourage her she'll back off on her own."

"I hope so." Jim licked the last of the icing from his fingers. "She's a dynamite worker. I've never heard her complain about the workload. Have you?"

"No. That's another thing." Marc frowned. "Now it sounds like I'm complaining because she never complains."

"You think about it. I'll back you and I know the others will, too. We all value your judgment. If what you think is true, sometime in the future it could turn into something that hurts the practice in general and you specifically."

Jim rinsed off his plate and put it in the sink. Marc followed him from the room determined to find a way to discourage Denise without causing the practice to lose a good nurse.

Fifteen

Cindy stared at the door long enough for Andrea to wait on two customers. Then she decided to take the coward's way out. She had to talk to Marc, but she didn't have to do it face to face. She went to her office, took a deep breath, picked up the phone, took another deep breath and punched in some numbers. She refused to allow herself to wonder why she had memorized the phone number.

"I need to speak to Marc," she said.

"Is this in reference to a patient?"

"No, it isn't."

"Well, Doctor Marc is very busy. He can't take personal calls right now."

The dial tone hummed in Cindy's ear. The woman on the office end must have flunked customer relations big time. As soon as Cindy hung up, the phone rang.

"Did you just call me?" Marc asked, throwing Cindy off so much that she forgot her prepared speech.

"I thought you were busy?"

"Not too busy to talk to you."

"Is she your girlfriend or something?"

"The 'or something' is right, but probably not what you mean. Denise is our LPN and she hasn't been working here for long. I'll take care of this problem. You can believe me, nothing like that will ever happen again."

"I don't want to interrupt. If this is a bad time, I can call back later."

"Don't be silly. I'll always have time for you. What's up?"

"I'm not coming to your house."

"Tomorrow night? For dinner? Why not? I already shopped."

"You know why."

"Because of a kiss? Aw, Cindy. Don't be silly."

"I'm not coming." She could imagine his head shaking, but she continued. "I think we should forget it. The whole plan, I mean. It was a crazy idea anyway."

"It was a great plan. It still is. We can't forget about it. We already put it in motion. If we back off now, they'll hound us until they drive us crazy. We have to continue. You have to come for dinner. How about if I promise that nothing will happen that you don't want to happen?"

"I'm not coming, Marc." That was her problem. She was afraid of what she did want to happen. And how much she would be hurt later if she did get involved.

"OK. We'll compromise. We'll go out for dinner, then. You name the place." She hesitated. He pushed. "As the commercial says, 'You gotta eat.'"

Cindy's possible answers tussled with each other. "No" lost the battle. "Ida's serves some good food."

"OK." He barely let her finish. "What time is good for you?"

Cindy was torn between "any time" and "never." She settled for six o'clock.

"Gotta go." Again Marc didn't leave a breath between her last word and his response. "See you tomorrow. No backing out, or I'll tell your mother to start looking again and you know how obsessed she can be. You don't know who she might pull out next. He might be worse than a doctor." He left a space but Cindy didn't fill it. "If such a thing exists," he continued. "Besides, then she'll get my mother going again and I won't get any peace either, and it will be all your fault. Tomorrow night at six. I'll come get you. If you're not ready, I'll wait." Marc hung up before Cindy could comment.

He tried using a quick relaxation technique, but gave up. Meditation wasn't going to cut it. This called for action. He called Denise into the office.

"Don't ever do that again." He shut the door.

"But you were busy."

"That's not for you to decide. Your job in this office is not to screen my personal calls nor anyone elses. Your job is to pick up charts, call patients from the waiting room, weigh them, take temps and blood pressure readings, draw blood and any other routine duties that working in this office entails. I appreciate you answering the phone if Marisha and Lisa are busy, but if you can't do that correctly, let the damn thing ring. I don't care what you do in your personal life, but don't you ever hang up on anyone on the phone in this office again. If I hadn't been walking past, I wouldn't have known it happened and if I hadn't hit redial I wouldn't have known that Cindy called." He stared at her. "Is this the first time you did something like this?"

"I . . . I never hung up on a caller before. Honest." Denise twisted her hands in front of her. "It was just"— she swallowed hard and started again—"I was just trying to . . ."

"Never again. Are you clear on that?"

"Yes, Marc."

"Good." He left the office and never looked back. If he had he wouldn't have liked the anger on Denise's face.

Who's he hooked up with to make him talk to me like that? How tight are they? Denise wiped her eyes. *I've bent over backward to please him. Who is this Cindy tramp that he's been kissing? Why can't he see that I would be good for him? All he has to do is give*

*me a chance to show him. If that woman wasn't in the picture, I'd
have a better chance. Then he'd realize that we'd be perfect together.*
She wiped her face again. *Who is she? What does she have to
make him beg her to go out with him?*

Denise rinsed her face with cold water. It had been a
long time since she had cried and it was Cindy's fault.
Who was she and what was she to Marc?

Cindy looked at the display of tiny ribbon bows. Every
color she had was jumbled in a pile as if waiting to be
thrown out instead of sold. She emptied the box and
started again putting each color in its section of the display container.

Who was that woman who had answered the phone?
Marc said the woman was just a nurse working in the office. If that was so, why did she act so proprietary? Cindy
frowned. She didn't need any problems. She was not getting tangled up in something that Marc already had
going. Trios were acceptable to her only where music
was concerned. She looked at the display of ribbon
bows. Now they looked as if they were inviting somebody
to buy them.

Why did Marc insist on inviting her to go out with
him? Why didn't he let it go? Why didn't he take his
nurse protector to meet his mother and drop this whole
charade? Cindy made her way to the craft section of the
store, but stopped in the beads section. The display
didn't need her attention. A new thought did. Maybe he
was just a player after all. There were a lot of them out
there, men who ego-tripped by seeing how many women
they could juggle at the same time. *Well, I won't be one of
them. I went through that one time already with . . .* She shook
her head. *No. I will not allow Harry to influence my life the
way he did in the past.*

She leaned against the wall. Was she being fair to

Marc? He said Denise only worked in the office. *Why can't I accept that? Why would I take a stranger's word over his?* As much as she wanted to deny it, Harry was still influencing her thoughts, and Marc was bearing the results of that influence. She shook her head. *I have to work harder to keep Harry out.*

She went to relieve Vera at the cash register. Maybe going out with Marc would be a good thing. Dinner at her house hadn't been too bad. Heat crept into her face as she remembered their kiss. Just the opposite. The problem was that the kiss had been too good. It had made her realize what she was missing; it had promised something; hinted at something that she had never experienced before. And her reaction to it had scared her. She frowned. Just thinking about it still did.

She wasn't sure if she wanted to be busy at the register to take her mind off her dilemma or if she wanted time to figure out a way to deal with it.

"I take it you talked to Denise." Jim sat at the table at lunchtime with the others. "She looked as if she had been crying."

"I did. I caught her hanging up on Cindy. I tried to keep my voice down, but I'm surprised you guys didn't hear me chew her out."

"That explains why she looked like somebody told her about the Easter Bunny and the Tooth Fairy at the same time." Sylvia frowned. "Do you think this will affect her work?" She leaned forward. "I have no complaints about the job she's doing, but if she's going to be trouble, maybe we need to talk about this."

"I think I made things clear to her. She swore that it never happened before, and I believe her." Marc shook his head. "I hate to fire her if things can be worked out."

"It's your call."

"Let's hold off."

"I'm glad you said that, old buddy, because the woman can cook. At least she can bake. I have never tasted a cake so good before."

"You'd better stop, Jim, or I'll tell Tomika on you," Sylvia said with a chuckle.

"Go ahead. Meka knows she's got nothing to worry about." He winked. "She knows the only other sweets that I'm interested in are of the baked variety." He smiled. "Heck, she'll probably tell Marc to ask Denise to bring an extra slice so I can take it to her." They all laughed.

"If I got through to her the way I hope I did, there won't be any more cake from her, or anything else that's not related to the office and its functions." He looked at Jim. "You can always ask her to bring some dessert for you. Of course, you'd better be prepared for her to read more into it than that."

"On second thought, I don't need that kind of trouble. I think I'll search the bakeries. One of them is bound to have cake just as good and the only strings attached to it will be those tied around the box." They laughed.

Marc had noticed the look on Jim's face when he mentioned Tomika. It was the same each time. *I want that.* After two kids and six years of marriage, Jim and Tomika still acted like newlyweds. Marc had teased them, but whenever he saw them together, envy sprouted inside him. *There's no reason I can't have that, too.*

The image of Cindy's face crept out and he smiled. They could have a future together. First he had to get her past her hang-up about his profession. Then the response that she showed to his kisses would have room to grow.

"What do you think, Marc?" Sylvia's voice called him back.

"Where were you, man?" Raheem asked.

"I'd guess, but that would take us to another whole subject. I'm no expert, especially since I've never seen you like this, but I think you got it bad, buddy."

Marc grinned sheepishly. Then he asked Raheem to repeat the presentation. This time he concentrated on the case.

Tuesday morning came at the usual time, but to Cindy, even though she had lain awake for hours waiting for it, it came too soon. Six o'clock loomed ahead like a hazard on a highway. She hoped she wouldn't have trouble navigating it. Dinner with Marc.

She searched her closet for the right outfit all the while she was trying to convince herself that it didn't matter what she wore. She was still trying to persuade herself when she put first one, then another and then a third outfit across her bed. Enough. She frowned at the dresses and put two back into the closet. Then she stared at the one left. The hot pink cowl-necked sweater dress lay spread out, waiting for her. Oh no. She shook her head. Hot anything was out. She put it back. If they still made potato sack dresses that would be the ideal solution.

She took out a deeper pink cashmere sweater from the back of her closet. This was a good fit when she was ten pounds heavier. She nodded and slipped a slate-colored skirt from a hanger. Then she stared at the sweater. *I don't care if it is loose, should I wear a sweater? Will that send the wrong message?* She frowned. *What message am I trying to send, anyway?* She sighed. Maybe that was the problem. She wasn't sure. She slipped the garment bag over the outfit and took it downstairs. She'd change at the store.

It was a good thing that she had gotten an early start this morning. If not, and if she had taken this long to decide on what to wear to work this morning, she would have been late enough to be fired if she weren't the boss.

As it was, she'd have to hurry to be ready by the time her mother picked her up.

She hurried her tasteless cereal, gulped her coffee that might as well have been hot water, and went to the door just as her mother pulled into the driveway. Cindy looked at her watch. *How does she do that? She's always exactly on time.* She shrugged. *Normally I don't have trouble, either.* Unfortunately, this was not normal times.

She got in the car wishing that six o'clock had come and gone and Wednesday morning was looking at her.

"I don't want to talk about tonight, Mom."

"Do you mean tonight, or this evening?"

"I should have driven."

"Then you'd either have to leave your car at the store or search for a parking spot near the restaurant."

"I know."

"It's only dinner. Imagine that it's me sitting across from you."

"You always gave me credit for having a great imagination, but, even on my best days, it was never that good."

"What exactly are you afraid of?"

"I don't know."

"They say, when you have an accident, you should get back behind the wheel of the car as soon as possible. Consider Harry your accident." She patted Cindy's hand. "You can't forget him, although that would be ideal. Instead, leave him were he belongs, tucked way back in the past. You can't change your bad marriage. You can learn from it." She squeezed Cindy's hand as she made her way down Lincoln Drive. "You're human. Humans make mistakes. It's expected of them. Harry was a big mistake. Let him go."

"I'm trying." Cindy sighed. "I can't take that kind of hurt again."

"Marc is a good person. Give him a chance. It's only

dinner." She smiled. "Look at it this way: You don't have to cook and it's not take-out. Did he say what he's cooking, or is it a surprise?"

"We're going to Ida's."

"He backed out of cooking for you?"

"I backed out of going to his house."

"Cindy, Cindy." Helen sighed as she shook her head. "That's OK. If you want to take small steps it's OK, baby. You'll get there in your own good time. I just want you to find your own happiness. 'Find your own shine' as the poet Tonya Marie says. You do it your way."

"I don't want to get hurt again."

"I don't want you to get hurt, either. Take one step at a time, no matter what size. Moving forward is what's important."

Traffic noises were the only sounds to interrupt the silence during the rest of the drive to the store.

"Don't worry, baby. Things will work out all right," Helen said as Cindy kissed her cheek. "Take care."

Cindy unlocked the door and got the store ready for customers. She kept her hands busy, but her mind kept jumping ahead to tonight. It was as persistent as a dog on a short leash after being pent up inside all day.

Mercifully, she was meeting with Mattie this morning. That should help the time pass, she thought as she went to Mattie's shop.

"Look at this." The woman waved a sheaf of papers. "Orders for six weddings." She laughed. "I will be sewing until my fingers are down to the nubs." She laughed again. "Thank you for allowing me to piggyback my shop on yours."

"No thanks necessary. We help each other." Cindy smiled at her. "I'm so happy for you."

She was still smiling when she left. It was nice that so many still believed in happily ever after. She frowned. Why not? Even if half of all marriages end in divorce, that meant that half stayed intact. She sighed. Why was she thinking about marriage anyway? She was going out to dinner. That was her only commitment. Dinner. She took a deep breath and made a calmness fill her. Dinner with Marc. A herd of butterflies galloped around inside her stomach like something had stampeded them. She shook her head. *Herd of butterflies. Galloping butterflies, yet. Maybe Mom was right about my imagination after all.*

"Marc is here, and I'm on my way out," Debbie called to Cindy.

"OK. I'll be out in a few minutes."

The day had crept along as Cindy had expected, in spite of the steady stream of customers. From the sort of things that were selling in the craft shop, it was obvious that many customers were working on holiday decorations and gifts. *I wish I could figure out how to catch some of that holiday spirit,* she thought as she pulled the sweater over her head. Then the holidays were the last thing on her mind.

She looked into the mirror fastened to the inside of the office door. Ten pounds had not been enough. She pulled the sweater away from her breasts in a futile effort to gain more room. *Got to stop using the chest press machine at the gym.* She shook her head and picked up the blouse she had just taken off. Maybe the paint spill wasn't so bad. She sighed at the splotch of red fabric paint that covered a third of the front of the blouse. Of all the days to be clumsy. She shook her head and put it back across the chair. *At least the skirt is full.* She pulled it on and fastened it. The full skirt swayed a little before it settled into place. *Maybe Marc won't notice how close the sweater fits.* She sighed. And maybe the sun will decide to do an encore. She got her purse and short red coat and went to meet Marc.

Maybe it won't be as bad as I thought. It's only a date. A first date. No pressure. It's part of a plan. Neither of us believes that it's for real. All part of our plan.

"Sorry you had to wait." She looked at Marc. His black leather jacket molded to his shoulders. Were they as strong as they looked? She wrapped the straps of her purse around her fingers.

"It was worth the wait." His gaze meandered down her body like a lazy stream, before it came back to her face. "Nice . . ." He smiled. She tensed. ". . . skirt." His smile widened. "Ready?" He lifted her coat gently from her arm and held it out. "It's cold outside," he said when she just stood in place.

Cindy walked toward him as if she were walking the last few steps of her last mile. She held her breath when he closed the space and waited for her to slip her arms into the sleeves.

It was going to be a long few hours. That's all we need. Get to the restaurant, eat dinner and then go home. Simple as that.

"OK." He straightened her coat onto her shoulders, but he didn't step away. Instead he pressed his mouth against the side of her neck. She gasped, but, instead of moving away, he moved his mouth up to the side of her face. When she didn't move, he gently turned her around to face him. "Just to set the mood. Don't read anything into it."

I can do without this coat, now. She shook her head. *Don't read anything into it. Ha.* "Lets go." Somehow her legs managed to not only support her, but also carry her out the door. If she wasn't still struggling to regain her equilibrium, she'd count that as a victory.

As they walked to Marc's Lexus, she wondered how she was going to manage to get through this ordeal. Then she wondered why it was such an ordeal?

"Anything exciting happen today?" Marc glanced at her before he pulled into traffic.

"Folks are working on holiday decorations."

"How about you? Do you make something new each year?"

"I usually don't bother to decorate." She shrugged. "It's only me."

"I think you deserve decorations even if nobody else comes to see them." He turned the corner. "Besides, what will I think when I come to your house for dinner during the holidays? That you have the 'Bah humbug' syndrome? Or maybe a bad case of Christmas decoration phobia? Besides, what would your customers say if they knew? They spend all of that money to buy supplies from your store to make Christmas and Kwanzaa decorations and the store owner herself doesn't even bother to decorate. He parked and they walked into the restaurant.

"Who said that you're coming to my house?" She frowned and tilted her head to the side. She was frowning as they followed the waiter to a table.

"It's part of the plan. A logical progression." He took her hand in his. "But we discuss it later." He touched her shoulder after she sat then he settled in his own chair.

The waiter came and Cindy's attention was on ordering instead of what might happen between her and Marc if he came to her house.

He can discuss it all he wants, she thought after they gave their orders. *I am NOT inviting him to my house for dinner.*

Sixteen

Marc gazed across the table more than he glanced at his plate. She was more compelling than any food. She was beautiful. No candlelight glimmered off reddish highlights in her hair to call his attention to it. Yet he wanted to stroke his way to the back of her head and unfasten the clip that held her hair tightly against her head. Didn't she ever let it free? He frowned.

He wasn't one of those men who got hung up on a woman's hair. His philosophy concerning that had always been: "Its her hair. She decides how she wants to wear it." Until now. His frown deepened. Even now it wasn't the hair, it was what it symbolized: Cindy's behavior was as uptight and standoffish as her hairstyle. They were both designed to make you believe that she wanted you to keep away. His frown deepened. He hoped that wasn't true.

"Is something wrong?" Cindy frowned and patted her hair.

"Do you ever wear it down?"

"My hair?" She shrugged. "Not in a long time. Why?"

Marc put a piece of steak in his mouth to keep him from saying what he wanted to. *Thank you, Mom, for teaching me not to speak with my mouth full. It kept him from asking if Harry had anything to do with her choice of hairstyle. He didn't know Harry, but already he didn't like him.* "I just wondered how you would look with it spread around your shoulders; soft, sensuous."

He was OK until he spoke that last word. He shook his head. He had been told on more than one occasion that sometimes he didn't know when to shut up.

Cindy glanced at her watch, but not before Marc saw desire flare up in her eyes as if she were going where his "sensuous" was leading.

"Sorry. I know that I was out of line with that last word."

"Why don't you look sorry?"

He stared at her.

"Is everything all right?" The waiter gave Marc time to find the right words. *I have to leave a really healthy tip.*

His stare never left Cindy, and he answered when the waiter left. "Because of the look that was left on your face when the shock of my last word went away." He reached for her hand, but pulled his back before he touched her. "I know you feel something between us. It might not be as strong as what I feel, but it's there. If you try to deny it, you're lying to yourself." His stare softened. "I'd never hurt you. We haven't known each other as long as it seems, but I hope you believe that about me." He smiled at her. "I can get references for you."

Her stare softened and a smile appeared. "Your references wouldn't be two old ladies, would it?"

"I'm going to tell our mothers that you called them old." His smile widened. He set his fork down on his plate. "I'll work hard at being patient. I've been where you are. In fact, I was there before I met you. Meeting you helped me move past the hurt with Tori." He leaned forward. "I'll wait until you're ready to take things further. I just don't want you to close the door on me before you give me a chance. I feel that we could have something special if we let it develop." This time he did touch the back of her hand. Tentatively, barely, giving her room to pull away if that was what she wanted. He released the breath that he wasn't aware he was holding when her hand stayed beneath his. His smile was gone, but the frown didn't come back. Hope kept them both away.

Cindy shrugged. "I . . . I guess we can see what happens. I guess it won't hurt." Her eyes were wide as she leaned forward. Her last sentence was a statement, but she looked as if she wanted assurance that she was right.

"It won't. I promise."

Will you leave me alone if I decide that I'm not interested in trying anymore?"

"I think I can do that. I have until the first of the year. That was our agreement."

"The end of the year we said."

"The end of the one year is the first of another. Nobody breaks up on New Year's Eve. It's—it's sacrilegious."

"New Year's Eve doesn't have anything to do with religion."

"Maybe not officially, but who can not be thankful for a new year; a blank slate? A chance to start over? And whom do you thank? Why, The Creator, of course."

"Becoming a lawyer must have been your second choice."

"I'm just being logical." His thumb moved in slow circles over the back of her head. "Come on. What's one more day?"

Cindy tried to follow his words, but, between what his thumb was doing and the fact that the furnace in the restaurant seemed to have suddenly gone crazy, her temperature felt as if it were soaring. She would think that she needed a doctor, but the doctor was causing the problem. "I guess one more day won't matter." She swallowed hard. She was lucky he had asked for only one more day. The way she felt, she wasn't sure what other suggestions she might have agreed to. She looked at his face and wondered if the same hungry look was on her own. *I should move my hand away from his. I really should.* She sighed. But what he was doing felt so right.

His thumb moved from tracing circles to making a path to the end of her index finger. It stroked along it before giving her other fingers equal attention. By the time he reached her thumb, her body had agreed that this was right. It prepared itself for more, to receive more of Marc, for things to go as far as possible between a man and a woman. Heat covered her face at the idea. She blinked, but she couldn't look away from him. Didn't her body realize that they were sitting in a restaurant surrounded by other people and not alone in a house? Was he feeling the same thing? *I'm in deep trouble.* Still, her hand stayed beneath Marc's.

Marc pulled away first. Cindy should have felt relieved. Instead regret flooded her. She swallowed hard. *What have I gotten myself into? And how do I feel about it?*

She forced her attention back to her food. Maybe, if she concentrated really hard, she could get her feelings back to normal, whatever that was. Say something, anything to break the spell.

What have I started? Marc felt his body react to what he was doing to Cindy's hand. How could touching her hand with only his own hand cause such a reaction in him? He had to fight with himself to take his hand away. That was preferable to dumping a glass of water into his lap in a few seconds and pretending that that was the only dampness. Not since his teenage hormones raged had he felt like this. He had never wanted anyone as much as he wanted her. He leaned back. Maybe putting more space between them would help. If he didn't gain control, he was going to scare her off.

Soft, intimate laughter from the couple at a nearby table reached him, but he didn't dare look at them. If he saw desire on their faces that just might push him over the edge. He wanted Cindy so bad his arms hurt from not holding her.

He frowned at his plate as if just now aware of it. He took a bite of steak because that was what was expected of him.

Say something. Anything.

"Tell me about . . ."

"How did you work the day off trade . . ."

"You first." Marc took a sip of water. Maybe he could cool off from within.

"I just wanted to know what day you had to give up to get tonight off."

"It's like sports. The agreement with Sylvia is for a day to be named later. It will probably be during the holiday week."

"Your turn." She smiled at him as if maybe, just maybe, he had a chance.

"I was just wondering how things are going at the shop."

"Fine." Her eyes reminded him of the glitter of stars. "Business is better than I dared hope for."

"Do you have things set for the next kids' workshop?"

"Felt bookmarks. The kids can decorate them anyway they want to." She looked at him. "Are you coming? With Kevin, I mean?"

"We wouldn't miss it unless the world ended." He met her stare and held it. "I have a favor to ask."

"What?"

"You're too young to sound so suspicious. It has nothing to do with any refuse container."

"That again."

"Actually, if I could think of how to do it, I'd thank the Dumpster." His stare heated up. "If not for it, we never would have met."

"Yes, we would." Her voice was a whisper. She swallowed. "Our mothers wouldn't have given up until we did."

"Neither of us would have been open to anything developing if we met under those circumstances." He smiled. "We met on our own and look at what a hard time you've been giving me." His smile deepened. "If whichever one of our parents managed to get us together and introduce us had mentioned the 'd' word, I know you would have shut me out and locked the door. Probably thrown away the key. On purpose." He nodded. "No, I have the Dumpster to thank. Do you think it would appreciate a big bow tied around it? Or maybe less trash for it to eat?"

"You are something else." She shook her head.

The man had a dimple in his left cheek. Did he know how out of place it was for a man to have a dimple? And how sexy? And how she wanted to taste it to see if it differed from the taste of the rest of his face? She blinked and dragged her attention from that direction.

"Of course I am. I just want you to take the time to find out all about me."

"What favor?" She had to get the conversation onto safe ground. It kept falling into quicksand, but she was the one who kept getting stuck.

"I'm going to start a series of parenting workshops at the halfway house on Broad Street after the first of the year. The residents are women who are recovering addicts. They have their children with them. It would be good to have an activity for the kids while I'm meeting with the mothers." He shrugged. "If you can't do it, it's all right. I know how busy you are. We can probable manage . . ."

"OK."

"One of the employees can probably"—he frowned—"Did you say OK?"

"I'll make room in my schedule as long as it doesn't conflict with my workshops at the store."

"I'll make sure it doesn't."

"Good." She smiled at him. "I'll just consider it a way for me to cultivate future customers." She nodded. "What you're doing is a great idea. My part will just be fun." She leaned forward. "How did you come up with the idea?"

"I can't take credit. The shelter approached us and we were already aware of the need. From time to time one of the partners has had a case of a parent not knowing basic parenting skills." He shrugged. "This is our chance." His smile returned. "I offered to do it; I didn't draw the short straw. I have more time than the other partners. Besides, it will be an attempt to give something back to the community. I was fortunate. My mom's mothering skills seemed to come naturally. Not everyone has that." He shrugged. "If it works out, I'll check the feasibility of doing something for the fathers. They should be part of their children's upbringing, too."

"That's true." She nodded. "What time will you have it?"

"From seven to eight. We'll have to wait until after those who work get off and after dinner. Then we'll schedule it early enough not to interfere with the kids' bedtime." He looked at her. "Thanks, Cindy. It will mean a lot to the program."

"I'm looking forward to it."

"Really?" He acted as if she had agreed to give him his life's desire.

"Really." She laid her napkin on her plate.

"Dessert?" The waiter appeared as if Cindy's napkin had been a green flag.

"None for me."

"Me neither." All he wanted was to take her with him. He frowned. Uh-uh. That wasn't all he wanted, that was only the beginning of what he wanted. What he really wanted . . .

The waiter put the check on the table and Marc picked it up right away. The distraction was what he needed to take his mind off what he wanted.

He helped Cindy on with her coat. Then he dared to leave his hand around her shoulder. It was killing him that that was all that he dared touch, but he took comfort in knowing that, if he was lucky, he'd get to touch her lips later. He squeezed her shoulders. Why did she live so far away?

Seventeen

He's going to kiss me when I get home just like he kissed me the last time. She was as sure of that as she was that tomorrow was Wednesday. *He's going to kiss me.* She sighed. *And I'll kiss him back just like the last time.* She felt warm thinking about the last time his lips had touched hers. And the time before that. "Touched" was not the right word for what had happened between them. *What if we don't stop there? What if we take it farther? Am I ready for that? I haven't known him long.* She frowned. *What does time have to do with anything?* She tried not to think ahead, but twenty minutes from now was staring her in the face.

Traffic was light as they made their way to Lincoln Drive. Cindy asked Marc about his first workshop for two reasons: She was curious about what he had planned and she was trying not to think about what might happen when they reached her house. She wasn't even sure what she wanted to happen.

"I'll mention basic things such as the need for rules and the consistency in enforcing them. I have brochures to distribute and discuss." He glanced at her and then back to the road. "There's an organization that has a set of leaflets about the different aspects of parenting. They were more than happy to provide them for me. I picked them up today after the lunchtime meeting." He glanced at her and smiled. "I'll spend the first session going over what we'll do in future sessions. One of the nurses in the office offered to come with me. She's off at six-thirty, but she's volunteering her time to help out."

"That's nice of her. That way you can concentrate on the workshop itself." She nodded. "Your plan sounds logical." *Where can I find some of that logic for myself?*

"What about you? Any ideas about what you will do? I know you haven't had time to think about it."

"I'll probably start with making pipe cleaner figures. They're easy enough to make and can be done by kids of a wide range of ages. After I meet with them and find out their ages, and what they're interested in, I can better plan the activities for the future workshops."

"You're planning on doing future activities?"

"Sure. I was considering adding general workshops at the craft store for those adults not interested in wedding projects, but I can add that later. This is needed. I think I can distract the kids so their mothers can get something out of your workshops." She smiled. "Of course, I'll continue as long as you need me."

"Then count on a long time."

Their glances met and held. Time seemed to stop to watch them. Then Marc, suddenly aware that he was driving, pulled his gaze back to the road. But most of his attention lingered with Cindy. *I shouldn't think about needing her. She was referring to the workshops. Nothing else. I haven't known her long enough to need her.* He frowned. Sometimes needs don't follow a timetable; they show themselves full grown and there is nothing you can do about it. He hoped the need wasn't just his.

Marc wasn't talking about the workshops and Cindy knew it. There were times when the twists and sharp turns of Lincoln Drive annoyed her. Tonight she was thankful for them. Marc slowed to take the curve ending at the light on Wissahickon Avenue. Cindy grabbed the opportunity to study him.

The fact that he was a doctor didn't matter as much

now as it had in the beginning. He was a good person. He had shown that from the first when he got into the infamous Dumpster to find a stranger's keys. Hers. He made her think that maybe they could have a relationship, that maybe it was time for her to let go of the past and find her future. Maybe it could be with Marc. She shook her head. *Don't jump too far ahead. He asked you to help with workshops because your help is really needed. Who knows how long his "long time" is?*

"You going to ask me in?"

Cindy looked around. They were parked in front of her garage in her driveway.

"What?"

"I could use a cup of coffee." He turned to face her. "We could discuss the workshop schedule."

"We already did that."

"How about: 'I'm not ready to leave you yet'? Will that work?"

"I only have instant."

"That's fine. A large glass of water would be fine." He smiled. "Large, so I can prolong my visit."

"Come on in." She got out before Marc could make it around to her side to open the door.

He followed her up the brick walkway leading to the door. The motion controlled lights on either side of the door came on when they reached the bottom step. He tried not to be impatient as she unlocked the door. *She won't uninvite me.*

"Let me hang up your coat." Cindy faced him but she didn't look at him.

"I can put it on this chair, if that's all right with you." *Is she apprehensive about me or herself?*

"Fine."

He watched as she shrugged out of her coat and held

it between them as if she needed a shield. He was glad that she didn't need his help in taking it off. He wasn't sure he could have touched only her coat. Would her other clothes come off just as easily? He stepped back. It was too soon to find out.

"It won't take me long. I can put some music on while you wait in the living room."

"I'll come with you."

Cindy shrugged. She was afraid that he would say that. She went into the kitchen, trying not to remember what had happened the last time they had been in this room together and trying not to think of what would probably happen later.

"I'll get the mugs. I remember where they are."

Cindy set the kettle on to heat. He probably remembered more than where she kept the mugs. She turned on the radio to help drown out her thoughts. Brian McKnight's yearning song was playing. This won't help at all. She reached to change the station.

"I like that song," Marc touched her hand. "It's a little old, but it's nice." Marc's stare told her that he wasn't talking about the melody.

"OK." Cindy tried to ignore the line about "You are the only one for me" but it reached her anyway. Maybe the fact that Marc's hand was still on hers had something to do with it.

The kettle whistled and Cindy wondered how long they would have stood like that if it hadn't.

She filled the mugs and Marc took his to the table. She followed, glad that she hadn't had to carry both of them. She held the mug in place on the tray so it wouldn't be as rattled as she was.

"How many mothers will be there? At the workshop, I mean? Do you have any idea?"

"I have an idea that you're just making conversation, but that's OK." His smile showed the dimple and as Brian

McKnight repeated the lyrics, her mind repeated her old idea about tasting it. Behave yourself, she thought.

Marc told her what he knew and she tried to follow his answer so she could ask questions along the way, but she was having a lot of trouble. The fact that Luther Vandross's "Just Let Me Love You Tonight" followed Brian McKnight only made things worse.

She said uh-huh from time to time and hoped she made sense. Then she sighed and drained her cup.

"Thirsty?" Marc set his cup down and stood. He walked around to her side of the table and all she could do was wait for him. He held out his hand and she took it. "Or waiting for this?" He eased her from her chair. She stood in front of him and waited for the inevitable. He was close enough for her to feel the heat coming from him. A hint of aftershave mixed with the essence of male teased her.

She licked her lips and desire flared up in his eyes. Her own grew within her. He stared at her for a few seconds longer. Then he eased her against him. She tilted her face up and his mouth captured hers. Her hands found the way around his neck and caressed his hair. His hands brushed their way to her back and stroked back and forth, kindling a fire that threatened to destroy her. His tongue touched her lips and she opened her mouth to let him in. She pressed her body against the length of him and the feel of his hardness against her softness stoked the fires inside her.

"I have waited so long for this." Marc kissed his way across her mouth and down the side of her neck. His hands found their way under her sweater and she was glad that it was such a loose fit. His fingers teased the already hard tip and she groaned as she leaned into his hand. A moan escaped into the room, but she wasn't sure if it came from her or him. She pressed her mouth against his chest. She didn't care.

She rubbed against his hand and he moved his hand back and forth to accommodate her. Her hands pulled at his sweater restlessly until they found the way to his skin. *Brown silk. He feels like brown silk only warmer.* His hand found the other peak and another moan escaped as desire filled her. She pressed her lips around the hard buttons on his chest and was rewarded by a groan from him.

He circled her ear with his tongue. Then he eased his head away. His body stayed pressed against hers.

"Look at me." He tilted her chin up so he could see her eyes. "Are you sure about this? Will you be sorry to-morrow?"

Cindy struggled for control. Was she sure?

She wasn't aware of it, but something about her must have answered "No." Marc eased his hands away. He smoothed her sweater down and moved his hands to safety against her back.

"There's no rush." He sounded as if he had just run a marathon up the Manayunk hills. She felt the same way. "We have time. When we make love, I want you to be as sure that it's right as I am right now." He brushed his lips across her forehead and stepped away. "Do you know how hard it was for me to put this space between us?"

"I'm sorry. I thought . . ."

"No apology necessary. This is a big step, not one that you can backtrack. I want you to be sure. I'm not into short-term relationships." He squeezed her shoulders. "I want . . ." He stepped further away. "Some other time we'll discuss what I want." Desire flared in his eyes again. "Besides you, I mean."

"Yes." Cindy struggled for air. He was two steps away, but she missed him.

"I'd better leave before I ignore my better judgment." He winked at her and went to the front of the house.

Cindy, surprised that her legs could still support her, followed.

Marc brushed his lips along her cheek. "I'll call you tomorrow. I would call after I get home, but I don't trust myself not to get back in my car and come back here and finish what we started." He touched the side of her face. "I'd wish you sweet dreams, but why should you get any sleep when I won't?" His chuckle rumbled and made Cindy's desire flare up all over again.

"Stay sweet," he said from the driveway before he drove away.

Cindy stood in the doorway long after the sound of his car had disappeared. If the city had a heat wave tomorrow, they could blame her. After a few minutes she realized that the cold outside could do nothing to cool off her insides, so she closed the door.

She went upstairs wondering how she was going to sleep. She smiled. She didn't care. Being in Marc's arms seemed so right. She sighed. She wouldn't see him until Saturday. Unless she went over to his office. Tomorrow. She smiled again. She'd bake a cake and take him a slice. Coconut with vanilla cream filling. She knew she didn't need an excuse to see him, but she wanted to do something. He had made her realize that she was ready to move on.

A lightness filled her as she got ready for bed. For the first time in several years, she had hope for what the new year held for her.

Eighteen

Cindy looked at the cake and shook her head. Eight o'clock in the morning and she had been up long enough to bake a cake. If she were in her usual state of mind, she would question how she could be so wide awake after so little sleep.

Her bed this morning had looked like a battle zone. She refused to let her thoughts dwell on when other activity could have resulted in the bed looking like it did.

The sun had barely shown itself when she hopped out of bed as if she had rested the recommended eight hours instead of enough time to only qualify for a long nap. Nevertheless, here she was, baking a cake to have a slice to take to Marc. Marc.

A giggle bubbled up in her and escaped. I don't giggle, she thought. Then another followed the first. She shook her head. Not usually. This was not as usual. *What is this I'm feeling for him?* She pulled the cake toward her without waiting for an answer.

Carefully, so as not to mix crumbs in with the chocolate icing, she covered the cake. It wasn't the coconut cake she had planned to make, since she had forgotten to buy more coconut, but she hoped Marc would like this cake anyway.

Is the way to a man s heart really through his stomach? She thought of the way he reacted to her when she was pressed against him and smiled. Whoever thought that was thinking too high.

Her smile widened and spread heat across her face with it. If they thought the same about a woman they were off, too. The things his hands did to her body were sheer magic. He gave real meaning to the saying "playing with fire," but neither of them had been playing.

The spatula slipped off the top of the cake and planted a glob of icing on the plate. Cindy scooped it up and put it where it belonged. She concentrated on covering the rest of the cake instead of thinking of when she and Marc would take things to the next level. The question was no longer if, but when. She smiled again. Her answer, "soon," repeated itself over and over as she drove to the store.

Cindy looked at the clock in her office. She had an hour before her ten o'clock store opening, but the clock hands had finally reached opening time at Marc's office. She cut a generous slice and slipped it onto a gold-trimmed plate from her special set of china. She smiled. A paper plate would have been all right, but this way Marc would have to come over to return it.

She covered it loosely, kept her smile on and hurried across the parking lot. She shook her head when she passed the Dumpster. Marc was right. There should be some way to thank it.

"Is Marc available?" Cindy shared her smile with the redhead sitting behind the receptionist's desk

"Do you have an appointment?" Then she peeked over the counter as if looking for a child.

"Just tell him that Cindy is here, please."

"May I help you?" A young woman came to the desk.

"I'm already taking care of this, Denise," the redhead said as she picked up the phone and called Marc.

Denise stared at the cake. She opened her mouth but

closed it without saying anything. Then she stared at Cindy before she slowly stepped away.

"Hi." Marc smiled and stopped right in front of her. "Did you rest well last night?"

"Slept like the famous log."

"Liar." He brushed his lips across her cheek. "Lisa," he pointed to the receptionist but his gaze stayed on Cindy, "said you wanted to know if I'm available." He stared into her face. "Most definitely for you." He stepped back to keep from pulling her against him. If he did, he'd forget where they were, that they had an audience. He'd forget everything except how perfect she felt against him. He took another step away from her, but his gaze stayed on her. A baby in the waiting room area cried and freed them both.

"I brought you something." Cindy handed him the plate. "Just a little something that I whipped up this morning. I hope you like it." She looked into his face and forgot to let the plate go. His hand covered hers as if the plate were suddenly too heavy for her to manage. And it was. Somebody behind them asked Lisa a question and Cindy stepped to the side.

"I will savor it, but you know that food doesn't really have that much to do with the way to a man's heart." His whisper tickled her ear as he bent closer. "There's a much better way."

Cindy smiled. The heat filling her face hinted to everyone who was looking at them the direction of Marc's comment, but she didn't care. "I came to that conclusion this morning, myself." If she got any hotter, she'd have to carry her coat back to the store. "I've got to go and you've got patients to care for."

"Want to do something tonight? I'm off at six." When Cindy's eyes widened at his words, he added, "I mean go somewhere, of course."

"I knew that. Sure. Come on over to the store when

you're ready for me." She shook her head quickly. "To go out, I mean."

"Of course that's what you meant. I knew that." He smiled and Cindy carried the image of his grin back to the store.

Time played games and pretended to be a snail. Cindy answered questions, hoped the answers were correct and tried to keep from thinking about later. She didn't know what he had in mind. She shook her head. *Yes I do. He has the same thing in mind that I do.* Her body went into the usual wanting mode that it switched to whenever she thought about Marc lately.

Marie was scheduled to come in later and Cindy took her turn at the register when they had a lot of customers. Finally lunchtime came. She wasn't hungry, but twelve o'clock meant that she was that much closer to going out with Marc.

After lunch she busied herself with the next two projects for the brides-to-be.

Tomorrow she would either show them three options for placecards or a centerpiece. She'd decide later which one she'd use but she'd make samples for all now. Making the centerpieces was complicated enough to almost keep her from watching the clock.

The clock quit playing games and reached six o'clock. She rushed to the front of the store and smiled when Marc came in.

"The cake was delicious." He kissed her cheek. "But not as delicious as you."

"I'm glad you enjoyed it," she frowned. "I mean liked it."

He laughed and took her hand. "I know that. I had to fight Jim over it. The man has a sweet tooth that borders on addiction."

"There's some left."

"More than one slice, I hope. I was planning to beg for a piece for my lunch tomorrow."

"There's half of the cake left. I was going to take it home." She shook her head. "Come on back to the office while I get it." She laughed. "I think that Jim is not the only one with a sweet tooth."

"Guilty."

"Tell me again about food not being the way to a man's heart." She laughed as she led him to her office.

"Don't get me wrong," he said as he followed her. "Food for the body is important and I do like sweets. Of all kinds." At his last words Cindy faltered. She shook her head, but she didn't look back at him.

After they reached the office, Marc turned her to face him. "I will admit that I do love desserts." His stare burned into her. "One kind more than others. In fact I have been aching for a particular dessert for what seems like a year." He cradled her shoulders with his hands and pulled her against him. His mouth claimed hers. "I've been waiting to do that all day." He kissed her again.

"Me, too." She barely found enough air to release her words after he pulled back from her.

"Cut the slices so we can get out of here." Again he captured her mouth with his.

"Good idea." This time she kissed him.

"I mean it." He caressed the side of her face. "If we don't leave this room, I know we'll discover other uses for your desk." He kissed her forehead. "Or your chair." He kissed the side of her face. "And I don't want our first time to be on top of a desk."

Cindy eased away from him as if it was the last thing that she wanted to do. And it was. The slices she cut looked as if a three-year-old had done it. She didn't look at him then or as she got her coat from the closet and started to put it on. If she did, he'd see that she wanted him as much as he wanted her and his desk idea would be put to the test.

"I think I can do this and still maintain my self-control." Marc took her coat and held it for her. After she slipped it on, he brushed his lips along the side of her face, but then he moved back. "So far, so good. We can do this."

He held the plate with the rest of the cake against him with one hand, took her hand with his other and led her to the front of the store. She gave last-minute instructions to Andrea, but Marc didn't let Cindy's hand go until they got to her car.

"I heard that you're interested in poetry," he said as he took the slice from her and handed her the cake plate.

"I used to go to readings all the time. I've been so busy lately." She set the plate on the floor in the back.

"Robin's bookstore on Sansom Street is having a reading tonight."

"I used to go there all the time before I opened the store. I love his programs. Larry is so supportive of poets, prose writers and our people in general."

"Good. I thought we could grab some dinner downtown and go hear what the poets have to say."

"Sounds great." She stared at him. "You like to go to poetry readings?"

"I like whatever you like." His manner was much lighter than the look he settled on her. Then he smiled. "Rather than trying to find two parking spaces downtown, let's take my car. We'll come back for yours before we go home."

"That makes sense." Cindy didn't let herself think about later. Now was too pleasant to rush it. As they walked to his office, Marc's arm was around her waist. It felt as if it belonged there.

"We just dropped by to give this to Jim," Marc said to Lisa. "Is he with a patient?"

"His next patient just went back so he probably has a minute. Let me check," Lisa said.

While they waited, Marc's hand traced circles over Cindy's back. Cindy was glad that Jim came back to meet them quickly. A little more of Marc's touch and he'd be mopping her up from where she had melted instead of introducing her.

"We brought you something," Marc said after he introduced Cindy to his blond partner. Jim and I were in med school together at Meharry. We kept in touch. When I moved here, we got together and decided to find two more partners and open a business. It was only recently that I noticed how bad his sweet tooth is."

"Say whatever you want. It got me this cake." He grinned at Cindy as he took the cake. "My favorite kind." He lifted the plastic wrap and sniffed. "I just met you and already I love you."

"I feel sorry for Tomika."

"She knows my weakness. She married me in spite of it." He laughed and looked at Cindy. "It's great to meet the woman who got Marc back into the stream of life. I was afraid he was going to be stuck on the bank for the rest of his life."

"You sound as if you should be going to the poetry reading tonight." Cindy stared at him.

"That's where you guys are going? Not to Robin's?"

"You know about Robin's?"

"I go every chance I get."

"Are you one of those closet poets?" Cindy asked.

"Afraid so."

"Closet poets?" Marc frowned.

"People who write poetry but keep it to themselves."

"That's not quite the case with me. I share it with Meka." He sniffed the cake again. "You kids run along and have fun."

"Not a problem." Marc put an arm around Cindy.

"Let's go before Jim tries to talk me into working for him so he can go listen to poetry with you." The three laughed and then Marc and Cindy left.

"I didn't know that Marc has a girlfriend." Denise came from the side hall and stared at the door after they had gone.

"There's probably a lot about him that you don't know." Lisa handed her some patient folders. "These patients are next."

Denise took the files, but she didn't move.

Marc refused the cake I brought him, yet he not only accepted a piece from her, he also comes back to bring Jim a slice. Her scowl made her look as mean as sin. *I know her cake isn't as good as mine.* She pushed her hair back behind her shoulders and it swayed against her back as she went to the examining rooms.

What is there about her? How did she get to him when I can't? My profession is in the same field as his. We understand each other. We could have something wonderful together. She frowned again. *She's into poetry.* Denise's nose wrinkled as if she had caught a whiff of something unpleasant. *Poetry. She tossed her hair back. It won't last. It can't. She's just a novelty for him.*

She slipped the files into the pockets on the outside of the examining rooms then went to call the first patient. He had to realize that Cindy was not the one for him.

Denise took the patient's weight and blood pressure and recorded them all the while she was trying to decide the best way to speed up Marc's realization of his mistake. Then she went to get the next patient.

"Denise." Raheem called her as he stepped from an examining room. "This is the wrong chart," he said when she reached him. "This isn't a regular patient of mine. If her weight wasn't so drastically different from what's on the chart from her last visit, it would have taken me longer to discover your mistake." He frowned at her. "The patient told me when I called her by the wrong name."

"I'm sorry." She took the file from him. "I'll get the right one." She took the folder from the next examining room. "I'll fix it right away."

"I'll fix it since I'm already with the patient." He took the file. "You have to be more careful."

"I will." Denise took a deep breath. *That Cindy is going to get me fired.* She checked the name on the file still in her hands. Then she put it into the pocket of the correct room. *I can't let that happen. I'd never see Marc again.*

As she processed the next patients, she double-checked the files before she recorded anything.

Nineteen

"I can't believe that I've stayed away from here for so long. I enjoyed all of the poets, but the group of women called 'In The Company of Poets' was fantastic. Not only are the poems stirring, but the way they perform them is equally impressive." She shook her head. "Wait," she said when Marc headed for the door. "I have to buy a couple of books. We have to keep Larry in business. No one else would do this." She picked up several books of poetry, and Marc found a couple that he wanted. Then they paid and walked to the car parked in the lot a block away.

"Can I assume that you enjoyed the reading?"

"How can you tell?" Laughter bubbled up in her. "I had fun." She looked at him. "Do you know how long it has been since I had real honest-to-goodness fun?"

"Too long." He kissed her forehead. "You should laugh more often. "It makes your face more alive. I think I even saw a hint of a dimple."

She shook her head. "Maybe a dimple wannabe." She touched his face. "Now if you want to see a real dimple, just look in the mirror." She rubbed a finger along his cheek.

"When I was old enough to notice girls, I complained to my mom about it. She said that any woman worth spending time with would love my dimple."

"Your mom is a wise woman." She eased his face to her and kissed his dimple. "I love your dimple."

Marc held her face when she started to ease away. He covered her mouth with his and Cindy forgot where she was. "Now that's a better use for a kiss." He moved back, but held her hand. "Let's go get your car."

As they rode to the store, Cindy kept the conversation going with discussions of the poetry they had heard, the poets who had read, the books they had bought, the bookstore itself, anything except what she knew would happen later that night.

After they got her car, Marc followed her home. She should have been more calm; he wasn't in the car with her. Instead she grew more nervous the closer she got to tonight.

"Do you want to come in?" She clutched the cake plate to her.

"Are you sure?"

"Positive. "

"No offer of a cup of coffee?"

"No." She fixed him with a stare.

"Good." He took the cake plate from her. "Coffee is not what I'm in the mood for."

"Me neither." Her voice was barely there.

"Let's go inside. I would mention how cold it is out here, but it's getting warmer all the time." He smiled. She stared at his smile. He eased the keys from her hand and unlocked the door, but he didn't push it open. "Don't you have to turn off the alarm?"

"Oh, yes." She blinked free and pushed the door open. "Come on in," she said a few seconds later.

"With pleasure." His voice rumbled. "I'll put this in the kitchen." He held up the cake plate.

"Good idea."

They both stood in the middle of the hall as if each was waiting for the other to make a move. Finally Marc shifted away from her. "I don't want to stand here all night holding this." He went to the kitchen. Cindy was still focused on "all night" when he got back.

Their gazes held as they each slipped off their coats. He moved toward her.

"It has been too long since we did this." He brushed his lips across hers, pulled back, then captured her mouth with his. He opened her mouth beneath his and moved closer still. The kiss deepened and she moved her hands to his chest. Is my heart racing like this? she wondered. Then she stopped wondering and just felt. His hands found their way beneath her blouse and stroked across her back, warming her. She didn't know whether to lean back to have more contact with his hand or press forward to feel more of his body against hers. He solved her problem by pressing her closer and increasing her contact with his hand. His fingers stroked across her bra strap at the back, slipped underneath to tease the skin, then moved to her waist.

Her hands found the buttons on his shirt and somehow, in spite of what his hands were doing to her senses, she managed to free them from the buttonholes. Firm muscles tightened as she stroked across his chest. He moaned when she curled her hands in the thick crisp hair. He moaned again and his hardness pressed against her mound when her hands traveled lower and rested on his belt buckle.

"Are you sure about this?" He gazed into her face. For a second her desire for him blocked her words.

"More than I have been about anything in a long time."

His smile caressed her as he pulled her close again. Slowly he kissed her cheek, her jaw, her other cheek; everywhere but her mouth. Cindy cupped her hands at the sides of his face and eased it to her.

"Not enough," she murmured. Her tongue darted out and traced little licks around his mouth. He covered her mouth again and, while their mouths were still tasting each other, his hands found the way to the front of her blouse. Strong fingers worked the buttons loose and Cindy wished she had chosen something with fewer buttons. She needed his hands against her skin, touching her, soothing her ache for him, releasing her. She needed him. She wanted him so badly that her fingernails ached.

Marc finally got the buttons loose and slipped her blouse down her arms. She copied his actions and slipped his shirt from his arms. Her stare found his eyes. Not just chocolate; hot chocolate pools met her stare. Desire and need filled his eyes. Cindy knew she was looking at a mirror image of what was in her own eyes.

Then, as if they had sent a message to each other, they moved slowly together. Cindy stopped when she filled the space he had left for her between his knees. The proof of his desire nudged against her softness. She shifted only enough to brush against it. Her movement was enough to fan the fire in his eyes. He took in a deep breath as if it would help cool him. If she thought it would work, she'd do the same.

Cindy's hands found their way around Marc's neck. She leaned her breasts against his chest and shifted slightly, only enough so she could feel the hairs on his chest brush across her nipples.

"You're driving me out of my mind." He stroked a hand down her back until he reached her bottom. His hands squeezed gently before he cupped her roundness and pulled her even closer to him. He lifted her into his arms as if she weighed no more than a rag doll. Then they found each other's mouths again. The kiss lasted the whole fifteen steps up to the second floor.

Marc lifted his mouth from hers and she felt the loss deep within. "I'm assuming that this is the right room."

"Yes." Cindy didn't take her gaze from him. Any room was the right one as long as he was with her.

"My favorite word."

Cindy didn't think she had space inside, but even more heat filled her when he smiled at her.

He eased her to the floor, but she didn't move away. Instead she leaned against him. There was no way her legs could support her without his strength against her.

"You haven't changed your mind, have you?"

"No."

"I now have a new favorite word." He kissed her eyes closed and feathered more kisses over the rest of her face. Then he fixed her with his stare as his hand slowly moved to her shoulders. Just as slowly he slid her bra straps down her arms. Her hands wrapped around his waist and her fingers found his belt buckle. They managed to undo the clasp.

Marc moved his hands to her back. After two misses, he managed to release the hooks. The bra fell to the floor in a whisper. Cindy's hands left Marc as she made a move to cover her breasts with her hands.

"Don't." Marc gently eased her hands to his side. "Let me look at you. Please."

Cindy obeyed the urgency of his request. She fixed her stare on his face as he looked at her. If the sight of her was doing to him what looking at him was doing to her, come morning she would need a new bedroom to replace the burned remains of this one.

She moved her hands back to his waist and managed to release the hook on his pants. She found the top of the zipper at the same time he decided that looking wasn't enough.

His fingers traced circles around the fullness of one breast. The circles got smaller as he moved closer to the tip, but the ache inside Cindy grew. His busy fingers skimmed over the tip and to the fullness on the other side.

Cindy gasped as he grazed the tip. She tugged the zipper down and slipped his pants off his hips. Marc's fingers returned to the aching tip and brushed back and forth over it.

"I love deep, dark chocolate." His words whispered as he bent his head to prove it. He took the hard tip into his mouth and tugged. A spear of lightning burned its way to her soft, moist, waiting center. Was it possible to die of want?

Marc pulled his head away and cool air surrounded her breast. She would be glad for the cooling, but it didn't cool her body, it only fanned her internal fires, making her need stronger.

"You have on too many clothes."

Marc unfastened her slacks and pushed them down her body, taking her lace panties with them. Then he stepped back only enough to let him see her. "You are more beautiful than I imagined." Without taking his gaze from her, he pushed one of his shoes off with his foot. The other followed.

"Not fair." She struggled to breathe. Her hands found the top of his underwear and traced along the waist, stopping at the middle. Her hands brushed down the front, barely touching, but making enough contact to harden him even more.

"Careful," he growled against the side of her face, "or this will be over before it reaches the interesting part." He touched the tip of her nose. "Don't go away."

As if she would. As if she could. Cindy watched as he fumbled to find his pants pocket. She smiled at him.

"If you looked at what you're doing, you wouldn't have so much trouble."

"Why would I want to look at pants when you present such a lovely"—he pulled out a handful of foil packets—"sensual"—he let the pants fall back to the floor—"sexy view." His gaze floated down her body and back up to her face. Her breast tightened even more under his gaze. Her entire body tingled impatiently. Her need for him to release her increased.

Then he stepped to her and didn't stop until his desire was prodding her hidden place. She widened her legs to let him get even closer. He lifted her and placed her in the center of the bed, then he eased himself, first beside her, then on top of her. "Do you know how much I want you?"

"Not as much as I want you." Cindy wiggled slightly beneath him. Then she frowned. "It's been a long time for me. I hope I don't disappoint you."

"Darling, you could never do that." He kissed away her doubts. "Wait." Marc's voice rasped. He groaned and eased away. Cindy knew he wasn't going to leave her, yet she felt abandoned until he came back. His fingers probed and she gasped when they entered her. She pushed into his hand.

"Now, please, Marc. Don't make me wait any longer."

"My Sweet Cindy." He kissed her and eased himself into her.

Cindy gasped, then sighed as her body closed around him, holding him inside her. Perfect fit, she thought.

Then Marc covered her mouth with his again and moved within her and she couldn't think at all; only feel.

They moved in rhythm as if they had practiced countless times to reach this perfection. They joined in a dance as old as time, yet new to them. Together they climbed to paradise, reached the top and flew off.

Later, neither knew how much later, but later, still joined together, Marc eased beside her and pulled her to him. She snuggled against him as if she had done so many times before.

Sometime later, she found the blanket and drew it over them. A little after that they shared love again and this time Marc had to pull the covers from the floor.

* * *

The sun opened one eye and Cindy and Marc came together for a third time before drifting off to sleep again.

"I'm gonna be late." Marc sat up in bed. "Please tell me that you set your clock early." He kissed Cindy and smiled.

"You have ten minutes more than you thought." She stretched and smiled back. "If somebody hadn't gotten frisky at daybreak he wouldn't be late."

"If somebody hadn't been beside me in all her sexiness," he brushed his lips across hers, "I could have gotten up." He smiled and his voice lowered. "I mean out of bed."

"Of course you do. You'd better hurry." She smiled at him. "And get ready." Her smiled widened. "For work, I mean."

Marc glanced at the clock again as if he hoped it had gone backward. "Oh, man. I have never been late since we opened the practice." He gathered his clothes, then looked at her and shrugged. "Of course, I never had a reason before." He started for the door, but came back. "Good morning, Beautiful." He stared at her before he blinked free. "Are you riding in with me?"

"I have another hour."

"But we have to talk."

"I thought we said everything last night. What more is there?"

"Don't start on last night or my partners will drop me because I will be spending my day here with you instead of with patients."

"Go. Use the shower down the hall."

"If I had time I'd suggest sharing."

"If you had time, I'd take you up on it."

Cindy watched him go. Then she pulled on her robe and went to the kitchen. Her smile widened.

She had never experienced lovemaking like that before, had never imagined that such intensity was possible. She sighed. When she went to sleep the last time, she had been tucked in Marc's arms. Still, a finger of fear nestled inside her: fear that daylight would find her alone with only a fantasy for company.

An ache started below her waist and spread through the rest of her body. It settled there as if it had no intention of leaving until it was appeased. She'd have to live with it, at least until tonight. It intensified. *Tonight. How many hours until then?*

She put water on to boil. *The least I can do is give him a cup of coffee to see him on his way.* She looked at the clock and quickly got out an egg. She could do better than that.

By the time Marc came into the kitchen she had an English muffin sandwich waiting for him.

"Breakfast?"

"The least I could do is help you replenish the energy you depleted."

"Especially since you helped me deplete it so wonderfully."

She nodded. "Especially since I helped."

"I have to call the office." He took a gulp of coffee before he made the call. "I'm running a little late," he told the person on the other end. He stared at Cindy. "Something came up."

She sputtered on her coffee. Then she shook her head. "You are terrible," she said after he hung up.

"I told the truth, but I used restraint and didn't say how many times." He kissed her. "And I hope you mean terribly good." He took a bite of sandwich and took a sip of coffee.

"You know it."

"I thought our first morning together would be different; more relaxed."

"If we had waited until you were off the next day, it would have been."

"Waited? I waited too long as it is." He fixed her with his stare. "Do you know how long I've wanted you? I was attracted to you the first time I saw you. The attraction grew each time I saw you after that."

"I'm glad you were persistent."

"Me too." He swallowed the last of his sandwich and drained his cup.

"Do you mean this isn't part of your plan?" She grinned.

"What plan? Do you mean the one I thought up out of desperation? Is that the plan you mean?"

"Just call me gullible."

"There are a lot of descriptions I could use for you, but gullible isn't on the list at all." He shook his head slowly. "If I had time, I'd not only go over them, I'd prove them to you."

"Interesting. Who do we petition for a bigger allotment of time?" They both laughed.

"Unless you are wearing your robe so you can be ready for me the next chance we get, I take it that you aren't riding in with me."

"I'll go in to work later."

"Are we on for tonight?"

"What do you have in mind?"

"Reruns are okay if you like the first time around."

"Then I guess reruns are definitely on the agenda." She brushed her finger down the side of his face. "Remember, I have my workshop tonight. I won't be finished until after eight."

"I'll wait however long it takes." He dropped a quick kiss on her mouth, stepped back and frowned, and kissed her again. "That's better. If I have a no-show I'm coming over to the store." He walked to the door opened it and turned around. "Clear your desk and keep your schedule loose just in case." He chuckled as the color on Cindy's face deepened. He walked back to her. "Bring an overnight bag with you. We'll go to my place?"

"OK." She nodded. "Go." She stood on tip-toe and kissed his cheek. "See you later."

"Absolutely." He stepped away from her as if he had to struggle against the pull of a strong rope. Then he forced himself out of the house.

Cindy locked the door behind him and watched from the window until she couldn't see him anymore.

"Wow." She said as she leaned against the door. "Double wow." The look on her face as she went up the stairs showed that, if there weren't any stairs, she could have floated up to the second floor. Her feeling was one of contentment mixed with a whole lot of anticipation. How was she supposed to get through the day until eight o'clock came? She frowned. Who decided that an hour should have sixty long minutes, anyway?

She took her shower and tried not to think of Marc. Her mind took over and sent her a fantasy of him in the shower stall with her.

When she picked out the marble stall with multiple water jets, the saleswoman mentioned in passing how large it was and made sure that she had enough room in her bathroom for it. She got it anyway, even though she thought she would be using it alone.

She smiled as the water cascaded over her. When would Marc share it with her? She shook her head. *Stop it or you'll have to take another shower right away.* She forced her mind to think about the workshop that evening and not move to what would happen afterward.

When she was back in the bedroom, she stared at her

bed and tried not to think of Marc and their lovemaking through the night, but the memory of his strong, brown arms around her, and his hard muscled chest and broad shoulders that she had clung to and his . . . Stop, she ordered her memory. Heat flooded through her. I do not have time for another shower this morning.

She stripped the flannel sheets off the bed and smiled. Who needed flannel sheets to keep warm? She dug in the back of the closet and pulled out the package of pretty satin sheets that she had bought on a whim a long time ago and that had never been opened. Red satin. Leftovers from another life. She smiled. Perfect for this one, she thought as she made up the bed.

As she got dressed, she tried not to think of Marc and how he had undressed her and what his hands had done to her body as he did so, and what his mouth had . . . Get out of the bedroom, she ordered herself. For once she listened. She went downstairs, didn't wait for the memories from there to show up, and left the house.

As she drove, she wondered. How in the world do people think they can concentrate on driving while they talk on cell phones when it's this hard with only memories to contend with?

Twenty

Cindy drove past her parking lot only once before she pulled in. She sat in the car, took a deep breath, then went inside.

"You look more than a little chipper this morning," Debbie said to her and grinned.

"I feel more than a little chipper this morning, and that's all I'm saying." Cindy knew that she wore a silly grin. She didn't care.

"Two more people called to ask if it was too late for them to take the workshop tonight. I added them to the list." She handed Cindy the paper. "Oh. And your mother called. She said she's bringing lunch over so don't make plans."

Cindy's face flooded with color as she thought about Marc's comment about her schedule.

"I'm not going to offer a penny because I know they are worth more." Debbie grinned. "In fact, I doubt if I could afford the price for you to tell me what you're thinking."

"You got that right. They're worthless to anyone else, but priceless to me." Cindy laughed as she went to her office. When she got there, she stood in the doorway staring at the desk. Her laughter fled, chased by more powerful emotions. Hunger filled her, but not for food.

She turned away before an image of her and Marc making love on top of her desk could show itself. She removed all the unnecessary clutter, but she didn't dare clear it completely. If she did, she'd never be able to focus on anything except the possibility of Marc and her . . .

She shook her head and took the empty bridal workshop materials container into the store and away from outrageous possibilities that seemed less outrageous by the second. Grinning, she gathered the materials for her workshop on making tiny basket centerpieces filled with pouches of potpourri. As she pulled the items from the shelves, she tried to concentrate on what she was doing, as if she had to make monumental decisions about each item instead of routinely gathering materials already decided upon.

She dragged out the task, but finally she was finished. She went back to the office and set the container on the credenza just as her private phone rang.

"Good morning again, Beautiful. I see you made it to your store all right."

"No thanks to you." She grinned. "Do you know how hard it was to concentrate on my driving?"

"I certainly do, because I had the same problem, but please don't use the word 'hard' in our conversation when we are not within touching distance of each other."

Although he sounded serious, Cindy laughed.

"I have a full schedule plus we had to squeeze an emergency in. You and I won't be able to get together until after your workshop."

"Don't say get together, or I might come over and request an emergency visit myself." She sighed. "I'll see you later."

"Too much later. Why don't you come to my house tonight? Even with the added patients, I'll finish before you will. I'll fix dinner."

"Sounds like a plan." She nodded as he gave her directions. After Marc had hung up, she still held the phone. How had she gotten so involved with him so quickly? She smiled and left her office. The how didn't matter. What did matter was that they had gotten involved.

She waited on customers when they were busy and found other things to do at other times.

"Hi, baby." Her mother hugged her and stepped back. "What is it?" She stared at Cindy.

"What did you bring for lunch?" Cindy led her back to the office without waiting for an answer.

"Meatloaf. Don't change the subject."

"I don't know what you're talking about." Cindy took twice as long taking the things out of the bag and putting them on the table than was necessary.

"It's not nice to lie at all, but especially to your mother." She stared at Cindy before she took out two plates. "If you can figure out how to package your glow, you could sell it as special Christmas tree decorations." She put her plate into the microwave, stared at Cindy again and shrugged. "Of course, you are entitled to your privacy." She smiled at her. "Are you ready for your workshop tonight?"

"It's Marc."

"Marc? As in Doctor Marc Thomas?"

"He's the only Marc I know."

"Evidently, he's the only one you need." At her mother's use of the word "need" Cindy reddened.

"OK." Helen nodded. "I will discreetly change the subject. Tell me about the workshop. What are you making tonight?"

Cindy kissed her mother's cheek as she went to warm own her food. "Ten women have signed up. Two of them called this morning and asked to be added to the list."

"That's a good number, isn't it?"

"More than I expected, but not too many for me to help if they get stuck. Anything over five I consider worthwhile." She got her plate and went back to her seat. Then she described the project.

"I have to go." Her mother stood forty minutes later. "My house on Sunday or yours, or do you and Marc have plans?"

"We haven't made plans." She knew her grin looked silly, but she was lost beyond caring. "My house; and I'll invite Marc and tell him to bring his mother."

"Take care, baby." Her mother kissed her cheek. Then they walked to the door together. "I know this was partly my idea, but you be careful, you hear?"

"I hear." Cindy sighed. It's too late. He already has my heart and I don't want it any other way.

"I think that's everybody." Cindy smiled at the eager faces focused on her. Now she understood their enthusiasm and their hope completely. She was far from engaged, but she knew how they felt about the future.

She distributed the materials and passed around a couple of finished baskets so they could examine them up close. Then she explained step by step how they were made. Next she went through each step and waited as they imitated it. Several times she allowed herself to imagine that she was working on centerpieces for her own wedding.

"According to your smile, we must be doing a bang-up job," one of the women said.

"You are."

And they were, but Cindy didn't tell them that her smile had nothing to do with what was happening at that moment. Instead she was already in the 8:01 mode. She backed up to the present.

"It's time for my usual speech. Your wedding will be much less expensive if you make as many decorations as you can. However, if you get stuck and need my help, please"—she held her hands in a prayer position—"I beg you, please do not wait until the last minute to ask me to

make them. This is not Santa's workshop and I am the
only elf in residence. I might suggest that you start a new
trend and have your wedding guests participate in a
make-it-and-take-it workshop." They all laughed as they
worked.

The workshop went well and the women were great,
but Cindy was glad when it was over. Her feelings had
nothing to do with the workshop.

She mentioned the next workshop and showed the
women the decorated glass candle holders that they
would make. The placecards she had planned would
wait until another time.

"You are so mean," one of the women said. Her smile
kept her words from stinging. "I thought I knew what I
wanted, and here you come with another great idea." She
released an exaggerated sigh. "Go ahead. Sign me up."

They all laughed as several others added their names
to the list. Then they started leaving the room.

"This is perfect for me," Connie said. "I don't need
to see anything else. Can I place my order now?"

"You sure can." Cindy followed them to the front of
the empty store.

As the others left, she processed Connie's order and
watched her go. Then she got her things and went to
meet Marc.

"I should have brought you a housewarming gift, since
this is my first visit." She set her overnight bag down and
shrugged out of her coat.

"You are my housewarming gift." He took her coat
and kissed her. "In fact, when we get together later," he
kissed the side of her face. "and I hope not too much
later," he kissed the other side, "I hope my house doesn't
burn down from the heat I expect us to generate." He
kissed her mouth again.

"I hope you intend to feed me dinner." Cindy stepped away enough so that she could form a coherent sentence.

"Of course I do. That's one of my intentions." He smiled and his dimple showed. "Do you want to guess what my other intentions are?"

"No contest. I know they match my own." She leaned up and kissed his dimple. "OK, enough. I'm ready."

"I am, too." He took her in his arms and covered her mouth with his.

"I mean for dinner." Cindy's words would have been a protest if she had managed to move away from Marc instead of wrapping her arms around his neck.

"I knew that." He eased her out of his arms and held her hand. "Come on, everything is ready." He smiled back at her. "And I do mean everything."

"Incorrigible."

"Only where you are concerned." He tugged her hand and she followed him into the large kitchen. "Should we eat in the dining room?"

"No," Cindy shook her head. "Why take everything into there, when we'll only have to bring them back in here."

"That's what I thought." He grinned. "I have a better use of time in mind." He held her chair out for her. "I guess our minds work in accord almost as well as our bodies." He kissed the side of her mouth. Then he shook his head slightly. "No, nothing can work just as well." He kissed her forehead. Then he eased away from her as if he were stuck in a pool of molasses and went to the stove.

"Something smells delicious."

"Salmon steaks with my special sauce over a bed of rice. I started to cook asparagus, but opted for green peas." He set a plate in front of her.

"I'm impressed." She took a taste. "This is delicious." Wonder filled her voice.

"You don't have to act so surprised. I discovered a long time ago that, no matter how good the food, you can get tired of eating out every night. That was when I bought a cookbook and got serious. No one was more surprised than I to learn that I like cooking." He sat across from her. "Now your turn. When and how did you learn to cook?"

Cindy stared at her plate. "A few years ago." Her words were barely strong enough to make it into the room.

"A few years ago?"

"Isn't that terrible?" She looked sheepish.

"Not particularly." Marc shrugged. "I am curious, though."

Cindy took a deep breath and chewed on her bottom lip. "Mom was such a good cook and I always had some activity to go to after school and on Saturdays so she always cooked." She shrugged. "I lived in the dorm at college. After I graduated. I was only home for a few months. Mom enjoyed cooking so much and I was so lazy; I let her do all the cooking." She glanced at Marc. "I should have, but I didn't bother to learn." She shrugged again. Her gaze slid away from Marc. "From there I got married. Harry had a housekeeper who cooked. Inez didn't like people in her kitchen." Cindy stared into the past. "When I tried to cook on her day off, Harry complained and Inez spent half a day after she returned putting things back the way they were supposed to be in her kitchen." She shook her head. "I stopped trying. After I left Harry I learned my way around the kitchen."

"From what I tasted when I ate at your house, you learned well." He touched her hand.

"Thank you." Her smile was slight.

"Harry was a jerk of the first magnitude."

Cindy's smile widened. "How would you like to meet him and tell him to his face?"

"Harry?"

"Tomorrow night is Cheyney's annual Wade Wilson Football Classic. I know Harry will be there. He can't resist the ego-stroking he gets. You know: Alumnus makes super good." She stared at him. "I love the atmosphere at a Cheyney football game, but I haven't been to one since the divorce. I usually just send a donation to the scholarship fund." She shrugged. "It's such short notice. You probably can't get off."

"What time?"

"Kick-off is at seven. A dinner dance follows."

"What time should I pick you up? Six? Will you change at the store? How do you want to do this?"

"You want to go?"

"You had me with the game. You know I love football. The fact that I get to hold you close in public is a bonus."

"Great." She smiled, but she quickly frowned. "I was kidding about you telling Harry what a jerk he is. You know that, right?"

"Don't worry." He squeezed her hand. "I won't make a scene." He smiled at her. "What I should do is thank him. If he hadn't been such a stupid jerk, I wouldn't have found you."

They settled the details. The conversation turned to college football, then to sports in general. Marc asked her about her day. Then he told about his. Both of them avoided mentioning what they both knew would happen when they finished eating.

"That was the best meal I had in a long time."

"Thank you. I aim to please."

"You did."

Their stares caught and held and time seemed caught up in it all.

"I'd better get this cleared away."

"I . . . I'll help." Cindy stood.

"Have you forgotten what happens when we get in the kitchen together? Or are you offering because you remember? Or maybe you're anxious to get this part out of the way?" He grinned.

"Stop it." She glared at him. He laughed.

"I'm just trying to understand your eagerness to clean up." He stilled her hands when she gathered the silverware. "I hope that's the only time you tell me that tonight."

The silverware clattered to the table and Cindy had to gather them back up. "You'd better be glad I wasn't holding the glasses."

"I hope that's not the only thing I have to be glad about tonight," his train of thought continued on the same track. He laughed and followed her over to the sink. "They go right into the dishwasher and that's it."

"You clean up as you go."

"Um-hm." He turned her toward him. "I have shown remarkable restraint this whole evening because I wanted you to have enough fuel to take you through the activities ahead." He kissed her. "I did not make dessert. I intend for you to be my dessert." He kissed her again and brushed his hands up and down her sides before they settled at the fullness of her breasts.

"I guess that makes you mine?"

"In every sense of the word. Let's go upstairs before we initiate my floor, which is too cold, or my table, which is no more comfortable than the floor."

He looked at her and she felt her heart skip a beat before it raced to catch up. He pulled her against him and inched his hand around to the front of her breast. His finger brushed across the hard tip and Cindy gasped at the fire that shot through her, settling in her place that was already prepared for him. She tightened her hands on his shoulders because that was the only way she kept from falling.

Their stares found each other. Cindy saw his desire for her that seemed to match her own.

Together, stares still locked, they climbed the stairs.

Their need for each other replaced any need for words. The only light in the bedroom was the soft moonlight filtering through the lace curtains at the huge window covering one wall.

They reached the massive mahogany four poster bed and Marc moved until his front was against her front. He kissed the sensitive spot just below her ear. He wrapped his arms around her, then he moved his hands to cup her breasts.

"They fit my hands perfectly," he said. He nibbled at her earlobe while his thumbs encircled the tips of her breasts, almost touching, but missing each time.

Cindy shifted, trying to ease the ache his not touching where she needed him to touch was causing. As she shifted her behind came in contact with Marc's front. He moaned into her ear. Then his fingers found the buttons on her blouse and undid them. All the while his mouth was working magic against her neck. She was working magic of her own as she rubbed against him.

Her blouse reached the floor and her bra followed. Marc let her go long enough to shed his sweater and add it to the pile of clothes. Cindy pulled at the hook at the top of his pants and he turned to face her so she could undo it.

"No belt," she whispered as the hook gave way and she eased his pants over his hips.

"One less step." He kicked off his pants and his shoes went with them. Then he slid her slacks and trousers down over her hips to join the rest of their clothes.

He picked her up and laid her on his bed. "I had every intention of taking it slow tonight to make up for the haste last night." His gaze was strong enough for her to feel it as it traveled over her. "Then I saw you, and I knew that my good intentions were lost." He reached into the nightstand and pulled out a gold-colored foil packet.

"I'd ask you to help me, but if you did, I wouldn't need it." He rolled the protection into place and lay beside her. Then he lifted her gently so she straddled his thighs. "Delightful."

His hands crept up her back and eased her down toward him until he could capture her breast with his mouth. A groan escaped from her as tension and desire and need threatened to destroy her.

He released her breast, licked his tongue across the tip one last time, then slowly lifted her onto his hardness until he was buried within her. "Still a perfect fit."

"Yes," was all she managed before he began lifting her up and down slowly, almost separating them, but not quite. "Oh yes." Then she learned that the movements were the same no matter their positions. Then neither words nor thoughts were necessary as they traveled to the place of wonder that they had visited the night before.

Twenty-one

Cindy stirred during the night and snuggled closer to Marc.

"Cold?" He wrapped his arm around her shoulders and pulled her even closer.

"A little." She nodded against him and smiled as his chest hairs tickled her face.

"Let's see what we can do about that." He eased her head away enough so he could see her face. "We have two options." He touched her lips quickly with his. "Option one: We can get the blankets from the floor where they magically ended up." He touched his lips to hers again, but this time the kiss was a bit longer. "Although, I must admit, the magic in this bed had nothing to do with blankets."

"And option two?" Cindy brushed her lips across the flat nipple hidden in the thicket on his chest.

"Evidently you have already figured out option two and begun without me."

She giggled before tasting his nipple. He groaned and she stopped to look into his eyes. "Is there an option three?"

"Do we need one?"

"Uh-uh." She moved her mouth back to his nipple. This time, instead of just sampling it, she pulled it between her lips.

Marc groaned as his whole body tightened against

hers. She shifted so the hardest part of his body was pushing against her softest part. She lifted her leg over his hip to allow him to enter her. He shifted slightly and accepted her invitation. He entered her place that was again ready for him and lay still.

Then he began his journey with his hands. Marc's hands teased her breasts, making the sensitive tips share their longing with another sensitive part of her body. He was already inside her, but she tried to get closer to him. She moaned and pulled his hips closer, but only his hands moved. He tugged her breast, moved his hands to her bottom, moving back and forth over the roundness. When he got to the fullest part, he pressed it gently so that she came even more in contact with him.

"Please." She moaned against his chest.

"Not yet." He moved one hand back to her breast and found the tip waiting tightly for him. While his hand on her bottom pushed and released, his fingers on her breast tugged and eased taking turns.

Cindy writhed beneath him. She tried to get closer to the alternating pressure of his hand on her bottom and his fingers on her breast. She pushed into whichever hand was moving, seeking, searching for release. Slowly he increased the speed of both hands. Cindy followed the changing speed. Marc replaced his hand on her breast with his mouth, but the tugging continued. His hand, free for a second, found the warm, moist place hidden in her thicket. His fingers found the nub and stroked it. Cindy's movements increased until it was impossible to tell where one ended and the next began as waves of release washed over her.

When she was able to open her eyes she stared at Marc.

"You didn't come with me." She saw the desire filling his eyes.

"That time was for you." His words rumbled.

"Is it your time now?"

"If you think you're ready, this time is for both of us."

"I'm always ready for you." His desire had rekindled hers.

Marc eased away, rolled protection into place again and quickly came back to face her. Then he entered her and they began moving together.

Trips with Marc were unlike any other she had ever taken. Their parts fit together the same way as they had before, but the journey was completely new each time. The movements duplicated those of before, but the feelings were deeper, more intense, different. The end was the same; soaring from this reality to one all their own.

"What time do you have to go in?"

"I assume you're asking about the office."

"You are impossible. What am I going to do with you?"

"The possibilities are endless although an encore would be just as satisfying." He rubbed a hand over her shoulders. "I don't see my first patient until late today. How about you?"

"I have to go now since I want to leave early for the game this evening."

"I guess this means separate showers again?"

"I'm afraid so." She eased to the side of the bed and tried to find enough nerve to stand without wrapping the sheet around her. *After what went on between us, this is ridiculous.* Still, it took an extra deep breath to find the bravery she needed to stand.

She avoided looking at him as she got her bag from beside the dresser.

"You shouldn't feel self-conscious. I'm in the same ultimate stage of undress that you are.

Finally she looked at him. A smile softened her face. "Yeah."

"Much better. Or is it worse?" Marc sat up and leaned against the headboard. The covers draped around his hips, hiding a lot, but not his broad, strong, sexy chest and well-muscled arms. Cindy's mouth watered as she stared.

"Between the way you are torturing me with the view of your delectable body and the hungry look on your face, you'd better hurry and leave the room before I try to change your mind."

She straightened and held her bag in front of her. "You can always look away, you know."

"No, I can't and you should know that."

Cindy shook her head and grinned. Then she hurried to the bathroom down the hall before she changed her own mind.

When she went back to the bedroom for the rest of her things after her shower, Marc was gone from the room. She smiled as she stared at the bed. The covers were rumpled as proof that very little sleeping had taken place. She warmed at the memory. If she touched the sheets, she would probably feel the residual heat from early last night. And late last night. Her smile widened even though an ache made her aware of certain body parts. And again early this morning. Would lovemaking always be this great with him? She sighed. She had no idea how long "always" would be with Marc. *Don't rush things,* she told herself. *Let this develop at it's own speed, as slowly as it needs to.* She grinned. Slow had been like that candy: indescribably delicious. She giggled. Fast had been, too.

She made her way to the kitchen and stopped just inside the door. The sight of Marc in his long green terry robe greeted her. He was fully covered, but her recent memories told her what was underneath and her body reacted as if it didn't know that she had to leave in a few minutes.

"If you keep on looking at me like that, this morning will be your turn to be late."

"It would give me great pleasure," she said. "But I really can't stay," she added when he took a step toward her.

He stared. "That will make it all the sweeter when we get together tonight." He handed her a cup of coffee. "Am I correct in assuming that we will be together after the dinner dance tonight?"

"If you want."

"Baby, you know that I want." They stared as if neither wanted to be the first to break contact. Then Cindy realized that she was holding her cup and Marc realized that he hadn't given her the breakfast sandwich he had made for her. They both smiled sheepishly.

"I can't send you away without sustenance to see you through the morning." He set the two plates on the table and got his own cup. "You sit there and I'll sit here and we'll see if we can get through breakfast without fooling around."

"If you stay over there and I stay over here, we might manage that." Cindy sat across from him and took a sip of coffee.

"I can try to do that." Marc took the seat across from her and picked up his sandwich. Cindy did the same with hers.

"When are you leaving?"

"Shortly after you do." He stared at her as he shrugged. "I have no reason to stay here if you're not with me."

"Poor Marc." Cindy patted his hand. He captured it with his. They finished the meal holding hands, both unaware of how the food had tasted.

"I gotta run." Cindy stood and stacked her dishes.

"Leave them. It will give me something to do after you abandon me."

She laughed and went to the front hall. Marc held her coat for her, turned her toward him and hugged her close. He placed a quick kiss on her mouth before he let her go.

"I'll see you at six?"

"Yes." He shook his head. "That feels like years away from now."

"Yeah." She brushed her lips across his mouth and left.

Marc stood at the door staring at it as if, if he stared long enough, she'd come back in. Then he shook his head and went back into the kitchen. This thing has grown so fast between us, he thought as he cleaned up the kitchen.

"I'll be right back." Denise dashed out the office door and across the parking lot as if afraid somebody would stop her.

Was Marc with Cindy? He usually came in early even when he didn't have a patient scheduled. Were they together?

She managed to erase her frown before she entered the store. She was trying to think of a good reason to ask for Cindy when she was saved from lying. Cindy was halfway down the aisle talking to some woman. Denise didn't have to fight this time to keep her frown from returning. She got copies of the workshop schedules and tucked them into her pocket as she hurried back to the office. At least he wasn't with her.

Six o'clock took much too long to arrive, but at last it did come. Cindy was waiting at the door when Marc came for her.

"I do like a prompt woman." He kissed her. "Of course I would like this woman even if she were hours late." He kissed her again. "Or weeks late." Debbie giggled at them, but again Marc kissed Cindy. "Or . . ."

"OK, I get the message." Cindy brushed a finger down his cheek, then stepped back. "We'd better go or we'll miss the kickoff."

They walked to his car with their arms around each other.

"What about your car?"

"I can leave it here until tomorrow. I'll catch a cab in."

"We'll work something out in the morning." He looked at her. "Mom said that she and your mom decided to have Thanksgiving dinner next week at my mom's house." Marc drove out of the parking lot and headed toward Temple University's football field, where the game would be held.

"Mom called me yesterday to tell me. I meant to mention it to you when I got to your house," she glanced at him, "but we were kind of busy."

"Busy doesn't begin to describe what occupied us last evening and again through the night." He headed for Broad Street. "I am so looking forward to being busy again later tonight."

"Me too." Cindy grew warm with anticipation.

"I'd better change the subject before we end up skipping the game." He glanced at her. "How come the game isn't played on Cheyney's campus?"

"They get more people to attend when it's held here in the city. So many alums still live around here. The dinner dance is at the Masonic Hall not too far from the field."

"I'm glad. The Masonic Hall is a lot closer to our houses than Cheyney is."

"Time to move the conversation back to neutral ground."

"Yeah. No sense in torturing ourselves."

"Yeah."

"There is something I meant to tell you. The week after Thanksgiving there's a conference in Pittsburgh. This year it's my turn to go." He stared at her. "If I could switch with one of the others, I would, but it's too short notice." He sighed. "I know because I tried."

"The whole week?"

"Just about. There's a preliminary session on Monday evening. I'm driving. I had planned to leave Sunday afternoon." He glanced at her. "Now I'm going to leave on Monday morning. I'll be back Friday night."

"So many days."

"And nights." He stared at her. "I would suggest that you come with me."

"I wish I could, but Marie is off that week. She and her husband are celebrating their fifteenth anniversary by going on a cruise." She sighed. "You know it's just as well. If I came with you, I doubt if you would attend enough sessions to make the trip worthwhile."

"And those that I managed to attend would be a waste of time since my mind would be on you instead of on the sessions." He parked in the lot. "Let's go watch Cheyney kick Lincoln's derriere."

Cindy laughed. "We Cheyneyites go to the football games for the ambience, not the game."

"Your team is that bad, huh?"

"It's a lot better than it was when I went to school. Back then our parting shot after each game was, 'That's OK. We'll get you in basketball.'" She laughed. "I haven't been to a game in a long time, but I keep track. The past few years have been winning seasons."

"Let's go watch them show off for the grads."

Cindy glanced around as she climbed to a bleacher about halfway up. No sign of Harry. Maybe he was too busy with Nurse Nina. A puzzled look covered her face. Then a smile replaced it. *I don't care. I honestly don't care.* She felt as if the years that had been pressing on her had suddenly lifted.

"Is he here?" Marc settled beside her.

"I don't see him." She didn't have to ask who he meant. She smiled at Marc. "And you know what? I don't care whether he's here or not." She laughed. Harry was no longer worth thinking about.

Then the teams ran onto the field and the game occupied most of their attention.

"See? I told you they would show off."

"So you did. I'm glad you were right." Cindy stood with the others. Everyone joined hands in tradition and sang the alma mater. The pride that always filled her as she sang the words that she knew she would never forget swelled in her. Then smiles were shared with others as they all made their way to the parking lot.

Soon they were getting out of their cars in the lot at the Masonic Hall.

"You go find us seats while I check our coats," Marc said when they got inside. He brushed his lips across hers. "It has been too long since I did that." He winked at her and left.

Cindy found two seats at a table that nobody had claimed yet. From the crowd at the game, she knew that it wouldn't be empty for long.

"I was wondering if you would be here."

Cindy stared at Harry. *Nothing. I feel nothing for him.* She smiled. Sometimes it was wonderful to feel nothing. "Why wouldn't I be here? It's my alma mater, too."

"I thought you might not want to take a chance on seeing me." He pulled out the chair beside her and sat down.

"Same old Harry. Don't flatter yourself."

"I was hoping to see you."

"And why is that?"

"It's not working out between me and Nina."

"And what does that have to do with me?"

"I realized as soon as you left that I had made a mistake."

"Funny. I realized my mistake before then."

"I still want you."

"You can't have me."

"Give me another chance. I know you still have feelings for me."

"I do have feelings for you, but they are not what you think." She stared at him. "Harry, I do not want you. The only thing I want as far as you are concerned is to thank you. If you hadn't shown yourself, I might still be stuck with you."

"Hey, baby," Marc gave her a quick kiss and caressed her cheek before he sat on the other side of her. "Did you miss me?"

"You know I did." She nodded toward Harry. "This is Harry."

Marc held out his hand. "I'm very glad to meet you. I want to thank you for releasing Cindy." He leaned to her and kissed her again. Then he held her hand. "So, Harry, did you have a good flight from Cleveland?"

Harry stared from one to the other before he focused on their clasped hands. "It was all right."

"Are these seats taken?" A woman with a group of older people asked.

"Do you need a seat for Nina?" Cindy asked Harry when he didn't answer.

"She's not here."

"Help yourself." Cindy smiled at the woman.

"Cora Williams, class of '62," she introduced herself as she sat opposite Cindy.

"Katherine Wilson, class of '65." One of the other women held out her hand and Cindy took it. The others introduced themselves.

"I'm an interloper," Marc said when they looked at him. "I'm with her." He squeezed Cindy's hand. "You folks make me wish that I had gone to Cheyney, though."

"You know the right thing to say, young man." Cora looked at Cindy. "He might be worth keeping even though he did choose the wrong school." They all laughed.

The president of the national chapter welcomed them and gave a brief report. He introduced the podium guests and, after they greeted everyone, the food was served.

During the meal Harry was quiet but the others discussed the game. Then the conversation moved to how campus life was when they were at the school.

"I must admit," one woman said, "that we went out to Cheyney this morning and took a walk with our memories as we circled the quadrangle." She sighed. "We didn't realize what we had at the time, did we?" The rest of the grads agreed.

Someone brought out a memory and shared it with the others. More memories followed.

"I remember Mr. Norvell Smith told us that, if we saw him on campus and complimented him on how nice his tie was, if we earned a 'c' we'd get a 'c.'"

"That's right," Estella said. "But do you know that some of those kids still tried to get over?" They all laughed.

"How about Dr. Oliver?" one of the men asked. "Who had him for English?" Several hands went up.

"I'm here to tell you, that man didn't play, either."

Marc glanced at the animated faces around the table and smiled. His smile was the widest and stayed the longest when he reached Cindy. She was so excited about her college days. It was as if it didn't matter that Harry had come into her life during that time. It didn't matter that he was sitting beside her today, either. Marc let out a deep breath. Maybe she was finally able to get past him.

Other names came up and more memories came out.

"I'm sorry we're being rude," Cora looked at Marc. "We've cut you out of the conversation completely."

"I'm enjoying it. Go right ahead."

"Tell us about your college years. Where did you go?"

Marc answered her question and the discussion turned to college experiences in general. It continued hopping around in comparisons as they finished eating and the table was cleared.

Soon the band was in place. The other couples left the table when the first song played.

"Remember that song? Why don't we dance to it for old times sake?" Harry turned to her and stood.

"There is nothing about our old times together that is not dead and buried. I have no desire to dig it up." She turned to Marc. "Want to dance?"

"I've been waiting all evening to hold you in my arms." He held out his hand and she took it and stood. With his arm around her shoulders he guided her to the dance floor. "How was it?"

"It is so true what they say: 'Revenge is sweet.'" She shook her head. "I don't know what I ever saw in him."

"Excellent answer." He eased her against him. As they moved to the crooning voice of the singer, they pretended that their main reason for being on the floor was to dance and not to just be in each other's arms. One song blended into another and they continued moving together.

When they returned to the table, they barely noticed that Harry was gone. They were too busy gathering their programs and making their way to the door.

Impatience and anticipation crowded them as they rode to Cindy's house. It stayed until they had satiated their desire for each other, at least for a little while.

Twenty-two

"I have to go." Cindy shifted against Marc and placed her hand against his chest.

Saturday morning had come so fast that she would swear that it skipped a lot of hours. Of course, the fact that she and Marc had been busy may have had something to do with it.

"I know." He brushed his lips across the top of her head. "I'm dropping you off at the store before I go pick up Kevin."

"You don't have time, do you?"

"I'll make time. It won't take long to shower since we have to do that separate thing again." He brushed his hand over her back before he sat up.

"I don't have a problem with taking a cab."

"And I don't have a problem with dropping you off." He got out of bed. "I would bet that I'll be ready before you, but for some reason, I don't feel up to a race this morning."

"I feel the same way." She smiled at him. "Must be something going around."

"I can think of a better explanation, and I could show you, but the demonstration will have to wait until later." He got fresh clothes and went into the bathroom.

Cindy felt a stirring inside as she watched him go. She shook her head. *I never knew that I could have such strong feelings.* She got her bag and took it into the master bathroom. *I could easily get used to this.* She sighed. *I want this for the rest of my life.* She blinked hard and clutched her bag to her. *I am in love. For the first time, I am in love. Honest-to-goodness, for-real love.*

She turned on the shower and stepped in. *Marc has to feel the same way that I do.*

They made do with yogurt and instant coffee for breakfast. During the ride to the store, Cindy kept the realization of her love to herself. She didn't want Marc to feel obligated to say the same thing. After all, it was less than an hour ago that her own feelings showed themselves to her.

"Here we are."

"Oh." Cindy glanced around at the familiar surroundings.

"You were preoccupied during the whole ride."

"Sorry."

"No apology needed. I was just making an observation." He leaned over and kissed her. "Do you know how lucky I am to have found you?"

"Not any luckier than I am." This time she brushed her lips across his.

"You'd better get going before we throw both of our schedules out the window." Marc straightened in his seat. "See you in a little bit."

"I can hardly wait."

"Bet you say that to all the guys." They laughed as he drove off.

As Cindy got out the materials for the kids' workshop, she wondered how deep Marc's feelings were for her. Whenever doubts tried to surface, she shoved them away. She couldn't be feeling this alone; it was too strong to be one-sided. Wasn't it?

By the time Marc arrived with Kevin she had reassured herself. Her love for him was so strong that it scared her into doubting her good fortune. That was the reason for her doubts. He had strong feelings about her, too. Maybe it wasn't love yet, but it would be.

Her eyes sparkled as she went to greet them.

"Hi, Kevin." She smiled at the boy whose smile was almost as wide as hers.

"I've been waiting all week for this. Can I sit down?"

"You sure can. The others will be here in a few minutes." She stared at Marc "You're a little early."

"I told that to Marc, but he said that it would be OK."

"He was right." She stared at Marc's mouth and then back to his eyes. "Whenever you get here is OK."

She knew from the sound that Kevin was moving away, but her gaze was stuck on Marc. She watched as he closed the space between them.

"Are you sure it's OK?" He traced a line around her mouth, warming wherever he touched as if he had used a warm match. She held his hand and pulled his finger into her mouth and quickly released it. His quick intake of breath and her quiet moan were synchronized. He shook his head slightly and took a step back. Their gazes promised each other: "Later."

The other workshop attendees arrived and took their seats. Cindy explained the personalized cups that she had decided upon instead of felt bookmarks.

"These are personalized cups. You design the picture that goes on it. You can use the paper on the table to try out different ideas. I cut it to the size needed so make sure that you fill the paper. You don't have to leave a border; we'll use the one that holds your design in place. We'll use markers instead of crayons so we can get brighter colors. When you're satisfied . . ." Marc cleared his throat loudly at the word "satisfied." Cindy smiled and shook her head, but she refused to look at him. Then she took a deep breath. "When you're satisfied that you have the picture that you want to use, we'll move to the next step of putting it in place and sealing it. These would make a nice Christmas gift."

They got started and she walked around the table checking the progress and making suggestions where needed.

When the workshop was over, she had the kids take turns holding up their cups so everyone could see. "Whoever is lucky enough to get your cup will be so pleased. They will keep it forever."

Every kid had a wide smile that stayed in place as they left.

"Where are you guys off to?" she asked Kevin.

"We're going to see my brothers play football. Their team is in the league playoffs." He grinned. "Maybe Buddy will catch a touchdown pass today." He stared at her. "Maybe you can go with us sometime? They play basketball, too, so we don't have to wait until next year." He smiled. "My brothers are good in all sports." He shrugged. "I just can't get into playing." His smile widened. "They said that's OK. They said that they need somebody to cheer for them and that's an important job, too." Again he shrugged. "They're good brothers."

"After the new year comes we shouldn't be so busy in the store. Maybe I can come to one of the games with you."

"Good." Kevin smiled. "After the game today we're going to the Rodin Museum. I've never been there." He nodded. "I'm thinking about trying some clay sculpture."

"I think you'd like that." She touched his shoulder. "You guys enjoy yourselves." Marc kissed her quickly and the two left.

The frown Cindy had kept hidden since she mentioned the new year came out. Marc's plan and her agreement stuck out in her mind. Was his involvement all part of his plan to convince their mothers that they were involved? It felt more real than any pretend could be. Did it feel the same way to him? I don't want to think about it, she told herself when her doubts tried to creep out during the rest of the day.

Evening came and brought Marc to her house for dinner. Jitters weren't just for new brides, she thought as she went to let him in. Then they were so busy that she didn't have time for doubts, nor room for anything but her growing love for Marc.

The days before Thanksgiving were busy. It was as if everybody had suddenly decided to make Christmas gifts instead of buying them and had decided not to wait until after Thanksgiving to do it.

Cindy closed early on Wednesday and Marc finished with his patients earlier than usual. She had just finished preparing the food when Marc came.

Throughout the meal they luxuriated in having more time together than usual. They ate slowly and talked about nothing special, but when they came together afterward, their speed increased. It was as if they had been apart for months instead of mere hours. The night sped past as it usually did.

"We are gonna be late if we don't hurry." Marc frowned at the clock. "I can't believe that's the time."

"Believe it, Honey. Even without the clock, that sunlight streaming through the window is a strong clue that the morning is almost gone." Cindy brushed a hand over Marc's chest. "At least you don't have to worry about keeping patients waiting."

"True." He covered her hand with his and moved it beneath the covers and to his waist.

"What happened to 'We're gonna be late if we don't

hurry'?" Cindy opened and closed her fingers as he moved her hand.

"It got lost in what you are doing to me."

"What?" The sparkle in Cindy's eye kept innocence from showing. "Do you mean this?" She eased her hand from his and dipped her fingers below his waist, slowly twirled through the hair tapering down and then returned to his waist before venturing below when the hair tapered off.

"Yeah. It's sort of like this." He circled the fullness of her breast, lightly scraping across the dark circle then skipping over the peak and to the other side.

Cindy eased her fingers below his waist again and rested her hand on his hardness. She held her hand still.

Marc countered by circling her breast in ever decreasing rings. This time when he reached the peak, he slowly captured it with his fingers and held it.

Cindy's hand squeezed gently only one time, but once was all it took. Marc hardened even more and pushed against her hand.

His fingers tugged gently on the sensitive tip. They both moaned and moved closer to each other at the same time.

"What time do we have to be there anyway?" Marc's voice sounded as if it were in trouble finding enough power to make sounds.

"Later." Cindy's voice was having the same problem, but it was all right. Neither needed words to express themselves right now, and right now was all that mattered.

The time, Thanksgiving dinner and everything else was forgotten as they focused on pleasing each other.

"Sorry we're late," Helen said as Jean let her and Cindy in. "Cindy was late picking me up."

"Hello, Miss Jean." Cindy avoided eye contact.

"No problem, girlfriend. Marc isn't here yet. He called and said he'd be late. You two come on in."

Cindy didn't even try to act surprised about Marc. She did try not to let her knowing fill her smile, but she was sure that her heightened color gave her away.

"Here are the pies I promised you." Helen handed Jean the pie holder that she was carrying.

"Hang up your coats and come on back."

"You know how I don't like to get in my child's business, so I won't ask her if she knows anything about Marc being late." Helen glanced at Cindy, but stared at Jean.

"I feel the same way. I'm sure it has nothing to do with her being late, too." She went toward the kitchen.

"Me, too." Helen followed.

"Teachers shouldn't gloat. It's bad for their image." Cindy went down the wide hall behind them.

"I don't have my teacher's hat on. Today I'm a mother and a friend and a woman who is about to enjoy the best Thanksgiving ever: good food, friends and hope for the future."

"I'll say amen to that," Jean said.

They had barely made it to the kitchen when the doorbell chimed.

"I'll get it. I have to warn Marc about you two." Cindy left the kitchen.

"A sassy mouth doesn't change the truth," her mother called after her. Helen and Jean's laughter skipped down the hall behind Cindy.

"Our mothers are at their peak today." Cindy raised her head, and her mouth met Marc's.

"Good afternoon, Gorgeous." He closed the door and hung up his coat. Then he drew Cindy against him. "Did you miss me as much as I missed you?"

"Probably more." She drew circles over his chest.

"Impossible." He brushed his lips across hers, pulled away and then covered her mouth again.

"We'd better go before they come looking for us."

"I wouldn't put it past them." He wrapped his hand around Cindy's waist. "Just don't say the word 'peak' again."

If their grins didn't give them away, Cindy's kiss-swollen mouth would. Neither had room inside themselves to care.

"Hi, Marc. I understand you had a little trouble and lost this morning somewhere."

"Hello, Miss Helen. Cindy warned me about you two." He smiled at Cindy's mother. "That's not true. I knew exactly where it was." He walked over and kissed his mother on her cheek. "Good afternoon, Mom."

"Even I, with all of my curiosity, am not going there." Jean patted his shoulder. "Why don't you young folks go see what's happening with the football game? Since some people were late, I have to warm up the vegetables." She smiled at him. "But I don't want you to feel guilty."

"I won't." Marc moved out of the way when she swatted at him. Then he took Cindy's hand and led her to the living room.

Cindy sat with him and tried to pay attention to the game, but she was too preoccupied with imagining being with Marc for the rest of her life. Don't jump so far ahead, she tried to caution herself and it worked for a little while. Then her imagination got back on the old track and settled in. She was still struggling when they were called to the table.

"What time do you open the store tomorrow?" The food had been passed around and full plates sat in front of all four of them.

"Too early; eight o'clock and we won't close until ten

tomorrow night." Cindy sighed. "You know how folks like to get an early start on Black Friday."

"I know." Her mother frowned. "Do you know that is one of the few positive images society has given to something black?"

"You got that right," Jean said. "Maybe one day." She sighed. Then she turned to Marc. "Do you have office hours tomorrow?"

"Yes, but we don't open until one and we don't have a lot of patients scheduled." He looked at Cindy and shook his head. "I could have followed a full schedule, if I had known . . ." He shrugged. "Raheem and Jim are off so Sylvia and I will be the only doctors on duty. Denise will be the only office personnel, but she'll be able to handle the phone and pull charts. If things go the way they did last year, we won't have any trouble handling the patients." He stared at Cindy. "I guess you have to work long hours on Saturday as well?"

"Gotta make it while we can." She stared back at him. Already she missed the chance for them to be together for a longer time. "Until the holiday we'll also be open on Sundays from ten until four." She sighed. "I set the hours a long time ago. Before . . ." She smiled at him. "Before I had any reason not to." She sighed again. "I'll know better next year." Her gaze slid away after she mentioned the future. She was getting way ahead of things again.

Cindy tried to enjoy the meal and Marc tried to do the same. Neither could forget the missed opportunity. Helen and Jean filled in with conversation as if they didn't notice how quiet Cindy and Marc were.

"Am I coming over later?" Marc stood at the door while Helen went to get leftovers from Jean.

"I hope so." She smiled at him. They were still smiling at each other when her mother came back to the door.

"OK, you can take me home so you young people can spend time together," Helen said as she came into the hall. "After all, it's been such a long time since you two have been alone together."

"I'm going to take Mom home before she really shows off."

"Just speaking the truth." Helen laughed.

"It's supposed to set you free." Jean and Helen high-fived as they laughed.

They were still laughing when Cindy and Helen got into the car. Even Cindy and Marc were smiling.

Twenty-three

"Hey, Baby." Marc kissed Cindy when she opened the door. "I wasn't sure, but I brought this just in case." He held up an overnight bag.

"Come on in. 'Don't heat up the outside,' as my grandmom used to say." Cindy locked the door behind him. "What do you mean you aren't you sure?"

"You have to get up early tomorrow."

"Yes." She nodded. "Six-thirty." She stared at him. "What's your point?" She led him into the living room.

"I wasn't sure if you wanted me to stay the night."

"What do you mean, you're not sure? Of course I do." She closed the space between them. The cold clinging to his coat spread to her when she leaned against him, but that was all right. Maybe it would cool her off. "You're always welcome in my house." She kissed him. "And in my bed." Always is a long time, poked at her, but she ignored it and pressed closer to Marc.

"Cindy, you know we have been late getting out of bed since our first time together." He wrapped his hands around her back and cradled her against him.

"So true." She brushed her hand down the side of his face. "We'll just have to set the alarm clock."

"For six-thirty."

"Yep." She frowned at him. "Is that too early for you to get up?"

He stared at her and a smile spread over his face. "With

you, there is never a time that is too early for me to get up." He rubbed his middle against hers. "Or too late."

"You are so bad." It was her turn to rub against him.

"Uh-huh." He flicked out his tongue and tasted her lips. "But in a good way.

"Definitely in a good way." She shook her head and laughed. Then she eased out of his arms. "How about some dessert?"

"You know I'm always ready for dessert."

"I'm talking about sweet potato pie. We were too stuffed to have any at dinner, so your mother put some in the goody bags that she gave me and Mom."

"I'm not going where the term 'goody bag' is begging to take me." Marc said.

"One track mind." Cindy slapped his arm.

"'When you find a good track,' I always say, 'no need to get off it.'" His kiss was long and thorough. When he pulled away Cindy had to set her own train of thought back on the track.

"Is that a 'yes' or a 'no' on the pie?"

"Do we have time?"

"Marc, it's only seven o'clock."

"But we have to get up." He grinned. "I mean we have to get out of bed at six-thirty."

She shook her head slowly and sighed. "I'd ask what I'm going to do with you, but I know what you would suggest."

"See? We're on the same track. At the proper time, we'll collide." He kissed her ear. "Some collisions are most welcome." He kissed the side of her face and then stepped back. "I think it's a good idea."

"What is?"

"You have to try harder to pay attention. You're too easily distracted. I think a piece of mom's pie would be good right now."

He chuckled as he smoothed out the crease that had

formed in Cindy's forehead. "Come on. My first dessert is calling my name." He took her hand and gently led her to the kitchen. He kissed her quickly before he let go. "I don't know how I can expect the pie to taste sweet after I've sampled your mouth."

"You do know the right thing to say. I'll get the pie, you pour the milk."

They sat at the kitchen table. "Tell me about the conference in Pittsburgh."

"OK, I'll try, but I've been trying not to think about being without you for so long." He brushed his hand over hers. "It's being held at Children's Hospital. Throughout the day they've scheduled workshops. A few of them offer the opportunity to see new procedures used. It seems as if there's some new breakthrough every few weeks."

As they ate dessert, he told her about some of the workshops in the past. Part way through describing a procedure, he stopped and frowned at her. "Are you sure you want to hear this, or are you just being polite?"

"I have to confess to being a science junkie. I read medical journals as if I'm in the field."

"I didn't know that."

"There's probably a lot about me that you don't know."

"Since we have both scraped our plates clean, I think I should use this opportunity to see if there's something new I can find out about you right now." He put the dishes in the sink. "A quarter to eight isn't too early is it?"

"It's never too early for me to be with you." Cindy took the glasses to the sink. Then they held hands as they walked upstairs to indulge in what had fast become a glorious habit.

A lot later, but not late enough for the two lovers, the alarm jarred them awake.

"Look." Marc nodded toward the window. "The sun

doesn't even want to get going this morning. If they can put people on the moon and into orbit, you would think somebody would invent a kinder and gentler alarm clock." He rubbed his hand over Cindy's back.

"Maybe it's up to us."

"The only up that should be in this conversation has to do with you getting out of bed."

Cindy groaned and slid away from him. "The sun's barely showing itself." She sat up. "Next year, please remind me of this when I set my store hours."

"I promise." He sat up and stroked a finger down her spine. He liked the idea of them still being together next year. He liked it a lot.

"How can rational people choose to get up this early to go shopping? Whatever they are looking for will still be there at eleven o'clock this morning.

"I can see that this is going to be a long day for you."

"It's going to be a long day for anybody who's up this early and has to stay at work until ten tonight." She got out of bed and grabbed her clothes. "You can go back to sleep if you want. What I'm going to wear is in the closet in the middle bedroom," she called as she left the room.

"As if I can get to sleep without you," he called after her.

He folded his hands behind his head and leaned back. *I am in this so deep that I couldn't get out if I wanted to. I wanted to get next to her.* He smiled. *And inside her, too.* He shifted as his body reacted as though Cindy were coming back to bed. *And I have.*

When he had suggested that they pretend for their mothers benefit, he figured that was a way to get Cindy to spend time with him. That was all. They would have a little fling and then move on. Now he was caught in his own net. He smiled. And he loved it. He frowned. Love? His face relaxed. Yeah, love. He nodded. This wasn't just lust.

That's what this was. Not a relationship that he knew would end somewhere in the future. He wanted her in his life forever. And she felt the same way. She had to. *I can't be feeling this all by myself.* He shook his head. Their mothers had been right.

He waited a little while as the truth settled in. He was in love with Cindy Larson. The thought weaved its way through his mind like an old dance line.

'Tis the season, he thought as he took his shower. For the first time in a long while he was looking forward to the new year. He smiled. It felt refreshingly good.

"I'll bring lunch over." Marc and Cindy stood outside her car. "Maybe that will help you get through the day."

Cindy nodded. "Good. I'll probably be too busy to eat, but I'll appreciate it. Especially since it means I don't have to wait until tonight to see you again." Then she laughed. "This is ridiculous. I am going to make money. Hopefully big money. I should be wishing for so many customers that I will be running ragged restocking shelves and waiting on them."

"Instead, we're both looking forward to tonight." He kissed her and opened her door. "You'd better leave while you can."

Later, as Marc drove to his house, he thought of every love song that he could. He sang at the top of his voice. When he couldn't remember the words, he made some up. *I wonder what kind of ring setting she likes.* Taking a second chance at love no longer made him wary. A new life in the new year beckoned to him. A life with Cindy.

"How's it going?" Marc didn't have to ask when he got to the store before going to the office. The lines at the registers were long and the aisles were full of customers putting things into their baskets as if afraid the items would disappear from the shelves.

"It's a madhouse." Cindy smiled at him. "A grand and glorious madhouse." She handed a customer a large bag. "Merry Christmas. Come again."

"So. The 'Bah humbug' spirit is gone."

"It was killed by the ringing of the cash registers." She spoke to the customer in front of her and began ringing up the purchases covering the counter.

"I brought this for you." Marc held up a Styrofoam platter. "I'll put it in your office."

"Thanks." She paused and looked at him. The customer shifted. Cindy shrugged and put her attention back on scanning items. Business or not, it would have been nice to have lunch with Marc. She smiled at him when he came back to the front of the store.

"I'll see you later." He kissed her cheek after she handed a customer her purchases. "Make sure you eat. You have to keep up your strength." He fixed her with his stare and chuckled when her face reddened.

"I know." She refused to make eye contact with him.

After Marc left, she looked at the item she had just scanned. Then she checked the receipt. She shook her head and voided the last two entries, she had scanned the item three times. Still, she smiled as she handed the bag to the customer.

It was just as well that she couldn't eat lunch with Marc. She would never have been able to keep her mind on business afterward.

Marie came back from lunch and the line of customers thinned as if people had decided to take a lunch break, too. Cindy ate, trying not to feel lonely. *Ridiculous. You've eaten meals without Marc before.* She shook her head. This time was different. This time there had been the possibility of sharing.

Later that evening Marc came in after he left his office. Cindy felt as if it had been days since she had seen him.

"Come over to my house when you leave here. I'll

have dinner ready." His smile warmed her and gave her new energy. In a few hours she'd see Marc again. She smiled as he left. If things went as they usually did, she'd do more than just see him.

When the last customer left at ten minutes after ten, Cindy allowed her tiredness to move in. They had done far better with sales than she had expected, but she was glad that the day was over. She locked the store and went to her car. The day might be over, but not the night.

She turned on the radio and found the Love Songs Just for You program. Before Marc, she used to either skip over it or allow herself to feel self-pity. Tonight she sang along.

"Your meal awaits." Marc greeted her at the door with a kiss. "I hope it meets your approval."

"I know it will." She followed him into the kitchen. Two tall candles provided the only light. It was more than enough.

"Sit down and permit Chef Marc to serve you."

He held her chair. After he slid it into place, he pressed his lips against her neck. Then he quickly placed their plates on the table. "I saw that," he said as Cindy covered a yawn.

"Sorry." She cut a piece of steak and put it into her mouth.

"You're entitled. Not only did you get up before daybreak, but somebody disturbed your sleep during the night."

"You'll never hear me complain about that."

"You do say the nicest things." He leaned forward. "How did your first Black Friday go?"

"It gave new meaning to the old saying: 'Black is beautiful.'"

"Great. How's your dinner?"

"Delicious." She lifted a forkful into her mouth.

"Did you get to eat lunch?"

"Some of it." She put down her fork. "It was sweet of you to bring it."

"I'm a sweet guy." They laughed together. "So tomorrow will be a repeat of today?"

"I open at the same time. Whether it will be a repeat will be up to the customers." She laughed, then covered another yawn. "Sorry. You know it's not the company." She rolled her shoulders.

"You are forgiven." He gathered the dishes and put them in the sink. "Let's get you upstairs." He blew out the candles and took her hand. "Are your shoulders sore?"

"A little. I've been pulling boxes from above the shelves."

"I can fix that." He wrapped his arm around her shoulders and led her to the steps. "Sounds as if you need the magic hands of Doctor Marc, masseuse extraordinaire."

"OK," he said when they reached the bedroom. "I'm not being fresh, but take off your blouse and skirt." He smiled. "For the time being, I have no ulterior motives. Lie down while I get the lotion."

"Yes, doctor." She grinned up at him before she complied.

"Relax." He straddled her and warmed some lotion between his hands. Then he began kneading her shoulders.

"That feels so good." She rested her head on her hands.

"Don't talk. Just enjoy."

"Um-hmm." She sighed as his hands rubbed across her shoulders and back.

Marc placed his mouth against her neck, then he massaged the tight muscles. He unhooked her bra and slipped the straps down her shoulders. She shifted but didn't say anything.

Then he slowly worked his way across her shoulders and

then down the middle of her back. His hands found their way around her neck where he kneaded the tightness away. He finished by making a slow path down her spine, circling every vertebrae before returning to her neck.

"How was that?" Marc got off her. When she didn't answer he brushed her hair aside and peeked at her. She was asleep. He smiled down at her. "I guess it did the job of relaxing you."

Cindy shifted when he gently eased her pantyhose off, but she didn't open her eyes. Marc placed a whisper of a kiss on her cheek. Then he got undressed, set the alarm clock and slid under the covers. Cindy turned toward him and shifted until her body was pressed against his and he wrapped his arms around her. He brushed his chin across her head. Then he tucked her closer still.

Her hands moved restlessly across his chest before they settled over his heart.

He smiled. I could get used to this, was his last thought before he brushed a hand across her back and drifted off to sleep.

Twenty-four

The buzz of the alarm clock was muffled by the pillow that Marc had placed on it. Cindy shifted her position and opened and closed her hand on Marc's chest as if trying to make the noise go away. Finally she frowned, gave up and opened her eyes. Her frown disappeared when she met Marc's gaze smiling down at her.

"Morning." He brushed his lips across hers. "Among other things," he kissed her again, "I do like the way you fight waking up."

Cindy frowned as she stared at him. "I fell asleep on you."

"Um-hmm."

"I mean I literally fell asleep on you." She shifted away from him. "I'm so sorry."

"Shh, no apology necessary." He touched a finger to her lips. "You were so tired. Something has been interfering with your sleep every night for a good while."

"You mean somebody and something and it hasn't been long enough." She smiled at him. "What time is it?"

"Time for you to get up." He smiled back at her and brushed her hair from her forehead. "Unfortunately I do mean out of bed and get dressed." He sat up taking her with him.

"I guess it would be bad for business for the store to open late because the boss didn't get there."

"Afraid so."

"I'd better leave this bed while I still can." She slipped out of bed and glanced back at Marc. Regret washed over her face before she got her things and went into the bathroom.

"No reason to stay here, Man," Marc said to the empty room. He pulled on his robe and was waiting in the kitchen when Cindy got there.

"You look beautiful in that emerald green." Marc nodded as he approved of the fitted wool dress that Cindy was buttoning up.

"You do say the nicest things," she said and smiled as he handed her a mug of coffee.

"I try." His smile warmed her even more. "Of course, you look beautiful in everything." His smile widened until his dimple showed itself. "And in nothing."

"I'll bet you tell that to all the women." She drank her coffee.

"Only you, Sugar, only you." He gave her a toasted English muffin. "You have to hurry. I forgot to build an extra ten minutes into the time."

"Um-hum." She took a bite of muffin and washed it down with the last of her coffee. Then she stared at him. "I've got to go." She stared at him a few seconds longer. Then she shook her head.

"Don't look so sad. We'll be together tonight, right?" He touched a finger to her forehead and brushed it along the length.

"Right. Want to come to my house?"

"We can come back here, since you don't get off until late again." He smiled at her. "Unless you are tired of Chef Marc's cooking."

"There isn't anything about Chef Marc that I could get tired of."

"You've got some good words of your own to bring out, don't you?"

"I try." She smiled. "Don't forget the workshop."

"I won't." He frowned. "Do you think you should have canceled it for today? You'll probably be so busy."

"I considered it, but the kids are off from school and they have so much fun. I did draft Mom to come in during the workshop time so that will be a big help."

"You're right about the kids. I know Kevin looks forward to it."

"I think Kevin would look forward to anything as long as you two were together." Her smile softened. "You guys really hit it off, didn't you? He is so lucky that you found him. What do you have planned for later?"

"Ice skating at Penn's Landing. I don't intend to set foot in any store except yours today." They laughed, then a serious look filled his face. "I think that I'm coming out ahead where he is concerned." He kissed her. "I've been lucky in a lot of things lately." He kissed her again. "You'd better go."

They walked to the door and he kissed her again before he helped her on with her coat. She waved once from his driveway and then she was gone. Marc stared out the window with a silly grin on his face for a long time before he went to get dressed.

When Marc and Kevin got to Cindy's store it was almost as crowded as it had been the day before. Helen, who had offered to help, smiled at him, waved, and called a quick hello before she went back to waiting on a customer. Marc hurried to the workshop room as eager to see Cindy as if they hadn't parted just a few hours ago.

Cindy showed the twisted paper angel project and patiently explained how to make it. Then she handed out the kits and the children got started.

As the people worked, her words were on the project, but her gaze kept creeping to Marc. She walked around the table, stopping at each person as she always did, but she couldn't help but linger a little longer whenever she got to Marc. The special smile he gave her when she did held her until she got to him again.

The workshop ended and Marc watched as the others left. Then he and Kevin stopped in front of Cindy, who was standing in the doorway.

"You're real busy again, huh?" Kevin asked.

"Afraid so, Kevin."

"Do you ice skate? That's where we're going."

"I used to skate a long time ago."

"Maybe, if we go again after the holidays, you can come with us."

"It's a date. I'd love to go out with two handsome men."

"Thank you. We're going to hold you to that." Marc kissed her cheek. "See you tonight. Same time as last night?"

"As soon as the last customer leaves."

"I'll be ready for you." He kissed her again, grinning at her deepened color. Then he winked as he and Kevin left.

Cindy was busy for the rest of the day. When the stream of customers slowed to a trickle, her mother left. By the time the last customer had been rung up, Cindy was almost as tired as she had been the night before. Almost but not quite.

She got her things and hurried to the front of the store. *I am not going to fall asleep on Marc tonight.*

She locked up and went to her car. At least not right away. She smiled. As she drove to Marc's house, she thought of how right it felt to wake up in Marc's arms and how perfect it would be to do so every morning.

"Hi, Sugar." Cindy wrapped her arms around Marc when he opened the door. "Miss me?"

"Every second that we've been apart." He eased her coat from her and kissed her neck before he stepped away.

"You do know how to make a lady feel welcome, don't you?"

"I try my best." He put an arm around her shoulders as they walked to the kitchen. "Tired?"

"Yeah, but not as tired as last night." She turned to him when they reached the kitchen. "Not nearly as tired." She eased his face to her and gave him a long kiss.

"Do you know what that does to me?" He pressed her closer to him. "Of course you do." Their kiss was longer and deeper. Then he led her to a chair and pulled it out. "Let's feed the more easily satisfied appetite first." He placed a quick kiss on her cheek before she sat. "Did you eat lunch or did you get right to work after we left?"

"You saw how busy we were." She shrugged. "I grabbed a yogurt."

"You're going to have to do better. Now that I've found you, I can't have you fading away to nothing."

"There's enough to me that there's little danger of that happening."

"We have to make sure." He stood straight. "The house special," he smiled at her. "I mean the house *food* special is shrimp scampi on a bed of rice pilaf with mixed vegetables on the side." He frowned. "I hope you like shrimp. You're not allergic to seafood, are you?"

"No I'm not and I love shrimp." She watched him prepare the plates. "I am impressed again. When you learned to cook, you went into it full force, didn't you?" He came to the table. "You'll make some lucky woman a good husband."

He stopped in front of her and their gaze locked. When he set the plates down and took his seat opposite her, neither had found words to move things forward.

The refrigerator clicked on and both of them blinked and picked up their forks.

"Delicious, as usual." Cindy chewed a forkful of scampi. "You seem to have a book full of menus.

"You'll have to stick around and sample all of them."
Marc fixed her with his stare.

"You know I'd love that." She smiled. "I'll be like a bad
case of chronic something; impossible to get rid of."

"I hope so."

They managed to finish their meal without looking at
their plates. They were too busy drinking in each other.

Soon, but not soon enough, they were in each other's
arms, trying to satisfy their needs for each other.

"OK, Princess." Marc kissed the top of her head. "I
gave you an extra ten minutes, and I hate to say it, but
you still better get up."

"OK." She stretched, and then she frowned. "We never
discussed how you're getting to the airport on Monday."

"Monday is a long way off." He rubbed her shoulder.
"Are you trying to get rid of me?"

"Never. I just want everything to be set. I'm taking you
to the airport."

"You'll be too busy."

"I already made arrangements for Debbie to shift her
lunchtime in case I'm not back in time. What time is
your flight?"

"The way things are at the airports, I planned to be
there by noon." He grinned at her. "I had planned to
catch an earlier flight, but I didn't want to leave any earlier than I had to. After all, there's nobody in Pittsburgh
that I want to spend time with." He kissed her and eased
away." We'd better get out of this bed before we throw
both of our schedules off." He patted her hip and left
the bed.

They hurried through their morning routines, but
already their thoughts were on tonight.

* * *

Too soon it was Monday morning. Both of the lovers were reluctant to leave their haven. Cindy turned to Marc.

"You're riding with me, right? Otherwise you'd have to leave your car at the office." She left the bed and got her bag.

"Sounds like a good plan." He stared at her. "One of these days we're going to see if one of my showers is big enough for two. Or one of yours. Or all of the above."

"It's a date."

He looked sheepish. "I'd better hurry and pack."

"You didn't pack when you got home last night?"

"I had other things on my mind." He smiled at her. "I always do lately. I'll gather my things. I can fix them neater when I get to the office."

She shook her head.

"What? I thought I was going to drive in later." He shrugged. "I didn't think about having to leave my car at the office. I already explained about what's going on in my mind lately. Well?" he said when she shook her head again. "You'd better hurry. You don't want to be late."

Much sooner than if they had showered together, they were on their way. Thoughts of being away from each other for four days were too strong to allow any conversation to intervene.

"I have three patients this morning. I'll be over when I'm through."

"I'll be ready." They kissed good-bye and went their separate ways. They were apart, but both Cindy and Marc had to struggle to keep their minds on their work, instead of each other.

Some nerve, Cindy thought as she opened the store. "You'll make some lucky woman a good husband," she mimicked herself. *You sounded as if you were hinting*.

She frowned and shook her head. *When we started this,*

we didn't make any conditions, no plans for the future, certainly not for a future together. She sighed as she hung up her coat. *Maybe he's not in this as deeply as I am. I have to let him take his own time getting where he wants us to go.*

I'm buying her a ring for Christmas. Marc nodded as he exchanged his coat for a white jacket. He smiled. A big, fat, but tastefully designed ring. He nodded. He should ask her first, but he knew what was in her heart. It was time. He went to meet his first patient.

"Wesley. When did you get to town?" Cindy looked up from the register and smiled as her cousin walked through the door.

"Yesterday. I stopped by to see Aunt Helen and she told me about this place." He glanced around and nodded. "You have done all right for yourself." He looked around again. "More than all right." He kissed her cheek and hugged her tightly. "You always did like making things." He laughed. "I remember you were always working on some craft."

"How mom used to fuss when my projects spilled out of my room and into the living room."

"And kitchen, and dining room and . . ."

"OK, OK." She tapped his arm. "Maybe I did tend to take over the house." She grinned up at him. "How long will you be in town?"

"Until after the new year. Aunt Helen already invited me to Christmas dinner. In fact she invited me to stay with her while I check out a job opportunity."

"Philly is a great place."

"So I hear. I also hear that you're involved with someone who helps makes it great."

"Mom does like to talk."

"From the glow on your face, I'd say that she wasn't exaggerating."

"Excuse me." Cindy went back to the register and waited on a customer. Then she went back to Wes.

"I'd better go and let you take care of business." He went to the door.

"I'll walk you out. I can't let you come here for the first time and not see you out."

She laughed and took his arm. "OK we're out." Wes turned to face her. They laughed together.

"When will I see you again?" Cindy stared up at him and smiled.

"How about this evening?"

"That will be great." She pulled him close and squeezed. "That should hold us until later." She laughed with him and watched as he got into the car. "See you tonight," she called. "I'm glad you're back." She watched as he drove away. Then she shivered and hurried back into the store.

Marc stood at the far end of the parking lot, held in place by what he had just seen, the suitcase in his hand forgotten. *She didn't even wait until I left.* He stared at the spot where she had destroyed his dreams for them. Then he turned and walked slowly back to the office.

He had been happy when his last patient canceled. Now he wasn't sure how he felt about it. Maybe it was true that what you don't know can't hurt you. He let out a deep breath. One thing he did know, what you did know could rip you apart.

He shook his head. *How many Tori act-alikes were there? And why did I have to find one of them?*

Twenty-five

Cindy waved good-bye to Wes once more and watched as his car left the parking lot. Then she hurried back inside. *It will be great to have Wes here. He and Marc will get along fine.* An ache teased her as she thought of Marc, but she smiled in spite of it. No sense in feeling frisky, you are on hold until Friday, she told herself when the ache tried to pull out desire. She went to help shorten the line of customers, grateful to them. Not only did they mean profits, but they'd help keep her busy. She did not let her sigh escape. *I don't need this as much now as I will later on; from now until Friday.* She rang up the purchases on the counter. Too many days until Friday.

"Come again," Cindy said to the customer as she handed her the bag of purchases and watched her leave. Then she rang up the next.

"Don't you want me to take over so you can go?" Debbie stood at the counter a while later.

Cindy looked at her watch and frowned. "Wow. Marc's going to be late." She closed out the register and Debbie moved into her place. Why hadn't he come over for me to take him to the airport? Did time get away from him? She smiled. *I wasn't there, so he can't blame me.* She looked at her watch again. "I'd better go see what's keeping him. Maybe he had an emergency or something."

She was still frowning as she walked over to his office. "Is Marc ready?" she asked Lisa. "Even if we leave right now, we're going to cut it awfully close."

"He already left." Lisa frowned.

"He left? For the airport? How long ago? We were busy in the store, but I had things worked out so I could take him."

"About half an hour ago. His second patient only took a few minutes and his last patient was a no-show." A puzzled look came over her face. "First he left with his suitcase and I assumed that he was going over to your store. Then he came back and said that you were busy and that he was going. to call a cab." She stared at Cindy. "That's when Denise offered to take him to the airport."

"Denise took him?"

"Maybe he thought you were too busy."

Cindy shook her head. "We worked out the arrangements this morning." Cindy stared at Lisa. "Denise, huh?"

"That girl has had a thing for him since he hired her." Lisa stared at Cindy.

"I figured as much." *Maybe that "thing" isn't all on her part.* Cindy said a hurried good-bye and swallowed the lump trying to dissolve into tears. She was still working hard at it when she got back to the store.

"What happened?" Debbie had just finished with a customer.

"He got a ride with somebody else." Cindy swallowed hard and ignored the question on Debbie's face. "Give me a few minutes and I'll relieve you. You can go to lunch at your regular time, if you want to." She hurried to her office before Debbie had a chance to put the questions on her face into words.

What's going on with him? He's never done something like this before. She frowned. *We were fine this morning. More than fine. What happened since then? How does Denise figure into this? Why didn't somebody else take him? Why didn't he call a cab? Before I offered to take him, that's what he was going to do. Why didn't he let me take him?*

The least he could have done was call and say he had changed his plans. She washed her face with cold water, giving extra attention to her eyes. *Just wait until he calls.*

She went back to the front of the store and relieved Debbie. *I hope we get a lot of customers today*, she thought as she rang up a purchase. *It's not just the money. I hope that we are so busy that I don't have time for what I'm thinking to develop any further.*

By closing time, part of Cindy's hope had come true. A steady flow of customers had come in and, at the times when she was busy, her questions stayed hidden. At other times, too many other times, they popped up as if maybe this time she had answers to them and would put them to rest.

After closing, she drove home, dreading the prospect of facing the rest of the evening. She should be able to laugh and she would if the hurt weren't so strong. Marc wouldn't be with her tonight even if she had been the one to take him to the airport. *Why does the idea of my empty house make me feel more lonely tonight than it should?* She shook her head. *I'm not dealing with that question, either, and I know the answer to that one.*

She wiped at her eyes and pushed the question away. She needed clear vision and all of her attention to negotiate the curves of Lincoln Drive.

When she entered her house, the loneliness assailed her. She tried to ignore it. *What is going on with Marc?* She glanced at the answering machine. There was no telltale red light. She frowned and went into the kitchen.

She opened a can of soup and tried to do justice .to it. Between spoonfuls she glanced at the telephone on the wall. Finally she dumped the soup, went into the living room and turned on the television. Maybe, between the sound and the pictures, it would help drown out her thoughts. Maybe television had enough magic tonight to keep her from thinking what she was thinking.

Many times she resisted the urge to pick up the phone and make sure there was a dial tone. But many times she did not.

At eleven-thirty she turned off the television and went upstairs. She did not check the phone on her night-stand. Instead she got ready for bed, slipped between the covers and tried not to think of the last time she was in this bed and whose arms had been wrapped around her. She turned out the lights and curled into a ball on what had become her side of the bed so quickly.

The next day she would put the flannel sheets back on and get out her flannel nightgown again. She wiped her eyes, which had finally decided to let go of the tears they were holding. *He never promised you forever. What did you expect? Didn't your experience with Harry teach you anything?* She shifted to her other side and released a hard breath. *He couldn't even wait until the new year.*

On Tuesday the customers had slowed to normal, and Cindy didn't have them to distract her. She met with Mattie as she did every few weeks to make sure that she had the supplies that Mattie needed for the wedding gowns she was making.

"I want to finish the gowns I'm working on before the new year." She smiled. "If things go the way they have been ever since I've been in this business, I'll get a whole slew of brides-to-be floating in here after Christmas, waving their left hands and wiggling their third finger, and pulling out their ideas of what they want for their weddings." She stared at Cindy and shook her head. "How come nobody ever gets engaged for Thanksgiving? Or the Fourth of July?" She laughed and Cindy managed to laugh with her, but Cindy's laughter disappeared when she left Mattie's shop.

She walked through the aisles straightening the shelves and refilling where needed and some places where it wasn't really needed.

By closing time Cindy was surprised that she had made it through the day; she didn't know how she had done it. She frowned. *I need to analyze this so I can do it again tomorrow. And the day after that, and . . .* She sighed. *I have the rest of my life to get through.*

When she got home, she kept her promise to herself and put the warmer sheets on the bed. She had just straightened the spread back into place when the phone rang. She tried not to let hope fill her as she rushed to answer it.

"Hi, Baby Girl." Her mother's voice threw Cindy's hope away.

"Hi, Mom." She failed at sounding cheerful.

"You sound just like I expected you to. Cindy, he's only been gone for one day."

"That's right." She couldn't tell her mother that it wasn't just one day, that it was the first day of a long, lonely string of days.

"I figured you'd be like this. Come on over for dinner tomorrow night. That will help you get over the hump day. It will be downhill to Friday from there." Her laugh came to Cindy and tried to tickle a laugh from her. It didn't succeed. "We'll see what we can do to help speed time along."

"I won't be very good company."

"It's not like I haven't seen you when you weren't very good company before." She laughed. "I'll make your favorite pot roast."

"OK."

"Come prepared to be beat in a cut-throat game of Black History Trivia."

"I'll see you tomorrow."

"Poor baby. You do have it bad. You didn't even pick up the challenge. I'll hang up because I know your mind's not on the conversation."

After they had hung up, Cindy wondered how she was going to get through the next day without telling her mother that she and Marc were finished. Then she realized that there was no reason for her mother not to know. When she didn't see Cindy with Marc anymore . . . Cindy shook her head. *I can't deal with that thought right now.*

She didn't bother to turn on the television. Tonight she couldn't even pretend to watch. She put on her long flannel nightgown and crawled between the flannel sheets. Usually she felt cozy, but tonight, in spite of the double flannel, she was cold.

She knew why the chill stayed with her and she couldn't do a thing about it; it was surrounding her heart and coming from inside her.

She curled on her side and lay with her back to the middle of the bed. Usually Marc snuggled against her back. Tonight only an empty space touched her.

She shifted to her back and closed her eyes. At least maybe they could rest. The rest of her body couldn't. The ache started in her heart and shared itself with the rest of her body. *How am I going to stand this for the rest of my life?* She turned back onto her side. *You only have to get through tonight, through the next minute and then the next. I read somewhere that a writer writes a novel word by word. You get through life minute by minute.*

When morning came Cindy was on the opposite side of the bed, the side where she usually curled up against Marc. She turned off the alarm before it could buzz. *Minute by minute.*

Even my car is lonely without him, she thought as she drove to work. She shook her head. *Even if things were all right between us, we still wouldn't be together today. He'd still be in Pittsburgh.* She sighed. Thinking that didn't help ease her loneliness at all.

Mattie, bless her, came into the office shortly before lunchtime.

"I just had to tell somebody and you got elected." She leaned against the wall. "I just had two, not one, but two women who called about having me make their gowns." She laughed. "One is engaged and the other expects a ring for Christmas. They heard about me and want to make sure that I'll have time to do the gowns for their weddings." She shook her head. "Can you believe it? The one without a ring wanted to come in, give me a deposit and look at pictures of gowns." She shook head again. "I persuaded her to wait until after she gets the ring. Isn't that something?"

"It sure is." Cindy managed to smile.

"You'd better be prepared. They both want consultants and they heard about you." She shook her head. "The one lady will be devastated if a ring doesn't materialize for Christmas." She frowned at Cindy. "Speaking of boyfriends, how is Marc doing?"

"He's doing OK." *If he weren't, Jean would have told me. That's the only way I would know. Or I could go next door and ask Denise.* She frowned. *Does Jean know? Did he tell her about Denise?*

"I can see that you're not here. I can understand that. I'd better leave you to your daydreams."

"I'm sorry, Mattie. Did you say something that I missed?"

"Only that I can imagine how much you miss him." She sighed and smiled at Cindy. "I'm not so old that I can't remember how young love feels." She left the office. Cindy stared at the door. It's not young anymore. It got old in a hurry. And it became one-sided. She swallowed hard. Maybe it was all along. She went to the front of the store to help.

She closed the store and headed to her mother's house. The trip wasn't long enough for her to figure out the best way to tell her mother about Marc. Cindy shook her head. There wasn't a trip that long.

"Come on in, Baby." Helen hugged her before Cindy could take her coat off. "Come on out to the kitchen." She patted Cindy's shoulder and squeezed it before she let go.

"I hope you didn't go to a lot of trouble. I'm not very hungry." She sat in her usual chair.

"I have worked my fingers to the bone fixing dinner. I don't want to hear about you not being hungry." She stared at her. "I'm sure you and Marc will work things out."

"Jean told you?" Cindy frowned. "Exactly what did she tell you?"

"Nothing much." She shrugged. "Jean said that Marc called Monday night to let her know that he arrived OK. Then he told her good-bye. When she teased him about hurrying their conversation so he could call you, he told her not to worry about that. He said he wouldn't be calling you." She stared at Cindy. "He didn't tell her anything else."

"There's nothing to tell." She sighed. "We didn't have an argument." She shrugged. "I guess he just got tired of me." She swallowed hard.

"That doesn't sound like Marc."

"I don't want to talk about this. OK?"

"Sure." She stared for a few seconds. "I'll fix your plate. After you eat a little, you'll feel better. I put mushrooms in with the vegetables just the way you like." She put a plate in front of Cindy and another in front of her own chair.

"Thanks, Mom." Cindy stared at her food. It was less than she usually ate, but it looked like a mountain of food.

"Eat what you, can while I tell you about my day." Helen settled into her chair. "Those kids' minds are not on school work and the closer we get to Christmas, the harder it will be to get through to them." She shook her head. "The week after New Year's Day won't be any better. I don't know which is worse: having them daydreaming about what they want for Christmas or having them thinking about what they got."

Her mother continued talking but Cindy wasn't following the conversation. Her mind was stuck back on the New Year's Day comment. *He convinced me to stick with the plan until after New Year's Day. What made him change his mind? Why didn't he tell me that the plan was off?*

She got through dinner and was glad when it got late enough to leave. Not that she had anywhere to go. She just needed to be alone with her misery.

Funny, she thought as she got ready for bed later that night. *Without Marc in bed with me, I should be able to catch up on some sleep. Instead I'm sleeping less than when I'm . . .* She shook her head. *Than when I was with him.*

Another day down, she thought as she got into bed.

Thursday morning came and again the alarm didn't have to do its job. Cindy got dressed and left the house.

"We got a call." Debbie stood in the office doorway late in the morning. "Somebody wanted to be added to the workshop list for tonight. I told her it wouldn't be a problem." She handed Cindy the slip.

"Thanks, Deb." She forced a smile as she put the paper on the desk without looking at it. It doesn't matter, she thought as Debbie left. *More women won't make it any harder.*

She went to gather the materials. *This is going to be more difficult than the earlier workshops. This time I allowed myself to believe that I could be like the women who attend. Now I know that's not true. I have to accept that and move on.*

"I have a couple of choices of candle centerpieces and favors for your guests." Cindy looked at the eight women. Their faces were so full of happiness that it radiated from them. Cindy was sorry that it wasn't contagious. She blinked and tried to focus on what she was doing. "All of these are made almost the same way, so I can cover all of them at the"—she frowned as Denise came into the room.

"Sorry I'm late. We had to squeeze in a couple of last-minute patients." She smiled at Cindy and sat at the opposite end of the table, facing her. "I hope I didn't miss anything."

"Are you a doctor?" The woman sitting beside her asked.

"No, I'm a nurse, but I work in the office with some great doctors." She giggled. "One in particular."

"You're going to marry a doctor? Why don't you just pay Cindy to make these things for you?"

"It will mean more if I make them myself." She giggled again.

"How long have you been engaged?" The woman on the other side of her asked.

"I'm not exactly engaged yet." Again her giggle escaped. "I expect that to be my Christmas present." She stared at Cindy. "I didn't mean to disrupt your workshop."

"No problem," she managed to get out. "We haven't started yet."

How can I feel as if I've been kicked in the stomach and still be standing and able to talk? She took a deep breath and looked at the direction sheet. She didn't need to consult it. She did need to avoid looking at Denise. She shook her head. *What was it with doctors' attraction to nurses?* She shook her head again. *There had to be a lot of doctors not involved with nurses.* She frowned. *Why do I always find the ones who are?* She stared at the first candle. *At least you found out before you got married this time.* She picked up the candle and started the workshop. Maybe she'd analyze her stupidity later.

She showed the samples and explained how they were made and the different possible variations of coordinating them with any color scheme.

When the workshop ended, she was glad. She was also pleased that she had made it through without breaking apart. She could do that later after she got home.

That night she set the alarm, trying not to think about the next day being Friday. Then she crawled into her cold bed.

Twenty-six

Cindy turned off the alarm that had been allowed to do its job for the first time in days. Friday morning's sun streamed brightly through the bedroom window as if, if it tried hard enough, it could lighten the load weighing Cindy down. It failed.

Friday. A week ago I couldn't wait for this day to come. Marc is coming back. She sat on the side of the bed. *Big deal. Not to me. He found his own Nina.* She got up and went to the bathroom. *It just started, but I'll be glad when this day is over.*

Why did he bother with me at all? she thought as she drove to the store. *Why not go right to Denise?* She left City Avenue and turned down Fifty-fourth Street. *Why did he change his mind?* She pulled into a parking space, but she didn't get out. *Maybe I'm way off the truth. Maybe he had only wanted me from the first because he couldn't have me.* She sighed. *I didn't make it too hard for him, did I? I didn't put up much of a fight at all. I fell right into bed with him like a love-starved . . .* She shook her head. *No. Not love anything. Love wasn't like this. It couldn't hurt this much.* She swallowed hard. *Truth time. What I had with Harry wasn't love, either.* It wasn't even lust. We were both ego-tripping: I had a doctor after me and he had his own private hero-worshipper.

She went into the store. *I'll bet Marc and Denise have a good time laughing about me.* She sighed. *Maybe love just isn't for me.*

Cindy struggled through the day. She had a rough time when she realized that it was time for Marc's plane to arrive, but she got over it. She could do this.

Her mother called late in the day and Cindy was glad for the distraction.

"Are we on for Sunday?"

"Only if you promise that it will be just the two of us."

"Jean said that Marc told her the same thing." When Cindy didn't answer, she continued. "It will be just the two of us, Baby Girl. Wes has other plans. We won't talk about anything that you don't want to talk about, starting with you and Marc."

"There is no me and Marc. There never was, really." She bit her lip. "It was all just an illusion." She sighed. "I'll see you on Sunday. I'm going to early service and the store is open until four, so I'll be over after I close."

As she was getting ready for bed at night, Cindy stopped just before she turned out the light. The next day was Saturday. Kids' workshop day. She sat on the edge of the bed. *Will he have the nerve to come or will he disappoint Kevin? What will he say to me? How will he explain what he did?* She got into bed, crossed her arms over her chest and leaned against the headboard. How dare he? The tears filling her eyes this time were from the anger seething through her, not any longing.

Whatever his excuse is, I don't want to hear it. Nothing can justify the way he hurt me. No explanation. Not even an attempt at rationalization.

She turned off the light and kicked the covers away. As hot as she was, she didn't need blankets. Her anger was a good substitute.

Early morning birds were letting the world know they were starting their day when Cindy finally drifted off to sleep.

I will not let him cause a scene in front of anyone, she thought as soon as she opened her eyes. *I am a professional and I have a business reputation to consider. I heard of several cases where personal relationships spilled out in front of customers.* She tightened her jaw. *Not in this case.*

She forced herself to remain calm as she got ready. Serenity was still in control as she drove to the store. By the time she was on her way to open the shop, her peaceful composure had faded and pain had replaced it. This was supposed to be a happy reunion, she thought as she hung up her coat. *We should have been together last night.* She shook her head. *If we should have been we would have been.*

She went to the front of the store to wait for her employees. She had a business to concentrate on.

Cindy glanced at her watch so often it was as if she were trying to catch it at something. When five minutes before ten finally came, she could only hope that she was as ready as the workshop room was.

She took her place at the door and greeted the kids and the few parents who would make today's project. She had just decided that Marc wasn't going to have the nerve to show when footsteps in the hall caught her attention. She turned back to the hall and there he was; too close, not close enough.

Time paused while their stares held together as if waiting for somebody to free them. Kevin released them.

"Hi, Miss Cindy, I'm sorry I'm late."

Cindy tore her gaze from Marc and it found Kevin. Her attention was having even more trouble. "No problem. At least you're here."

"I don't like being late, but I had trouble finding my hat and Mama Margie wouldn't let me leave without it. We have a new kid living with us, now, named Hakim, and he had it. He's only five, so he doesn't exactly know about taking things that don't belong to you."

"You're not late. We haven't started yet. Come on in."

She purposely didn't look at Marc. "You know, sometimes not even grown-ups follow the rules."

Kevin hurried to his seat. Marc paused in front of her and his aftershave nudged her attention. She didn't want to, but she glanced at him as he passed her. The anger in his eyes was in the wrong place. It was supposed to be in hers. *How dare he look at me as if I'm the one who's wrong.*

"What are we going to make today?" Lynn looked eagerly at her. "These?" She held up a kit that was in the middle of the table.

"Why you always got to touch things before you're supposed to? Why can't you be patient like the rest of us?" Janice glared at Lynn from across the table.

"You're not the boss of this. Miss Cindy is." Lynn glared back.

"Are we going to make something today or are you two going to argue the time away?"

"Make something," everybody answered.

Cindy picked up a flower pot kit. *The only one here who has a right to be angry is me.* She took a deep breath and let it out slowly. Then she showed some examples.

"You're going to make up your own design. I wanted you to see the possibilities."

Possibilities with painting flower pots were safe. Too bad some possibilities had to be experienced before you learned that they weren't real after all. She shook her head. Concentrate on the project, not on what might have been.

"Is this OK?" Janice held up her pot so the drawing could be seen.

"Any design is OK. Didn't you hear Miss Cindy say so?" Lynn answered before Cindy could.

"I wasn't talking to you. I was talking to Miss Cindy."

"If that's what you want, it's OK." Cindy made the mistake of glancing at Marc. In the past, when Janice and

Lynn got into it, he had shared a smile with her. Not this time. This time he looked as if he wasn't the one who had pretended to want her and then changed his mind.

She walked around the table, checking on the projects. She paused at everyone except Marc. Him she tried to ignore. It was a good thing for her that she was better at business than she was at ignoring.

Twelve o'clock came and the workshop was over. She wouldn't have to see Marc until the following week. A week seemed to have too few days. She pulled her attention back to this workshop.

"We have one more workshop before Christmas."

"Aw, how come only one more?"

"Because a second one would take us to close to Christmas and this place will be a madhouse. Those last few days, I'll be so tired, I'll probably fall asleep as soon as I hit the bed."

The kids murmured, but the noise that grabbed her attention wasn't from the kids; it was the sound of Marc's quick intake of breath. Again their stares found each other. Was he thinking of the night she fell asleep while he was giving her a back massage? Was he remembering how that was the first time after they had found each other that they didn't make love before going to sleep? Or was his mind on the night before that or the night after that when their lovemaking had taken them to a special place? A place where only the two of them ever went? He couldn't be reacting to the word "bed" or to the fact that they hadn't shared a bed since Monday. She swallowed the lump, hoping to keep tears from escaping. The fact that she and Marc would never share a bed again was his doing.

"Miss Cindy?" Lynn's voice rescued Cindy from the pain of her thoughts. "What are we going to make next Saturday?"

"Origami. Does anybody know what that is?" Many

hands went up, but not all. Cindy was glad for the ones that didn't. It gave her something to do.

She explained the paper-folding process and told them the history of it. "We'll make Christmas ornaments and decorations using only one sheet of paper for each." She was proud of herself when she managed to smile. "See you next week." She focused on each person who left and tried not to think about the ones still in the room.

"We're going to the art museum again today." Kevin stood in front of her. "I guess you can't come this week either, huh?"

"I'm sorry, Kevin."

"Maybe some other time?" He looked so hopeful. Cindy wished she could let him keep his hope. But she couldn't. Neither could she tell him that Denise would more than likely be the one to go with him and Marc.

"I don't like to make promises that I don't intend to keep."

"Neither do I. Not even unspoken ones." Marc, who hadn't said a word since his mumbled "hello," spoke as he glared at her. What did he have to glare about? "Have you decided where we're going to eat lunch?" The way he looked at Cindy, anyone who didn't know better would think he was talking to her instead of to Kevin. Luckily for them both, Kevin knew that he was supposed to answer and he did.

Marc pulled his attention away from Cindy just as he had last Monday only today it hurt a little less because she expected it.

As he walked away with Kevin, Cindy couldn't help but wonder if he compared his special place with her to the one he now shared with Denise.

She looked at the trash scattered over the table that she had neglected to collect. By the time she finished he'd be gone from the store. Then she would see him only one more time during the rest of her life. She frowned. Surely he wouldn't have the nerve to sign up for the next series of workshops? She sighed. He would find somebody else to help with the workshops at the shelter. As she cleared the table she wondered. Was all of that good or bad?

Marc walked to his car parked outside the office as if he was late for something. How dare she act like the wounded one, as if she were the victim and he the bad guy. She was the one sneaking around. *She couldn't wait until I left before she turned to another man.* He snatched open the car door as if he had expected it to be stuck. *Does he sleep on the same side of her bed that I do?*

He and Kevin got into the car, but Marc didn't start it. Instead he stared straight ahead. He didn't want them to, but memories of her in his arms, giving her little moans, sharing her heat with him crashed over him. Did she compare him to her new man?

"What's wrong, Marc?" Kevin broke through the memories.

"I was just remembering something." He took several deep breaths and let them out slowly. *She's moved past what I thought we had. I have to learn to do the same.* He stared out the windshield. *I only have to see her one more time.* Then he took another deep breath to help him regain control. *Only one more time,* he thought as he started the car and left the parking lot. Other craft stores have workshops for kids. I can take Kevin to them. He tried to be happy about that as he drove down Kelly Drive and to the art museum.

That night the memories that had politely stayed away while he was with Kevin returned. When he opened the door to his house, he could swear that a faint smell of Cindy's perfume greeted him. He blinked and just stood in the hallway. *Just my imagination.* When she was in his arms, the perfume was so subtle that he had to nuzzle her to catch it.

He locked the door and leaned against it as sharp memories hit him: Cindy's hand against his chest, undoing the buttons of his shirt while he did the same to her blouse. The smile she gave him as if she was sharing something with him that she had never shared with anyone else. Heat spread through him.

Cindy, skin to skin with him, her breasts burning his chest, her mouth searing his.

His hands ached as if needing to feel the fullness of her breasts, as if it was vital for his fingers to brush across the tip that hardened before he even touched it. He bit his lip to keep from missing the taste of the two chocolate tips. He closed his eyes to make the image of the heat that flared in her eyes whenever he stroked her place that was a secret to everyone except him.

He pushed off from the wall and shook his head. That was a lie. Already she had found somebody else.

He went upstairs to his bedroom. More memories were waiting for him there and they rushed to greet him as he stepped into the room. He had changed the sheets before he left. The smooth surface of the spread lay in front of him, but that wasn't what he saw. He was remembering Cindy in his bed among tousled covers, reaching for him, waiting until he protected them; waiting for him to join her so she could join with him as they journeyed to their place.

He pictured him and Cindy, in his bed, in each other's arms as if they would share a bed and wake up together for the rest of their lives.

He stared at the bed waiting for the memories to quit so the pain could stop. Then he got tired of waiting and left the room.

Maybe tomorrow night, he thought as he went into the bedroom across the hall. Or next week. He frowned.

Surely by the end of the year? He stood in the doorway. Please let it be before the new year.

He got undressed, trying not to think of how he had thought the new year would be the beginning of their new phase, not a time to look back on what had never been real.

Twenty-seven

"See you after you close?" Helen stood in front of Cindy in the sanctuary after the end of the early service and stared at her as if looking for something.

"I'll be there." Cindy sighed.

"No going home first and then calling me to say that you changed your mind, OK?"

"No, Ma'am." She shook her head.

"Good." Her mother hugged her. "'Cause I know where you live and I'd come to get you. You know that, don't you?"

"Yes, Mom." Cindy's laugh was weak, but it was a laugh.

"That sounded good." Her mother nodded and patted Cindy's arm. "See you in a little bit."

Cindy made her way out of the church and to her car. *I hope she keeps her promise about not talking about Marc. He's taking up too much space in my mind already. I don't need for her to bring him up, too.*

She drove to the store wishing that she could discover a way to delete Marc from her mind like a bad file on a computer disk: painlessly and leaving no scars nor any trace. She sighed. For all of the scientists' declarations about how superior the human mind was to a computer, in this case she wouldn't mind being as unfeeling as machine.

The customers were numerous enough so it wasn't a waste of time to open, yet she and Debbie were enough staff. The sales weren't enough, however, to keep Marc out of her thoughts. A dull ache hurt just as much as a sharp pain.

At four, Cindy locked up and went to her mother's, glad for the company.

"Everything is ready." Her mother greeted Cindy at the door. "The pot roast is cooked just the way you like it and I baked an apple pie yesterday." She hugged her. "The Eagles have a late game today, so we didn't miss as much as we usually do."

"OK." Cindy stood in the hall as if waiting for something, or afraid of something.

"It's just the two of us, Baby Girl." Helen touched Cindy's arm. "I kept my promise. Wes is out with some friends. He got tickets for the Black Nativity and he's going with them." Helen gasped and grabbed Cindy's arm. "I'm so sorry." She shook her head. "I . . . I wasn't thinking."

"It's OK, Mom. We can't avoid talking about places because of . . ." She took a deep breath. "It's OK. Really." *At least I hope it will be.* She followed her mother into the kitchen.

"I set us up in here. You just fix your plate from the stove." She held up her hand. "And don't remind me of how I drilled into you the importance of putting food into serving bowls and platters." She laughed. "I won't tell the protocol police if you don't." She laughed again. "Go on. Help your plate before the food gets cold." She nodded when Cindy picked up her plate. "Good. Did I tell you that Mrs. Long has us learning a couple of new songs? We're going to sing them for Christmas Eve service, if we get them right." She chuckled. "Knowing Mrs. Long the way I do, we will get them right."

"Tell me about the songs."

Cindy took her plate to the stove, grateful for something else to talk about besides what was filling her mind. She tried to follow her mother's words, but it was hard. Marc kept getting in the way. He kept derailing her train of thought all during dinner. Just as he had been doing since last Monday. She frowned. *I have to try harder.*

"Let's take our dessert into the living room." The table had been cleared, Cindy had managed to do justice to her mother's cooking, leftovers had been put away and Marc's name hadn't come up once.

"I don't know what went wrong. Nothing happened." Cindy set her dessert plate on the coffee table. She was breaking her own rule. "I thought we were fine. Then"—he shrugged—"I have no idea what went wrong." She frowned. "We were set for me to take him to the airport." She looked at her mother. "He had kissed me good-bye before he walked over to his office." She shook her head. "It didn't seem like a good-bye kiss." She stared, trying to analyze that last kiss as she had already done too many times. "Denise took him to the airport." She stared at her mother again. "I went over to hurry him along, and Lisa told me that he had already gone with Denise."

"No explanation?"

"No explanation. No note. No nothing." Her jaw tightened. "Just as bad as Harry. Worse. I cared more about him than I ever did Harry. Harry made me mad. That's what hurt with him. This, this thing with Marc . . ." She shook her head. "I knew I shouldn't have gotten involved. I knew it. But I went against my better judgment and look what happened." She leaned back. "I never told you about his plan, did I?"

"What plan?"

Cindy explained what she and Marc had decided. "It was his plan. After he talked me into going along, I said only until Christmas. He said 'no,' we'll make it until after the new year." She shook her head slowly. "He lost interest a few weeks before Christmas."

"Oh, Cindy." Helen patted her hand. "I'm so sorry. I feel responsible. All the times Jean and I tried to get you two together . . ." She sighed. "It's my fault. Jean and I should have left it alone. I feel just awful."

"It's not your doing. I met him before I knew who he was. Or what he was. To keep seeing him afterward was my decision." *If seeing was all that went between us, I wouldn't be hurting so much.*

"Jean said Marc didn't say anything about why you two broke up."

"He's probably too ashamed. It's not that he broke things off. I wouldn't expect him to keep things going if he . . . he didn't want me anymore." She wiped her eyes. "It's how he did it. He didn't even tell me." She wiped her face again. Then she took a deep breath. "Let's watch the game. I've let Marc take up too much of my time already."

"Sure, Baby."

A few hours later, Cindy stood. "Thanks, Mom." She put on her coat. "I'm glad you made me come."

"I never make you do anything." She grinned. "Sometimes I'm just a little heavy-handed in my urging." She nodded. "It will get better. I promise. It won't always hurt this much. Wait a minute." Helen went to the kitchen and returned with a plate in her hand. "Tomorrow's dinner."

"Thanks again." Cindy sighed. "I'd better get going. I've got another busy day ahead of me tomorrow." She managed a weak smile. "At least I hope so."

As she drove home, she hoped her mother was right: that the ache would ease as time passed. She was skeptical. It hurt just as much now as it had six days ago.

Monday morning was gray. It looked as if the sky was in mourning. Cindy slowly got up and faced the day. She was glad that she owned a business. Glad that she had something to occupy her time now that Marc had moved on. Her face hardened. *I will not think of him today. I know he isn't thinking about me.*

By the end of the business day, she was pleased by the number of customers. She was not pleased that she couldn't keep her promise not to think about Marc.

She went home and it was as if he had tagged along with her. She warmed up the leftovers her mother had given her and wondered what Marc was eating. Had he gone to his mother's house the day before for dinner and had he taken Denise? Cindy shook her head. No. If he didn't talk to Miss Jean about breaking up with Cindy, he wouldn't have taken Denise over there.

Cindy picked at her food as if suddenly she didn't like her favorite meal. Maybe they stayed at his house. Her thoughts flew to the last time that she and Marc made love.

The ache grew and mixed with desire. She swallowed the lump. How could she still want somebody who didn't want her? But she did. Heaven help her, she did.

Her body warmed as she remembered how Marc had reacted when she mirrored what he was doing to her. As his hands caressed her breasts and teased her nipples, she had done the same to him. From his reaction, his body responded the same as hers. From there their hands had explored their way lower, teasing, taking turns with their tongues, which were busy with the nipples. Her breasts tingled and hardened as if, any minute now, Marc would be there and they could repeat their actions.

She closed her eyes as her body readied itself to receive him. Why did he break things off?

Cindy cleared the table and turned on the television. Maybe she could find something to take her mind off Marc and making love with him, and waking up during the night to make love with him again.

She surfed the channels looking for something to take her mind off love, period. She shook her head. You used to be able to depend on sitcoms to be safe. Now they were as much fools about love as about everything else.

She turned to another channel and then another. Finally she stopped at a channel for kids. That should be safe. A coyote trying to catch a bird had nothing to do with love.

A while later, she glanced at the clock. *How much longer before I can go to work?* She shook her head. *Too long. I haven't even gone to bed and pretended to expect to have a restful night's sleep yet.*

She went to the kitchen. It had been a long time since she had reorganized the pots and pans. She sat on the floor and pulled everything out of the cupboard. She tried not to notice each time she pulled out a pan that she had used to cook something for Marc.

By the time it was late enough for her to go to bed, she had straightened every lower cabinet in the kitchen. She sighed as she stood.

I'll save the top cupboards for tomorrow. I'll need something to do then just as much as I do now.

Twenty-eight

Cindy got through Tuesday and was working on Wednesday the same way she got though Monday: with a lot of heartache trying to overwhelm her. By the following evening, every cabinet and cupboard in her home could have passed the toughest inspection. Still, it wouldn't be enough to keep thoughts of Marc away permanently. She tried to be grateful for the few minutes at a time when he didn't bother her. She processed a couple of orders and did routine things as if everything was normal, as if she always felt like this. In the late afternoon Debbie opened the wound without knowing it.

"What do you have planned to make tomorrow night?" Debbie's question, asked innocently, felt like a punch.

"Bouquets. I'll be back in a minute."

Cindy rushed to her office as if enthusiasm drove her rather than the need to not let Debbie see her cry. *How am I going to do this? How am I going to face those happy women who have found love?* She shook her head. It wasn't that long ago that she had fit right in with them.

She leaned against the closed office door. Tears poured from her eyes as if tired of being hidden. Cindy let them come out.

When they finally stopped, she wiped her face and held a cold washcloth to her eyes for a minute. She sighed. She had done this before. She had to find some way not to do this again. She shook her head. A waste of tears. She looked in the mirror. *I hope Debbie and the others are kind enough not to ask what's wrong.*

She got the three different sample bouquets from the shelf, took a deep breath, and went into the workshop room. She refused to look at the chair where Denise had sat. *If I'm lucky, she won't show up tomorrow.* She sighed. *With less luck than that, I can win the lottery and I don't even buy tickets.*

She went back to the front of the store. *I will not think about tomorrow night until tomorrow night.*

In spite of her promise, thoughts of the next night stuck with her and rode home with her. There they stayed in the front of her mind for the rest of the evening, keeping those of Marc company.

They were back in place as soon as she woke up, as if afraid she'd forget about the workshop if other thoughts got through. Regardless of how busy Cindy was or what she did, the workshop thoughts stayed stuck in place throughout the day.

By the time six o'clock came, Cindy was relieved. She just wanted to get through it. She smiled as the women came into the room. She even managed to smile at Denise. It wasn't as strong as the smiles she gave to the others, but it was more than Denise deserved.

"Excuse me," Cindy said when Denise found an excuse to mention Marc for what seemed like the hundredth time. "I'll be back in a minute." Cindy smiled and left the room. She took a few deep breaths. When it didn't help, she went to her office and closed the door.

"If that woman mentions Marc one more time I will make her eat whatever is in her hand at the time," Cindy said to the empty room. "I hope it's something sharp: like floral wire. Or scissors." She clinched her teeth together. "Then I will call the police and tell them what I did." She picked up the paperweight from her desk and put it down. Then she picked up the desk organizer and put it back down. "When the jury hears my story they will decide that it's justifiable homicide." She straightened the already neat piles of papers on her desk. Then she went back to the workshop.

Denise got through the rest of the workshop alive only because Cindy kept singing the "Twelve Days of Christmas" over and over in her head. By the time eight o'clock came, Denise was still alive, thanks to the partridges and pears and maids and lords and all of their company parading through Cindy's mind keeping her from making tomorrow's headline. Cindy congratulated herself on her self-control. She even managed to smile at the women.

"Remember, no more workshops until after the new year." Her voice broke on the words, "new year," but the women didn't seem to notice. Cindy wished them happy holidays and smiled as they left talking with each other about Christmas.

Denise, the last to leave, stopped in front of her. "I'm sorry this is the last workshop for awhile. I'm so looking forward to the next one." Her look was more of a smirk than a smile. "Wait until I show Marc what we made tonight." When Cindy didn't respond, Denise moved on. Cindy took a little pleasure in Denise's disappointment. She shook her head as she stared at the woman's back.

She doesn't have a clue as to how lucky she is to still be breathing. Cindy closed the door and went to the front of the store.

Too bad I don't have some kit on a shelf to help me get through the next few weeks.

Through the days that followed, Cindy never caught the holiday spirit from the people who came into the shops. She did manage to keep her pain down to a level that she could manage. In some ways the days flew past, but in other ways they dragged on. There had been a time, not too long ago, when she had been looking forward to Christmas and, for once in a long time, to a new year. Now it stretched ahead just as lonely as the last one and the ones before that. She knew that not every new year brought a change, but it still hurt to face that this was the case this year, too.

We had planned to end things on New Year's Day, anyway. Marc just ended it early. She tried to rationalize.

"My house for Christmas dinner, right?" Helen asked Cindy after church the Sunday before Christmas.

"Yes."

"I thought I'd better make sure, since I haven't seen you for dinner for weeks."

"I've been busy."

"I won't put you on the spot by asking for details. I don't want to make you lie in church."

"I have cleaned every closet in the house."

"Uh-oh." She shook her head. "A bad sign. Did you get to the third floor?"

"Not yet."

"Come over to the house today so I won't have to eat alone."

"What about Wes?"

"He got tickets to the game. He swears that the Eagles are going to the playoffs again this year."

"He may be right." Cindy sighed. "I'll be over."

"Good. Maybe we'll see Wes in the stands. He promised to keep his shirt on and not to paint his face green and white." She laughed. "He said that he's perfectly happy with his brown face and he doesn't need to change its color to show his loyalty."

Cindy cringed at her mother's words about taking off shirts, even though the image of Marc's broad strong chest popped up, bringing an ache with it. She had barely controlled her reaction to that when her mother mentioned loyalty. She stared at her mother's back, wishing the kitchen were a block away.

Cindy ate dinner with her mother and every now and then, for a minute or so, she got so involved in their conversation that she didn't think about Marc.

She was surprised when it was time to go home.

The few days before Christmas passed in a flurry of customers who had decided to give craft kits and supplies for gifts.

Christmas morning came and Cindy tried to feel something, but she couldn't. She put on a red dress for the occasion, not because she felt festive, but because it was an appropriate color for the holiday.

"I have decided to take the job," Wes announced at the table. "I'll relocate to Philadelphia in March. I have a good feeling about this."

"It will be great having you back here. Remember the year you got a skateboard for Christmas?"

"Yeah, and you begged to try it?"

"And scratched up the entire middle of your face," her mother finished. They laughed. "You can laugh now, but you can count yourself blessed that you don't have a scar running from your nose to your chin." They laughed again. Then somebody else pulled out another memory to share.

They spent the rest of the day taking turns with Wes sharing some special past Christmas memories from the time he had been away.

By the end of the day, Cindy was pleased that she had gotten through it.

"What time do you open tomorrow?"

"The regular time. Folks will be coming to spend gift

certificates as if afraid I'll go out of business before they can use them. Others will want to spend money they got for Christmas." She shrugged. "Whatever their reasons, I'll be glad to welcome them into the shop."

She drove home thinking, that wasn't as bad as I thought it would be. She got ready for bed thinking, I can get through this.

The next day came cold, but bright. Cindy forced herself from under the warm covers. How many days until spring? She frowned. First you have to get through New Year's Day and what might have been.

"It has been a very merry Christmas." Mattie danced into Cindy's office at the end of the day. She waved a loose-leaf notebook and twirled around. "The salespeople in the jewelry stores must have been busy working overtime." She waved the notebook in front of Cindy again. "I got orders for six weddings so far." She held up her hand. "Don't ask me how I'm going to do it." She laughed. "As soon as I can, I'll pin all of the newly engaged down as to the wedding gown and attendants' outfits. A couple of women came with pictures. All of them knew what their color schemes would be." She laughed again. "Even the two who were surprised by the proposals and the rings." She sighed. "I guess, in spite of the progress women have made, girls still dream of their weddings."

"I guess so."

"Smile. This means more business for you, too. Most of the women asked about your workshops. I told them to ask when the new schedule will be ready." Happiness filled her face. "If this keeps up, I'll have to hire somebody to help me do the sewing." She did a few dance steps. "Maybe a couple of somebodies." She held up her hand. "I'm not complaining, mind you." She shook her head. "I have never had this many orders at one time before."

"I'm glad for you."

Cindy watched as Mattie went back to her shop. Some women did believe in finding the right man. She swallowed hard. She hoped it worked out all right for them.

Twenty-nine

Cindy closed the store early on New Year's Eve, not because she had someplace to go, but because she was sure that everybody else had something more interesting and exciting to do than to go to a craft store. Crafters would be resting their eyes and hands after making the holiday crafts.

She frowned as she drove home. Any woman interested in the bridal shop would probably spend tonight with her lover. A few weeks ago she thought that was how she'd be spending tonight. She blinked away the tears. Her ache was just as strong as it had been when she found out . . . She shook her head. *I'm not going over that ground again.* She sighed. How could he do that to her?

She went into the house without noticing the snowflakes that had started to escape from the sky. She didn't notice anything except how lonely her house felt again.

After a light dinner of soup and a grilled cheese sandwich, she went upstairs to get ready for bed. She pulled on her red flannel nightgown. That sexy lingerie store founder would have a heart attack if she could see this outfit, Cindy thought as she zipped on her long blue velvet robe over it. Who was Victoria anyway? Probably the real name was Victor. Most of the things she had seen in the window of the store didn't look like anything a woman would design. She shook her head. Those supposed-to-be clothes were for women who had a man who would see the outfits. She swallowed hard. *Before he undressed her.* She sighed. Not long ago she was one of those women. She frowned. At least she thought she was. She shook her head. *Not tonight. I won't let Marc ruin tonight.*

She sighed. It would take nothing short of a miracle to let her keep that from happening. She went back downstairs hoping for just such a thing.

Popcorn and hot chocolate. With lots of little marshmallows. That's how she would celebrate. She wouldn't even turn on the television and wonder how those people could find it fun to stand out in the cold of New York City surrounded by strangers and have their feet freeze while they waited for some silly fake silver ball to slide slowly to the ground.

She went into the living room and lit the wood stacked in the fireplace. *I'd rather watch the fire.* She sighed. *And listen to music. I need music. Lots of music to give me something else to think about.*

She sorted through her collection of LPs that she had begged from her mother. It wasn't easy finding albums with all upbeat music. She sighed. *I'll do the best I can.* That's all she could do about anything.

She put a stack on the old record player and turned it on. By the time she had made her popcorn and cocoa and taken them into the living room, Little Richard was singing about "Tutti-Fruitti." *That should do it. If Little Richard can't get my spirits up, I don't know who can.* She picked up the stack of books waiting beside her big overstuffed armchair. *I can finally get some reading in.*

Marilyn Tyner's latest book was on top. Cindy shook her head. *No romance. I can't read any romance right now.* She had to go through books by Kayla Perrin, Beverly Jenkins and just about every writer whose covers she could relate to, before she got to one that was safe to read.

Ken Follett was always an interesting read. He might

even keep her mind off the person she wasn't supposed to think about.

Twenty pages into the thriller and she had to start over. She had no idea what she had just read. She glanced at the clock. Eight-thirty. Those planning to go out to celebrate were still at home. She'd go to bed, but that would be worse than sitting up in a chair. Her bed held too many memories.

The new year was coming and bringing the same old baggage with it. The twelve months ahead would be just like the last twelve. She shook her head. No, they wouldn't. The first few months of the new year would be a lot different from the last few of this one.

The doorbell rang and she rushed to the door. *Maybe Mom decided to come over even though I told her that she didn't have to bother.*

Cindy peeked out the small window at the top of the door and stared.

"What are you doing here?"

"Open the door." Marc shifted from one foot to the other. "It's cold out here." He turned his collar up around his scarf.

"Then go home."

"We have to talk." He hunched his shoulders around his ears.

"So *now* you want to talk." She glared at him through the window. "Well it's a little late for that."

"Cindy, let me in. I'm freezing."

She stared through the window a few seconds longer. *May as well let him in and get this over with.* She let out a harsh breath. *If I don't let him in, he's stubborn enough the stay out there and I don't want to have to explain to the police why there's a frozen body on my porch.*

She opened the door. "Well?"

Marc dashed inside as if he was afraid she was going to change her mind.

She reached around him and closed the door, trying not to notice the tiredness around his eyes. She frowned and shook her head. He's probably too busy with Denise to get enough sleep. That's all it is. She tried not to remember when she and he together didn't get much sleep either.

"What do you want?" She glared at him and folded her arms across her chest.

"I'll start by saying that I want to talk to you." He walked past her and into the living room. His aftershave swiped at her as he passed.

"There's nothing to talk about."

"Why did you do it? I have to know. I thought I could let it go, but I can't." He shrugged out of his coat and laid it on the back of her favorite chair. Then he turned to glare at her.

"Why did I do what? You're the one who asked Denise to take you to the airport. You're the one who decided to throw out our so-called plan without telling me. You're the one with Denise. You have a ton of nerve acting as if I'm to blame."

"I didn't ask Denise. She offered."

"I'll bet she did. I'll bet she offered you more than that. She's been trying to jump your bones since she met you."

"Who told you that?"

"It doesn't matter who told me, if it's true. Is it?"

"That doesn't have anything to do with us."

"There isn't any us. You saw to that. You ended whatever we had going when you started with Denise." It was hard, but she kept her voice from shaking. She would not let him know how. much he had hurt her.

"What are you talking about?" His puzzled look almost made Cindy believe that he didn't know. She stared at him as he continued. "I didn't start anything with Denise or anybody else except you. Besides, you're the one with a lot of nerve. You're the one who was kissing on that man. I thought we had something serious growing between us." He shook his head. "And then that."

"What man? The only man I've been kissing on is you and that was a colossal mistake. I should have known better. As if there aren't enough new mistakes, I have to repeat an old one." Cindy's voice would have reached somebody on the third floor if anyone had been up there.

"Don't try to deny it. I saw you myself. Right outside your shop that Monday. You couldn't even wait a few more hours for me to leave before you turned to somebody else." Marc's voice matched Cindy's in volume. His glare matched hers.

"You must be crazy. I did not kiss . . . Oh." She stopped in the middle of her sentence and covered her mouth.

"Aha. Figured out how I saw you, did you? I don't know why you're surprised. You were right in plain sight for anyone and everyone to see." He glared at her. "You weren't expecting me to come to the store so soon, were you? I had a patient no-show and was on my way over to you so we could leave early for the airport, maybe grab something to eat on the way since we hadn't had time for a decent breakfast." His voice had run out of strength by the time he got to the part about them and breakfast.

Twin flares of desire showed in both pair of eyes. Both of them managed to gain control.

"That was Wes." Cindy's voice had dropped to its normal level.

"I don't care what his name is. You were kissing on him." Marc's voice had turned up the volume again.

"He's my cousin."

"Your cousin? Yeah, right." He frowned and stared at her, taking time to analyze exactly what he had seen that morning. A kiss on the cheek and a hug. That was all. The rest was in his head. His frown eased. "He was your cousin." Marc's voice was back to normal. He looked as if a heavy load had been lifted from his shoulders. "Your cousin. Wes." He smiled at her.

Cindy was far from smiling. "He still is, but Wes doesn't have anything to do with what you did. I'd better tell you something that you must not know about me." She put her hands on her hips. "There are some things I don't share. A man is at the top of the list." He glared at him. "Let's talk about almost-engaged Denise. Did you give her the ring she was expecting for Christmas or is she going to help you pick it out?" Cindy was proud of the control in her voice despite sharp edges of pain poking her.

"I don't know what you're talking about. Denise works for us. That's all. There is nothing between her and me. I told you that a long time ago." He stared at her. "He's your cousin?"

"Don't try to change the subject. Denise has been to two of my workshops chattering and bragging about you and the wedding you two will have."

"She *what?*" Marc stared at Cindy with wide eyes.

"'Marc is so understanding,' she said. 'He wants me to have the kind of wedding that would make every woman envious,' she said." Cindy did her best to capture Denise's voice, but she couldn't get the evil in it right.

"All Denise is to me is a soon-to-be ex-employee of our practice."

"Uh-huh."

"Cindy, listen to me. I am not now nor have I ever been involved with Denise. She's not my type." He shook his head. "I thought you were involved with that man."

"Wes. His name is Wes." Her frown was back, but it was different. "How could you think that about me after what we had together?" Her anger had dissolved. She wanted to believe him, needed to believe him. Did she dare?

"The same way you could think that about me." He

took a step closer to her. "Oh, Cindy, I could never be involved with Denise or anybody else besides you."

Was that really desire for her that she saw in his eyes or was her imagination creating something that no longer existed? "I want to believe you."

"Why can't you?" He closed the rest of the space between them but he didn't touch her. "Why can't you believe that you're the only one I want, the only one I will ever want; the one I will always want."

"I . . . I'm afraid of getting hurt again." Why didn't he touch her? Why didn't he wrap his arms around her and chase away her fears? Why didn't he show her how he felt instead of telling her?

"I could never hurt you. I love you." Finally he touched her. He folded her into his arms where she belonged and held her close. Her hands found their old spot over his heart and settled in as if they were home.

"You love me?" She held her breath. What if she had imagined those words. What if he hadn't said them at all?

"I love you more than I ever thought possible." He brushed his lips across hers so gently that it barely happened. "If you let me, I'll spend the rest of my life proving it."

"You love me? You're sure?" Wonder covered her face. Was it time for her to love again? She shook her head. To love for the first time. What she had felt with Harry wasn't love, but a poor imitation instead.

"More sure than I've ever been about anything else in my life." He kissed the side of her mouth.

"I love you, too." Her breath was having trouble keeping steady. "I love you so much that it scares me. I feel as if I'm hanging from a limb high up on a tree and I can't see what's below."

"I'm there. I'm below. Let go. I'll catch you." He kissed the other side of her face. "And after I do, I'll never let you go."

"I know that, now. I . . ." No other words followed. They were swallowed by Marc's kiss before they could reach the air.

Their arms tightened around each other and they tried to give each other all of the missed kisses of the past weeks. Finally Marc lifted his mouth from hers. "When we open the office on Saturday, Denise will have to look for another job. Do you want to come over and hear the truth from her?"

"No." Cindy shook her head. "I don't need to. I know you'll take care of it. I trust you." She stared at him and finally allowed her love for him to show itself. "I don't want to talk about her. I don't want to talk at all." She opened several buttons on his shirt and pressed her mouth against his chest.

"I don't want to talk, either." Marc smiled at her. "I like your outfit." He moved his hand to the top of the zipper at her neck. "I'll like it even better when it's off you." He eased the zipper down as if there was no hurry.

"My grandmom had an old saying." Cindy unfastened the rest of the buttons on his shirt and slid it down his arms. It fell beside her robe. She caressed her way across his chest, giving into the temptation to gently squeeze the flat nipple hiding in his thick chest hair. She smiled as she was rewarded with a gasp from Marc.

"What was that?" Marc brushed his hand slowly over the front of her gown. His hand stilled when it reached the fullness of her breast. "I missed this." He stroked his finger over the tip and Cindy tried to lean into his hand, but he pulled back. Before she could protest his moving away, his mouth found the hard tip. The fabric between her breast and his tongue didn't prevent the warmth from flaring up inside her and spreading to the place that had waited too long for him.

He tugged gently, and the fires leapt within her as if trying to consume her. He kissed his way back to her face. "We have to get you out of your gown. One side of the front is wet." He smiled at her. "What did she say?"

"Who?"

"Your grandmom." He smiled at her and the dimple that had been hidden from her for too long showed itself. "You have to concentrate."

"I am. I have something better than a conversation to focus on."

She brushed her hand to his waist and hesitated before gliding lower. She smiled at him as she rested her hand over his fullness. She squeezed gently once and Marc groaned. Then she eased her hand around to his back and pressed him even closer to her. "She used to say that whatever you're doing when the New Year comes is what you'll be doing for the rest of the year." She opened and closed her hands over his backside.

"What time is it?" Marc's words struggled to be heard.

"The clock hasn't chimed midnight yet." Her words were ragged as if she had just run a marathon. She pressed her lips against his chest and brushed back and forth over his nipple.

"Good. We still have time." He lifted her into his arms covered her mouth with his. Then he carried her up the stairs.

"Is this what you intend to do for the rest of the year," Cindy whispered as he let her feet touch the bedroom floor.

"For the rest of my life, if you let me." He touched her lips with his and then looked at her. "Marry me? I know somebody who can help you plan all the trimmings."

"I don't need any trimmings." She smiled up at him. "All I need is you. Just you." She feathered a kiss against his chest. "Now." She kissed him again. "And for always."

Marc lifted her chin and covered her mouth with his. Then he pulled back and shook his head. "A flannel nightgown?"

"And sheets, too. My bed was cold without you."

"Did they help?"

"No. They couldn't substitute for you."

"Good. I'd hate to be replaced by a nightgown and sheets."

"Nothing and noone could replace you."

He kissed her again. "Let's get rid of this. You won't need it anymore." He helped her ease it off.

"You might need these again, but for now, while we're playing 'off with the old,'" she touched his pants, "let's get rid of these, too." She unfastened his pants and freed his hardness. His clothes quickly covered her gown on the floor.

"If what your grandmom said is true," he said as he placed her on the bed. "My partners will have to find a replacement." He rolled on protection, lay down beside her and gathered her into his arms. Their lips met as if the other times had been weak rehearsals.

A short while later, when the city welcomed midnight, neither Marc nor Cindy noticed the time. They were locked in each other's arms declaring their love in the way they knew best.

Once during the night Cindy stirred. Marc's arms tightened around her. "Happy New Year." He kissed her forehead.

"You do know how to bring in the new year right, don't you?" Cindy touched the side of his face.

"We'll have to practice during the year to see if we can improve for next year."

"You can't improve on perfection, but we can have fun trying." She drew his face to hers and kissed him.

"And again the next year." His kiss for her was longer.

"And the next." Her kiss surpassed his in intensity. "Maybe we should start practicing now?"

"I agree."

"Happy New Year," she said before she was too busy to say anything else.

And it was.

Dear Reader,

Cindy and Marc, like so many others today, were so hurt by their bitter divorces that they vowed never to love again.

Fortunately, their mothers, long-time friends, are tired of being the only ones in their crowd who are not grandmothers. They are convinced that if Cindy and Marc would only meet, they would fall in love. Cindy and Marc resist but fate takes pity on their mothers and steps in.

I am embarrassed to admit that a little of Jean and Helen are based on myself. Although I didn't have a woman in mind for my son to marry, I did ask him if it wasn't time for him to find somebody and get married so I could have grandchildren while I was still able to play with them.

Fortunately, he hasn't had the bad experiences that Cindy and Marc had with their marriages. Tony and Clara have been married more than fifteen years. I have two grandsons and a granddaughter.

Keep reading and I'll keep writing. You may visit my Web site www.alicewootson.net or you can contact me at agwwriter@email.com or by U.S. mail: P.O. Box 18832, Philadelphia, PA 19119.

If you write, please include an SASE.

Sincerely,

Alice

ABOUT THE AUTHOR

Alice Wootson has been a reader for as long as she can remember. She left Rankin, Pennsylvania, to go to Cheyney University and remained in the Philadelphia area.

After years of reading other authors and after her three sons were grown, she decided to try her hand at writing. Her first two novels were historicals and have not yet been published. Her first contemporary was accepted by Karen Thomas for Arabesque two days after Alice received a particularly mean rejection from an agent who stated that Alice's style was too poetic to have commercial value.

To Love Again is her fifth novel and will be followed by *Escape to Love* in June 2003.

She is still in awe of knowing authors whom she only knew through their books.

She writes so the people in her head will shut up.